WINGS IN THE NIGHT

———

The Weird Works of
Robert E. Howard,
Volume Four

THE WEIRD WORKS OF ROBERT E. HOWARD

Shadow Kingdoms
Moon of Skulls
People of the Dark
Wings in the Night
Valley of the Worm
Gardens of Fear
Beyond the Black River
Hour of the Dragon
Black Hound of Death
A Thunder of Trumpets

WINGS IN THE NIGHT
The Weird Works of Robert E. Howard, Volume Four

———

ROBERT E. HOWARD

Edited by
Paul Herman

Introduction by
Paul Herman

WILDSIDE PRESS

WINGS IN THE NIGHT

———

Publication History:

First Paperback Printing: January 2007

Wildside Press

www.wildsidepress.com

For more information, contact **Wildside Press**.

ISBN: 0-8095-5791-6

TABLE OF CONTENTS

INTRODUCTION: REVENGE

How does one justify violence? Robert E. Howard ("REH"), as an author, almost always preferred to create stories based on physical conflict. And as REH wanted to constantly expand his skills and improve his workmanship, REH faced the challenge of utilizing new and different reasons for the violence and strife he preferred in his works. By the year 1932, REH had already used boxing, the fall of civilizations, treachery, survival and even Lovecraftian horror. But now he would come up with a reason that he could turn into a great set of stories: Revenge! Revenge works well for the short story format, as the situation is quickly created, the evil deed done, and the revenge unleashed, strongly justified, to the hero if not to the reader. First used so skillfully in the incredible "The Dark Man," REH in short order turned out a focused number of new gems, each of which regularly make fans Top 20 lists of REH stories. These include "Wings in the Night," "Worms of the Earth," "The Scarlet Citadel," and "The Tower of the Elephant," all of which are presented in this volume.

"Wings in the Night" may be REH's ultimate presentation of the failed and now angry and avenging angel story. REH's religious hero, Solomon Kane, goes clean berserk, and finds a way to destroy an entire race, in what is arguably the best of the Solomon Kane stories. "Worms of the Earth" sees REH moving away from the simplicity of the hero being the executioner, and instead making the hero become the catalyst to set the revenge in motion. In "Worms of the Earth," Pictish king Bran Mak Morn unleashes unspeakable evil to kill a single man, a Roman leader. Then in "The Scarlet Citadel" and "The Tower of the Elephant," REH's greatest hero, Conan, is the unwitting catalyst for the revenge of others, though of course it works out to his benefit as well.

REH would wind his way through other justifications for violence as his skills evolved, though revenge would remain a touchstone he would return to again and again, including in several of his Crusader and El Borak stories.

The other two stories in this volume show some other story types REH was working on. "The Cairn on the Headland" is almost contrary to revenge, as the man who hates so much, and wants to kill, in the end tries to save, his love of humanity rising in the face of supernatural risk. It makes for an interesting counterpoint to "Worms of the Earth," in which the hero recognizes the risks that will be unleashed, and does it anyway. What it says about REH's fans, that "Worms of the Earth" is sometimes considered the best REH story ever, and "Cairn" is not among the Top 20, would be an interesting bit of analysis.

"Phoenix on the Sword" is the historically important first Conan story. While it started life as a rewrite of an unsold Kull story, "Phoenix" establishes the very unique character of Conan, and sets in place the history and many of the attributes of the Hyborian Age, from which all the later stories would flow. Conan would consume REH for a couple years, with REH generating an enormous volume of work based on the character.

This volume also contains the last of REH's poetry that would be published in *Weird Tales* during his lifetime. REH quit sending poetry to *Weird Tales*, as he was paid by the word, and he quickly found out that a simple 16 line poem doesn't pay nearly as well as a 10,000 word story, especially when the editor will only include one work per author per issue.

All stories and poetry in this volume have been restored to the first published version. So you will get to read them just as the pulp readers of the 1930s did. It is hoped you will find them as exciting, fascinating, and emotionally gripping as they and innumerable later fans have found them to be.

Paul Herman
Plano, Texas

WINGS IN THE NIGHT

Weird Tales, July 1932

---

1. The Horror on the Stake

Solomon Kane leaned on his strangely carved staff and gazed in scowling perplexity at the mystery which spread silently before him. Many a deserted village Kane had seen in the months that had passed since he turned his face east from the Slave Coast and lost himself in the mazes of jungle and river, but never one like this. It was not famine that had driven away the inhabitants, for yonder the wild rice still grew rank and unkempt in the untilled fields. There were no Arab slave-raiders in this nameless land—it must have been a tribal war that devastated the village, Kane decided, as he gazed somberly at the scattered bones and grinning skulls that littered the space among the rank weeds and grasses. These bones were shattered and splintered and Kane saw jackals and a hyena furtively slinking among the ruined huts. But why had the slayers left the spoils? There lay war spears, their shafts crumbling before the attacks of the white ants. There lay shields, moldering in the rains and sun. There lay the cooking-pots, and about the neck-bones of a shattered skeleton glistened a necklace of gaudily painted pebbles and shells—surely rare loot for any savage conqueror.

He gazed at the huts, wondering why the thatch roofs of

so many were torn and rent, as if by taloned things seeking entrance. Then something made his cold eyes narrow in startled unbelief. Just outside the moldering mound that was once the village wall towered a gigantic baobab tree, branchless for sixty feet, its mighty bole too large to be gripped and scaled. Yet in the topmost branches dangled a skeleton, apparently impaled on a broken limb. The cold hand of mystery touched the shoulder of Solomon Kane. How came those pitiful remains in that tree? Had some monstrous ogre's inhuman hand flung them there?

Kane shrugged his broad shoulders and his hand unconsciously touched the black butts of his heavy pistols, the hilt of his long rapier, and the dirk in his belt. Kane felt no fear as an ordinary man would feel, confronted with the Unknown and Nameless. Years of wandering in strange lands and warring with strange creatures had melted away from brain, soul and body all that was not steel and whalebone. He was tall and spare, almost gaunt, built with the savage economy of the wolf. Broad-shouldered, long-armed, with nerves of ice and thews of spring steel, he was no less the natural killer than the born swordsman.

The brambles and thorns of the jungle had dealt hardly with him; his garments hung in tatters, his featherless slouch hat was torn and his boots of Cordovan leather were scratched and worn. The sun had baked his chest and limbs to a deep bronze but his ascetically lean face was impervious to its rays. His complexion was still of that strange dark pallor which gave him an almost corpse-like appearance, belied only by his cold, light eyes.

And now Kane, sweeping the village once more with his

searching gaze, pulled his belt into a more comfortable position, shifted to his left hand the cat-headed stave N'Longa had given him, and took up his way again.

To the west lay a strip of thin forest, sloping downward to a broad belt of savannas, a waving sea of grass waist-deep and deeper. Beyond that rose another narrow strip of woodlands, deepening rapidly into dense jungle. Out of that jungle Kane had fled like a hunted wolf with pointed-toothed men hot on his trail. Even now a vagrant breeze brought faintly the throb of a savage drum which whispered its obscene tale of hate and blood-hunger and belly-lust across miles of jungle and grassland.

The memory of his flight and narrow escape was vivid in Kane's mind, for only the day before had he realized too late that he was in cannibal country, and all that afternoon in the reeking stench of the thick jungle, he had crept and run and hidden and doubled and twisted on his track with the fierce hunters ever close behind him, until night fell and he gained and crossed the grasslands under cover of darkness. Now in the late morning he had seen nothing, heard nothing of his pursuers, yet he had no reason to believe that they had abandoned the chase. They had been close on his heels when he took to the savannas.

So Kane surveyed the land in front of him. To the east, curving from north to south ran a straggling range of hills, for the most part dry and barren, rising in the south to a jagged black skyline that reminded Kane of the black hills of Negari. Between him and these hills stretched a broad expanse of gently rolling country, thickly treed, but nowhere approaching the density of a jungle. Kane got the impression of a vast upland plateau, bounded by the curving hills to the east and by the savannas to the west.

Kane set out for the hills with his long, swinging, tireless stride. Surely somewhere behind him the black demons were stealing after him, and he had no desire to be driven to bay. A shot might send them flying in sudden terror, but on the other hand, so low they were in the scale of humanity, it might transmit no supernatural fear to their dull brains. And not even Solomon Kane, whom Sir Francis Drake had called Devon's king of swords, could win in a pitched battle with a whole tribe.

The silent village with its burden of death and mystery faded out behind him. Utter silence reigned among these mysterious uplands where no birds sang and only a silent macaw flitted among the great trees. The only sounds were Kane's catlike tread, and the whisper of the drum-haunted breeze.

And then Kane caught a glimpse among the trees that made his heart leap with a sudden, nameless horror, and a few moments later he stood before Horror itself, stark and grisly. In a wide clearing, on a rather bold incline stood a grim stake, and to this stake was bound a thing that had once been a black man. Kane had rowed, chained to the bench of a Turkish galley, and he had toiled in Barbary vineyards; he had battled red Indians in the New Lands and had languished in the dungeons of Spain's Inquisition. He knew much of the fiendishness of man's inhumanity, but now he shuddered and grew sick. Yet it was not so much the ghastliness of the mutilations, horrible as they were, that shook Kane's soul, but the knowledge that the wretch still lived.

For as he drew near, the gory head that lolled on the butchered breast lifted and tossed from side to side, spattering blood from the stumps of ears, while a bestial, rattling whimper drooled from the shredded lips.

Kane spoke to the ghastly thing and it screamed unbearably, writhing in incredible contortions, while its head jerked up and down with the jerking of mangled nerves, and the empty, gaping eye-sockets seemed striving to see from their emptiness. And moaning low and brain-shatteringly it huddled its outraged self against the stake where it was bound and lifted its head in a grisly attitude of listening, as if it expected something out of the skies.

"Listen," said Kane, in the dialect of the river-tribes. "Do not fear me—I will not harm you and nothing else shall harm you anymore. I am going to loose you."

Even as he spoke Kane was bitterly aware of the emptiness of his words. But his voice had filtered dimly into the crumbling, agony-shot brain of the black man. From between splintered teeth fell words, faltering and uncertain, mixed and mingled with the slavering droolings of imbecility. He spoke a language akin to the dialects Kane had learned from friendly river-folk on his wanderings, and Kane gathered that he had been bound to the stake for a long time—many moons, he whimpered in the delirium of approaching death; and all this time, inhuman, evil things had worked their monstrous will upon him. These things he mentioned by name, but Kane could make nothing of it for he used an unfamiliar term that sounded like *akaana*. But these things had not bound him to the stake, for the torn wretch slavered the name of Goru, who was a priest and who had drawn a cord too tight about his legs—and Kane wondered that the memory of this small pain should linger through the red mazes of agony that the dying man should whimper over it.

And to Kane's horror, the black spoke of his brother who had aided in the binding of him, and he wept with infantile sobs, and moisture formed in the empty sockets and made tears of blood. And he muttered of a spear broken long ago in some dim hunt, and while he muttered in his delirium, Kane gently cut his bonds and eased his broken body to the grass. But even at the Englishman's careful touch, the poor wretch writhed and howled like a dying dog, while blood started anew from a score of ghastly gashes, which, Kane noted, were more like the wounds made by fang and talon than by knife or spear. But at last it was done and the bloody, torn thing lay on the soft grass with Kane's old slouch hat beneath its death's-head, breathing in great, rattling gasps.

Kane poured water from his canteen between the mangled lips, and bending close, said: "Tell me more of these devils, for by the God of my people, this deed shall not go unavenged, though Satan himself bar my way."

It is doubtful if the dying man heard. But he heard something else. The macaw, with the curiosity of its breed, swept from a nearby grove and passed so close its great wings fanned Kane's hair. And at the sound of those wings, the butchered black man heaved upright and screamed in a voice that haunted Kane's dreams to the day of his death: "The wings! The wings! They come again! Ahhhh, mercy, *the wings!*"

And the blood burst in a torrent from his lips and so he died.

Kane rose and wiped the cold sweat from his forehead. The upland forest shimmered in the noonday heat. Silence lay over the land like an enchantment of dreams. Kane's brooding eyes ranged to the black, malevolent hills crouching in the distance and back to the faraway savannas. An ancient curse lay over that mysterious land and the shadow of it fell across the soul of Solomon Kane.

Tenderly he lifted the red ruin that had once pulsed with life and youth and vitality, and carried it to the edge of the glade, where arranging the cold limbs as best he might, and shuddering once again at the unnamable mutilations, he piled stones above it till even a prowling jackal would find it hard to get at the flesh below.

And he had scarcely finished when something jerked him back out of his somber broodings to a realization of his own position. A slight sound—or his own wolf-like instinct—made him whirl. On the other side of the glade he caught a movement among the tall grasses—the glimpse of a hideous black face, with an ivory ring in the flat nose, thick lips parted to reveal teeth whose filed points were apparent even at that distance, beady eyes and a low slanting forehead topped by a mop of frizzy hair. Even as the face faded from view Kane leaped back into the shelter of the ring of trees which circled the glade, and ran like a deer-hound, flitting from tree to tree and expecting each moment to hear the exultant clamor of the braves and to see them break cover at his back.

But soon he decided that they were content to hunt him down as certain beasts track their prey, slowly and inevitably. He hastened through the upland forest, taking advan-

tage of every bit of cover, and he saw no more of his pursuers; yet he *knew*, as a hunted wolf knows, that they hovered
close behind him, waiting their moment to strike him down
without risk to their own hides. Kane smiled bleakly and
without mirth. If it was to be a test of endurance, he would
see how savage thews compared with his own spring-steel
resilience. Let night come and he might yet give them the
slip. If not—Kane knew in his heart that the savage essence
of the Anglo-Saxon which chafed at his flight would make
him soon turn at bay, though his pursuers outnumbered
him a hundred to one.

The sun sank westward. Kane was hungry, for he had not
eaten since early morning when he wolfed down the last of
his dried meat. An occasional spring had given him water,
and once he thought he glimpsed the roof of a large hut far
away through the trees. But he gave it a wide berth. It was
hard to believe that this silent plateau was inhabited, but if it
were, the natives were doubtless as ferocious as those hunting him. Ahead of him the land grew rougher, with broken
boulders and steep slopes as he neared the lower reaches of
the brooding hills. And still no sight of his hunters except for
faint glimpses caught by wary backward glances—a drifting
shadow, the bending of the grass, the sudden straightening
of a trodden twig, a rustle of leaves. Why should they be so
cautious? Why did they not close in and have it over?

Night fell and Kane reached the first long slopes which
led upward to the foot of the hills which now brooded black
and menacing above him. They were his goal, where he
hoped to shake off his persistent foes at last, yet a nameless
aversion warned him away from them. They were pregnant

with hidden evil, repellent as the coil of a great sleeping serpent, glimpsed in the tall grass.

Darkness fell heavily. The stars winked redly in the thick heat of the tropic night. And Kane, halting for a moment in an unusually dense grove, beyond which the trees thinned out on the slopes, heard a stealthy movement that was not the night wind—for no breath of air stirred the heavy leaves. And even as he turned, there was a rush in the dark, under the trees. A shadow that merged with the shadows flung itself on Kane with a bestial mouthing and a rattle of iron, and the Englishman, parrying by the gleam of the stars on the weapon, felt his assailant duck into close quarters and meet him chest to chest. Lean wiry arms locked about him, pointed teeth gnashed at him as Kane returned the fierce grapple. His tattered shirt ripped beneath a jagged edge, and by blind chance Kane found and pinioned the hand that held the iron knife, and drew his own dirk, flesh crawling in anticipation of a spear in the back.

But even as the Englishman wondered why the others did not come to their comrade's aid, he threw all of his iron muscles into the single combat. Close-clinched they swayed and writhed in the darkness, each striving to drive his blade into the other's flesh, and as the superior strength of the white man began to assert itself, the cannibal howled like a rabid dog, tore and bit. A convulsive spin-wheel of effort pivoted them out into the starlit glade where Kane saw the ivory nose-ring and the pointed teeth that snapped beast-like at his throat. And simultaneously he forced back and down the hand that gripped his knife-wrist, and drove the dirk deep into the black ribs. The warrior screamed and the raw acrid scent of blood flooded the night air. And in that instant Kane was stunned by a sudden savage rush and beat of mighty wings that dashed him to earth, and the black man was torn from his grip and vanished with a scream of mortal agony. Kane leaped to his feet, shaken to his foundation. The dwindling scream of the wretched black sounded faintly *and from above him*.

Straining his eyes into the skies he thought he caught a glimpse of a shapeless and horrific Thing crossing the dim stars—in which the writhing limbs of a human mingled namelessly with great wings and a shadowy shape—but so quickly it was gone, he could not be sure.

And now he wondered if it were not all a nightmare. But groping in the grove he found the ju-ju stave with which he had parried the short stabbing spear which lay beside it. And here, if more proof was needed, was his long dirk, still stained with blood.

Wings! Wings in the night! The skeleton in the village of torn roofs—the mutilated black man whose wounds were not made with knife or spear and who died shrieking of wings. Surely those hills were the haunt of gigantic birds who made humanity their prey. Yet if birds, why had they not wholly devoured the black man on the stake? And Kane knew in his heart that no true bird ever cast such a shadow as he had seen flit across the stars.

He shrugged his shoulders, bewildered. The night was silent. Where were the rest of the cannibals who had followed him from their distant jungle? Had the fate of their comrade frightened them into flight? Kane looked to his pistols. Cannibals or no, he went not up into those dark hills that night.

Now he must sleep, if all the devils of the Elder World were on his track. A deep roaring to the westward warned him that beasts of prey were a-roam, and he walked rapidly down the rolling slopes until he came to a dense grove some distance from that in which he had fought the cannibal. He climbed high among the great branches until he found a thick crotch that would accommodate even his tall frame. The branches above would guard him from a sudden swoop of any winged thing, and if savages were lurking near, their clamber into the tree would warn him, for he slept lightly as a cat. As for serpents and leopards, they were chances he had taken a thousand times.

Solomon Kane slept and his dreams were vague, chaotic, haunted with a suggestion of pre-human evil and which at last merged into a vision vivid as a scene in waking life. Solomon dreamed he woke with a start, drawing a pistol—for so long had his life been that of the wolf, that reaching for a weapon was his natural reaction upon waking suddenly. And his dream was that a strange, shadowy thing had perched upon a great branch close by and gazed at him with greedy, luminous yellow eyes that seared into his brain. The dream-thing was tall and lean and strangely misshapen, so blended with the shadows that it seemed a shadow itself, tangible only in the narrow yellow eyes. And Kane dreamed he waited, spellbound, while uncertainty came into those eyes and then the creature walked out on the limb as a man would walk, raised great shadowy wings, sprang into space and vanished. Then Kane jerked upright, the mists of sleep fading.

In the dim starlight, under the arching Gothic-like branches, the tree was empty save for himself. Then it had been a dream, after all—yet it had been so vivid, so fraught with inhuman foulness—even now a faint scent like that exuded by birds of prey seemed to linger in the air. Kane strained his ears. He heard the sighing of the night-wind, the whisper of the leaves, the faraway roaring of a lion, but naught else. Again Solomon slept—while high above him a shadow wheeled against the stars, circling again and again as a vulture circles a dying wolf.

2. The Battle in the Sky

Dawn was spreading whitely over the eastern hills when Kane woke. The thought of his nightmare came to him and he wondered again at its vividness as he climbed down out of the tree. A nearby spring slaked his thirst and some fruit, rare in these highlands, eased his hunger.

Then he turned his face again to the hills. A finish fighter was Solomon Kane. Along that grim skyline dwelt some evil foe to the sons of men, and that mere fact was as much a challenge to the Puritan as had ever been a glove thrown in his face by some hot-headed gallant of Devon.

Refreshed by his night's sleep, he set out with his long easy stride, passing the grove that had witnessed the battle in the night, and coming into the region where the trees thinned at the foot of the slopes. Up these slopes he went, halting for a moment to gaze back over the way he had come. Now that he was above the plateau, he could easily make out a village in the distance—a cluster of mud-and-bamboo huts with one unusually large hut a short distance from the rest on a sort of low knoll.

And while he gazed, with a sudden rush of grisly wings the terror was upon him! Kane whirled, galvanized. All signs had pointed to the theory of a winged thing that hunted by night. He had not expected attack in broad daylight—but here a bat-like monster was swooping at him out of the very eye of the rising sun. Kane saw a spread of mighty wings, from which glared a horribly human face; then he drew and fired with unerring aim and the monster veered wildly in midair and came whirling and tumbling out of the sky to crash at his feet.

Kane leaned forward, pistol smoking in his hand, and gazed wide-eyed. Surely this thing was a demon out of the black pits of Hell, said the somber mind of the Puritan; yet a leaden ball had slain it. Kane shrugged his shoulders, baffled; he had never seen aught to approach this, though all his life had fallen in strange ways.

The thing was like a man, inhumanly tall and inhumanly thin; the head was long, narrow and hairless—the head of a predatory creature. The ears were small, close-set and queerly pointed. The eyes, set in death, were narrow, oblique and of a strange yellowish color. The nose was thin and hooked, like the beak of a bird of prey, the mouth a wide cruel gash, whose thin lips, writhed in a death snarl and flecked with foam, disclosed wolfish fangs.

The creature, which was naked and hairless, was not unlike a human being in other ways. The shoulders were broad and powerful, the neck long and lean. The arms were long and muscular, the thumb being set beside the fingers after the manner of the great apes. Fingers and thumbs were armed with heavy hooked talons. The chest was curiously misshapen, the breastbone jutting out like the keel of a ship, the ribs curving back from it. The legs were long and wiry with huge, hand-like, prehensile feet, the great toe set opposite the rest like a man's thumb. The claws on the toes were merely long nails.

But the most curious feature of this curious creature was on its back. A pair of great wings, shaped much like the wings of a moth but with a bony frame and of leathery substance, grew from its shoulders, beginning at a point just back and above where the arms joined the shoulders, and extending halfway to the narrow hips. These wings, Kane reckoned, would measure some eighteen feet from tip to tip.

He laid hold on the creature, involuntarily shuddering at the slick, hard leather-like feel of the skin, and half-lifted it. The weight was little more than half as much as it would have been in a man the same height—some six and a half feet. Evidently the bones were of a peculiar bird-like structure and the flesh consisted almost entirely of stringy muscles.

Kane stepped back, surveying the thing again. Then his dream had been no dream after all—that foul thing or another like it had in grisly reality lighted in the tree beside him—a whir of mighty wings! A sudden rush through the sky! Even as Kane whirled he realized he had committed the jungle-farer's unpardonable crime—he had allowed his astonishment and curiosity to throw him off guard. Already a winged fiend was at his throat and there was no time to draw and fire his other pistol. Kane saw, in a maze of thrashing wings, a devilish, semi-human face—he felt those wings battering at him—he felt cruel talons sink deep into his breast; then he was dragged off his feet and felt empty space beneath him.

The winged man had wrapped his limbs about the Englishman's legs, and the talons he had driven into Kane's breast muscles held like fanged vises. The wolf-like fangs drove at Kane's throat but the Puritan gripped the bony throat and thrust back the grisly head, while with his right hand he strove to draw his dirk. The bird-man was mounting slowly and a fleeting glance showed Kane that they were already high above the trees. The Englishman did not hope to survive this battle in the sky, for even if he slew his foe, he would be dashed to death in the fall. But with the innate ferocity of the fighting Anglo-Saxon he set himself grimly to take his captor with him.

Holding those keen fangs at bay, Kane managed to draw his dirk and he plunged it deep into the body of the monster. The bat-man veered wildly and a rasping, raucous screech burst from his half-throttled throat. He floundered wildly, beating frantically with his great wings, bowing his back and twisting his head fiercely in a vain effort to free it and sink home his deadly fangs. He sank the talons of one hand agonizingly deeper and deeper into Kane's breast muscles, while with the other he tore at his foe's head and body. But the Englishman, gashed and bleeding, with the silent and tenacious savagery of a bulldog sank his fingers deeper into the lean neck and drove his dirk home again and again, while far below awed eyes watched the fiendish battle that was raging at that dizzy height.

They had drifted out over the plateau, and the fast-weakening wings of the bat-man barely supported their weight. They were sinking earthward swiftly, but Kane, blinded with blood and battle-fury, knew nothing of this. With a great piece of his scalp hanging loose, his chest and shoulders cut and ripped, the world had become a blind, red thing in which he was aware of but one sensation—the bulldog urge to kill his foe. Now the feeble and spasmodic beating of the dying monster's wings held them hovering for an instant above a thick grove of gigantic trees, while Kane felt the grip of claws and twining limbs grow weaker and the slashing of the talons become a futile flailing.

With a last burst of power he drove the reddened dirk straight through the breastbone and felt a convulsive tremor run through the creature's frame. The great wings fell limp—and victor and vanquished dropped headlong and plummet-like earthward.

Through a red wave Kane saw the waving branches rushing up to meet them—he felt them flail his face and tear at his clothing, as still locked in that death-clinch he rushed downward through leaves which eluded his vainly grasping hand; then his head crashed against a great limb and an endless abyss of blackness engulfed him.

3. The People in the Shadow

Through colossal, black basaltic corridors of night, Solomon Kane fled for a thousand years. Gigantic winged demons, horrific in the utter darkness, swept over him with a rush of great bat-like pinions and in the blackness he fought with them as a cornered rat fights a vampire bat, while fleshless jaws drooled fearful blasphemies and horrid secrets in his ears, and the skulls of men rolled under his groping feet.

Solomon Kane came back suddenly from the land of delirium and his first sight of sanity was that of a fat, kindly black face bending over him. Kane saw he was in a roomy, clean and well-ventilated hut, while from a cooking-pot bubbling outside wafted savory scents. Kane realized he was ravenously hungry. And he was strangely weak, and the hand he lifted to his bandaged head shook and its bronze was dimmed.

The fat man and another, a tall, gaunt, grim-faced warrior, bent over him, and the fat man said: "He is awake, Kuroba, and of sound mind." The gaunt man nodded and called something which was answered from without.

"What is this place?" asked Kane, in a language he had learned, akin to the dialect the black had used. "How long have I lain here?"

"This is the last village of Bogonda." The fat black pressed him back with hands gentle as a woman's. "We found you lying beneath the trees on the slopes, badly wounded and senseless. You have raved in delirium for many days. Now eat."

A lithe young warrior entered with a wooden bowl full of steaming food and Kane ate ravenously.

"He is like a leopard, Kuroba," said the fat man admiringly. "Not one in a thousand would have lived with his wounds."

"Aye," returned the other. "And he slew the akaana that rent him, Goru."

Kane struggled to his elbows. "Goru?" he cried fiercely. "The priest who binds men to stakes for devils to eat?"

And he strove to rise so that he could strangle the fat man, but his weakness swept over him like a wave, the hut swam dizzily to his eyes and he sank back panting, where he soon fell into a sound, natural sleep.

Later he awoke and found a slim young girl, named Nayela, watching him. She fed him, and feeling much stronger, Kane asked questions which she answered shyly but intelligently. This was Bogonda, ruled by Kuroba the chief and Goru the priest. None in Bogonda had ever seen or heard of a white man before. She counted the days Kane had lain helpless, and he was amazed. But such a battle as he had been through was enough to kill an ordinary man. He wondered that no bones had been broken, but the girl said the branches had broken his fall and he had landed on the body of the akaana. He asked for Goru, and the fat priest came to him, bringing Kane's weapons.

"Some we found with you where you lay," said Goru, "some by the body of the akaana you slew with the weapon which speaks in fire and smoke. You must be a god—yet the gods bleed not and you have just all but died. Who are you?"

"I am no god," Kane answered, "but a man like yourself, albeit my skin be white. I come from a far land amid the sea, which land, mind ye, is the fairest and noblest of all lands. My name is Solomon Kane and I am a landless wanderer. From the lips of a dying man I first heard your name. Yet your face seemeth kindly."

A shadow crossed the eyes of the shaman and he hung his head.

"Rest and grow strong, oh man, or god or whatever you

be," said he, "and in time you will learn of the ancient curse that rests upon this ancient land."

And in the days that followed, while Kane recovered and grew strong with the wild beast vitality that was his, Goru and Kuroba sat and spoke to him at length, telling him many curious things.

Their tribe was not aboriginal here, but had come upon the plateau a hundred and fifty years before, giving it the name of their former home. They had once been a powerful tribe in Old Bogonda, on a great river far to the south. But tribal wars broke their power, and at last before a concerted uprising, the whole tribe gave way, and Goru repeated legends of that great flight of a thousand miles through jungle and swampland harried at every step by cruel foes.

At last, hacking their way through a country of ferocious cannibals, they found themselves safe from man's attack— but prisoners in a trap from which neither they nor their descendants could ever escape. They were in the horror-country of Akaana, and Goru said his ancestors came to understand the jeering laughter of the man-eaters who had hounded them to the very borders of the plateau.

The Bogondi found a fertile country with good water and plenty of game. There were numbers of goats and a species of wild pig that throve here in great abundance. At first the black people ate these pigs, but later they spared them for a very good reason. The grasslands between plateau and jungle swarmed with antelopes, buffaloes and the like, and there were many lions. Lions also roamed the plateau, but Bogonda meant "Lion-slayer" in their tongue and it was not many moons before the remnants of the great cats took to the lower levels. But it was not lions they had to fear, as Goru's ancestors soon learned.

Finding that the cannibals would not come past the savannas, they rested from their long trek and built two villages—Upper and Lower Bogonda. Kane was in Upper Bogonda; he had seen the ruins of the lower village. But soon they found that they had strayed into a country of nightmares with dripping fangs and talons. They heard the beat of mighty wings at night, and saw horrific shadows cross the stars and loom against the moon. Children began to disappear and at last a young hunter strayed off into the hills, where night overtook him. And in the gray light of dawn a mangled, half-devoured corpse fell from the skies into the village street and a whisper of ogreish laughter from high above froze the horrified onlookers. Then a little later the full horror of their position burst upon the Bogondi.

At first the winged men were afraid of the black people. They hid themselves and ventured from their caverns only at night. Then they grew bolder. In the full daylight, a warrior shot one with an arrow, but the fiends had learned they could slay a human and its death scream brought a score of the devils dropping from the skies, who tore the slayer to pieces in full sight of the tribe.

The Bogondi then prepared to leave that devil's country and a hundred warriors went up into the hills to find a pass. They found steep walls, up which a man must climb laboriously, and they found the cliffs honeycombed with caves where the winged men dwelt.

Then was fought the first pitched battle between men and bat-men and it resulted in a crushing victory for the monsters. The bows and spears of the black people proved futile before the swoops of the taloned fiends, and of all that hundred that went up into the hills, not one survived; for the akaanas hunted down those that fled and dragged down the last one within bowshot of the upper village.

Then it was that the Bogondi, seeing they could not hope to win through the hills, sought to fight their way out again the way they had come. But a great horde of cannibals met them in the grasslands and in a great battle that lasted nearly all day, hurled them back, broken and defeated. And Goru said while the battle raged, the skies were thronged with hideous shapes, circling above and laughing their fearful mirth to see men die wholesale.

So the survivors of those two battles, licking their wounds, bowed to the inevitable with the fatalistic philosophy of the black man. Some fifteen hundred men, women and children remained, and they built their huts, tilled the soil and lived stolidly in the shadow of the nightmare.

In those days there were many of the bird-people, and they might have wiped out the Bogondi utterly, had they wished. No one warrior could cope with an akaana, for he was stronger than a human, he struck as a hawk strikes, and if he missed, his wings carried him out of reach of a counter-blow. Here Kane interrupted to ask why the blacks did not make war on the demons with arrows. But Goru answered that it took a quick and accurate archer to strike an akaana in midair at all and so tough were their hides that unless the arrow struck squarely it would not penetrate. Kane knew that the blacks were very indifferent bowmen and that they pointed their shafts with chipped stone, bone or hammered iron almost as soft as copper; he thought of Poitiers and Agincourt and wished grimly for a file of stout English archers—or a rank of musketeers.

But Goru said the akaanas did not seem to wish to destroy the Bogondi utterly. Their chief food consisted of the little pigs which then swarmed the plateau, and young goats. Sometimes they went out on the savannas for antelope, but they distrusted the open country and feared the lions. Nor did they haunt the jungles beyond, for the trees grew too close for the spread of their wings. They kept to the hills and the plateau—and what lay beyond those hills none in Bogonda knew.

The akaanas allowed the black folk to inhabit the plateau much as men allow wild animals to thrive, or stock lakes with fish—for their own pleasure. The bat-people, said Goru, had a strange and grisly sense of humor which was tickled by the sufferings of a howling human. Those grim hills had echoed to cries that turned men's hearts to ice.

But for many years, Goru said, once the Bogondi learned not to resist their masters, the akaanas were content to snatch up a baby from time to time, or devour a young girl strayed from the village or a youth whom night caught outside the walls. The bat-folk distrusted the village; they circled high above it but did not venture within. There the Bogondi were safe until late years.

Goru said that the akaanas were fast dying out; once there had been hope that the remnants of his race would outlast them—in which event, he said fatalistically, the cannibals would undoubtedly come up from the jungle and put the survivors in the cooking-pots. Now he doubted if there were more than a hundred and fifty akaanas altogether. Kane asked him why did not the warriors then sally forth on a great hunt and destroy the devils utterly, and Goru smiled a bitter smile and repeated his remarks about the prowess of the bat-people in battle. Moreover, said he, the whole tribe of Bogonda numbered only about four hundred souls now, and the bat-people were their only protection against the cannibals to the west.

Goru said the tribe had thinned more in the past thirty years than in all the years previous. As the numbers of the akaanas dwindled, their hellish savagery increased. They seized more and more of the Bogondi to torture and devour in their grim black caves high up in the hills, and Goru spoke of sudden raids on hunting-parties and toilers in the plantain fields and of the nights made ghastly by horrible screams and gibberings from the dark hills, and blood-freezing laughter that was half-human; of dismembered limbs and gory grinning heads flung from the skies to fall in the shuddering village, and of grisly feasts among the stars.

Then came drought, Goru said, and a great famine. Many of the springs dried up and the crops of rice and yams and plantains failed. The gnus, deer and buffaloes which had formed the main part of Bogonda's meat diet withdrew to the jungle in quest of water, and the lions, their hunger overcoming their fear of man, ranged into the uplands. Many of the tribe died and the rest were driven by hunger to eat the pigs which were the natural prey of the bat-people. This angered the akaanas and thinned the pigs. Famine, Bogondi and the lions destroyed all the goats and half the pigs.

At last the famine was past, but the damage was done.

Of all the great droves which once swarmed the plateau, only a remnant was left and these were wary and hard to catch. The Bogondi had eaten the pigs, so the akaanas ate the Bogondi. Life became a hell for the black people, and the lower village, numbering now only some hundred and fifty souls, rose in revolt. Driven to frenzy by repeated outrages, they turned on their masters. An akaana lighting in the very streets to steal a child was set on and shot to death with arrows. And the people of Lower Bogonda drew into their huts and waited for their doom.

And in the night, said Goru, it came. The akaanas had overcome their distrust of the huts. The full flock of them swarmed down from the hills, and Upper Bogonda awoke to hear the fearful cataclysm of screams and blasphemies that marked the end of the other village. All night Goru's people had lain sweating in terror, not daring to move, harkening to the howling and gibbering that rent the night; at last these sounds ceased, Goru said, wiping the cold sweat from his brow, but sounds of grisly and obscene feasting still haunted the night with demon's mockery.

In the early dawn Goru's people saw the hell-flock winging back to their hills, like demons flying back to Hell through the dawn, and they flew slowly and heavily, like gorged vultures. Later the people dared to steal down to the accursed village, and what they found there sent them shrieking away; and to that day, Goru said, no man passed within three bowshots of that silent horror. And Kane nodded in understanding, his cold eyes more somber than ever.

For many days after that, Goru said, the people waited in quaking fear, and finally in desperation of fear, which breeds unspeakable cruelty, the tribe cast lots and the loser was bound to a stake between the two villages, in hopes the akaanas would recognize this as a token of submission so that the people of Bogonda might escape the fate of their kinsmen. This custom, said Goru, had been borrowed from the cannibals who in old times worshipped the akaanas and offered a human sacrifice at each moon. But chance had shown them that the akaana could be killed, so they ceased to worship him—at least that was Goru's deduction, and he explained at much length that no mortal thing is worthy of real adoration, however evil or powerful it may be.

His own ancestors had made occasional sacrifices to placate the winged devils, but until lately it had not been a regular custom. Now it was necessary; the akaanas expected it, and each moon they chose from their waning numbers a strong young man or a girl whom they bound to the stake. Kane watched Goru's face closely as he spoke of his sorrow for this unspeakable necessity, and the Englishman realized the priest was sincere. Kane shuddered at the thought of a tribe of human beings thus passing slowly but surely into the maws of a race of monsters.

Kane spoke of the wretch he had seen, and Goru nodded, pain in his soft eyes. For a day and a night he had been hanging there, while the akaanas glutted their vile torture-lust on his quivering, agonized flesh. Thus far the sacrifices had kept doom from the village. The remaining pigs furnished sustenance for the dwindling akaanas, together with an occasional baby snatched up, and they were content to have their nameless sport with the single victim each moon.

A thought came to Kane.

"The cannibals never come up into the plateau?"

Goru shook his head; safe in their jungle, they never raided past the savannas.

"But they hunted me to the very foot of the hills."

Again Goru shook his head. There was only one cannibal; they had found his footprints. Evidently a single warrior, bolder than the rest, had allowed his passion for the chase to overcome his fear of the grisly plateau and had paid the penalty. Kane's teeth came together with a vicious snap which ordinarily took the place of profanity with him. He was stung by the thought of fleeing so long from a single enemy. No wonder that enemy had followed so cautiously, waiting until dark to attack. But, asked Kane, why had the akaana seized the black man instead of himself—and why had he not been attacked by the bat-man who alighted in his tree that night?

The cannibal was bleeding, Goru answered; the scent called the bat-fiend to attack, for they scented raw blood as far as vultures. And they were very wary. They had never seen a man like Kane, who showed no fear. Surely they had decided to spy on him, take him off guard before they struck.

Who were these creatures? Kane asked. Goru shrugged his shoulders. They were there when his ancestors came, who had never heard of them before they saw them. There was no intercourse with the cannibals, so they could learn nothing from them. The akaanas lived in caves, naked like beasts; they knew nothing of fire and ate only fresh raw meat. But they had a language of a sort and acknowledged a king among them. Many died in the great famine when the stronger ate the weaker. They were vanishing swiftly; of late years no females or young had been observed among them. When these males died at last, there would be no more akaanas; but Bogonda, observed Goru, was doomed already, unless—he looked strangely and wistfully at Kane. But the Puritan was deep in thought.

Among the swarm of native legends he had heard on his wanderings, one now stood out. Long, long ago, an old, old ju-ju man had told him, winged devils came flying out of the north and passed over his country, vanishing in the maze of the jungle-haunted south. And the ju-ju man related an old, old legend concerning these creatures—that once they had abode in myriad numbers far on a great lake of bitter water many moons to the north, and ages and ages ago a chieftain and his warriors fought them with bows and arrows and slew many, driving the rest into the south. The name of the chief was N'Yasunna and he owned a great war canoe with many oars driving it swiftly through the bitter water.

And now a cold wind blew suddenly on Solomon Kane, as if from a Door opened suddenly on Outer gulfs of Time and Space. For now he realized the truth of that garbled myth, and the truth of an older, grimmer legend. For what was the great bitter lake but the Mediterranean Ocean and who was the chief N'Yasunna but the hero Jason, who conquered the harpies and drove them—not alone into the Strophades Isles but into Africa as well? The old pagan tale was true then, Kane thought dizzily, shrinking aghast from the strange realm of grisly possibilities this opened up. For if this myth of the harpies were a reality, what of the other legends—the Hydra, the centaurs, the chimera, Medusa, Pan and the satyrs? All those myths of antiquity—behind them did there lie and lurk nightmare realities with slavering fangs and talons steeped in shuddersome evil? Africa, the Dark Continent, land of shadows and horror, of bewitchment and sorcery, into which all evil things had been banished before the growing light of the western world!

Kane came out of his reveries with a start. Goru was tugging gently and timidly at his sleeve.

"Save us from the akaanas!" said Goru. "If you be not a god, there is the power of a god in you! You bear in your hand the mighty ju-ju stave which has in times gone by been the scepter of fallen empires and the staff of mighty priests. And you have weapons which speak death in fire and smoke—for our young men watched and saw you slay two akaanas. We will make you king—god—what you will! More than a moon has passed since you came into Bogonda and the time for the sacrifice is gone by, but the bloody stake stands bare. The akaanas shun the village where you lie; they steal no more babes from us. We have thrown off their yoke because our trust is in you!"

Kane clasped his temples with his hands. "You know not what you ask!" he cried. "God knoweth it is in my deepest heart to rid the land of this evil, but I am no god. With my pistols I can slay a few of the fiends, but I have but a little powder left. Had I great store of powder and ball, and the musket I shattered in the vampire-haunted Hills of the Dead, then indeed would there be a rare hunting. But even if I slew all these fiends, what of the cannibals?"

"They too will fear you!" cried old Kuroba, while the girl Nayela and the lad, Loga, who was to have been the next sacrifice, gazed at him with their souls in their eyes. Kane dropped his chin on his fist and sighed.

"Yet will I stay here in Bogonda all the rest of my life if ye think I be protection to the people."

So Solomon Kane stayed at the village of Bogonda of the Shadow. The people were a kindly folk, whose natural sprightliness and fun-loving spirits were subdued and saddened by long dwelling in the Shadow. But now they had taken new heart by the white man's coming and it wrenched Kane's heart to note the pathetic trust they placed in him. Now they sang in the plantain fields and danced about the fires, and gazed at him with adoring faith in their eyes. But Kane, cursing his own helplessness, knew how futile would be his fancied protection if the winged fiends swept suddenly out of the skies.

But he stayed in Bogonda. In his dreams the gulls wheeled above the cliffs of old Devon carved in the clean, blue, wind-whipped skies, and in the day the call of the unknown lands beyond Bogonda clawed at his heart with fierce yearning. But he abode in Bogonda and racked his brains for a plan. He sat and gazed for hours at the ju-ju stave, hoping in desperation that black magic would aid him, where the white man's mind failed. But N'Longa's ancient gift gave him no aid. Once he had summoned the Slave Coast shaman to him across leagues of intervening space—but it was only when confronted with supernatural manifestations that N'Longa could come to him, and these harpies were not supernatural.

The germ of an idea began to grow at the back of Kane's mind, but he discarded it. It had to do with a great trap—

and how could the akaanas be trapped? The roaring of lions played a grim accompaniment to his brooding meditations. As man dwindled on the plateau, the hunting beasts who feared only the spears of the hunters were beginning to gather. Kane laughed bitterly. It was not lions, that might be hunted down and slain singly, that he had to deal with.

At some little distance from the village stood the great hut of Goru, once a council hall. This hut was full of many strange fetishes, which Goru said with a helpless wave of his fat hands, were strong magic against evil spirits but scant protection against winged hellions of gristle and bone and flesh.

4. *The Madness of Solomon*

Kane woke suddenly from a dreamless sleep. A hideous medley of screams burst horrific in his ears. Outside his hut, people were dying in the night, horribly, as cattle die in the shambles. He had slept, as always, with his weapons buckled on him. Now he bounded to the door, and something fell mouthing and slavering at his feet to grasp his knees in a convulsive grip and gibber incoherent pleas. In the faint light of a smoldering fire nearby, Kane in horror recognized the face of the youth Loga, now frightfully torn and drenched in blood, already freezing into a death mask. The night was full of fearful sounds, inhuman howlings mingled with the whisper of mighty wings, the tearing of thatch and a ghastly demon-laughter. Kane freed himself from the locked dead arms and sprang to the dying fire. He could make out only a confused and vague maze of fleeing forms, and darting shapes, the shift and blur of dark wings against the stars.

He snatched up a brand and thrust it against the thatch of his hut—and as the flame leaped up and showed him the scene he stood frozen and aghast. Red, howling doom had fallen on Bogonda. Winged monsters raced screaming through her streets, wheeled above the heads of the fleeing people, or tore apart the hut thatches to get at the gibbering victims within.

With a choked cry the Englishman woke from his trance of horror, drew and fired at a darting flame-eyed shadow which fell at his feet with a shattered skull. And Kane gave tongue to one deep, fierce roar and bounded into the melee, all the berserk fury of his heathen Saxon ancestors bursting into terrible being.

Dazed and bewildered by the sudden attack, cowed by long years of submission, the Bogondi were incapable of combined resistance and for the most part died like sheep. Some, maddened by desperation, fought back, but their arrows went wild or glanced from the tough wings while the devilish agility of the creatures made spear-thrust and ax-stroke uncertain. Leaping from the ground they avoided the blows of their victims and sweeping down upon their shoulders dashed them to earth, where fang and talon did their crimson work.

Kane saw old Kuroba, gaunt and bloodstained, at bay against a hut wall with his foot on the neck of a monster who had not been quick enough. The grim-faced old chief wielded a two-handed ax in great sweeping blows that for the moment held back the screeching onset of half a dozen of the devils. Kane was leaping to his aid when a low, pitiful whimper checked him. The girl Nayela writhed weakly, prone in the bloody dust, while on her back a vulture-like thing crouched and tore. Her dulling eyes sought the face of the Englishman in anguished appeal. Kane ripped out a bitter oath and fired point-blank. The winged devil pitched backward with an abhorrent screeching and a wild flutter of dying wings and Kane bent to the dying girl, who whimpered and kissed his hands with uncertain lips as he cradled her head in his arms. Her eyes set.

Kane laid the body gently down, looking for Kuroba. He saw only a huddled cluster of grisly shapes that sucked and tore at something between them. And Kane went mad. With a scream that cut through the inferno he bounded up, slaying even as he rose. Even in the act of lunging up from bent knee he drew and thrust, transfixing a vulture-like throat. Then whipping out his rapier as the thing floundered and twitched in its death struggles, the raging Puritan charged forward seeking new victims.

On all sides of him the people of Bogonda were dying hideously. They fought futilely or they fled and the demons coursed them down as a hawk courses a hare. They ran into the huts and the fiends rent the thatch or burst the door, and what took place in those huts was mercifully hidden from Kane's eyes. And to the frantic white man's horror-distorted brain it seemed that he alone was responsible. The black folk had trusted him to save them. They had withheld the sacrifice and defied their grim masters and now they were paying the horrible penalty and he was unable to save them. In the agony-dimmed eyes turned toward him Kane quaffed the black dregs of the bitter cup. It was not anger or the vindictiveness of fear. It was hurt and a stunned reproach. He was their god and he had failed them.

Now he ravened through the massacre and the fiends avoided him, turning to the easy black victims. But Kane was not to be denied. In a red haze that was not of the burning hut, he saw a culminating horror; a harpy gripped a writhing naked thing that had been a woman and the wolfish fangs gorged deep. As Kane sprang, thrusting, the bat-man dropped his yammering, mowing prey and soared aloft. But Kane dropped his rapier and with the bound of a blood-mad panther caught the demon's throat and locked his iron legs about its lower body.

Again he found himself battling in midair, but this time only above the roofs of the huts. Terror had entered the cold brain of the harpy. He did not fight to hold and slay; he wished only to be rid of this silent, clinging thing that stabbed so savagely for his life. He floundered wildly, screaming abhorrently and thrashing with his wings, then as Kane's dirk bit deeper, dipped suddenly sidewise and fell headlong.

The thatch of a hut broke their fall, and Kane and the dying harpy crashed through to land on a writhing mass on the hut floor. In the lurid flickering of the burning hut outside, that vaguely lighted the hut into which he had fallen, Kane saw a deed of brain-shaking horror being enacted—red dripping fangs in a yawning gash of a mouth, and a crimson travesty of a human form that still writhed with agonized life. Then in the maze of madness that held him, his steel fingers closed on the fiend's throat in a grip that no tearing of talons or hammering of wings could loosen, until he felt the horrid life flow out from under his fingers and the bony neck hung broken.

And still outside the red madness of slaughter continued. Kane bounded up, his hand closing blindly on the haft of some weapon, and as he leaped from the hut a harpy soared from under his very feet. It was an ax that Kane had snatched up, and he dealt a stroke that spattered the demon's brains like water. He sprang forward, stumbling over bodies and parts of bodies, blood streaming from a dozen wounds, and then halted baffled and screaming with rage.

The bat-people were taking to the air. No longer would they face this white-skinned madman who in his insanity was more terrible than they. But they went not alone into the upper regions. In their lustful talons they bore writhing, screaming forms, and Kane, raging to and fro with his dripping ax, found himself alone in a corpse-choked village.

He threw back his head to shriek his hate at the fiends above him and he felt warm, thick drops fall into his face, while the shadowy skies were filled with screams of agony and the laughter of monsters. And Kane's last vestige of reason snapped as the sounds of that ghastly feast in the skies filled the night and the blood that rained from the stars fell into his face. He gibbered to and fro, screaming chaotic blasphemies.

And was he not a symbol of Man, staggering among the tooth-marked bones and severed grinning heads of humans, brandishing a futile ax, and screaming incoherent hate at the grisly, winged shapes of Night that make him their prey, chuckling in demoniac triumph above him and dripping into his mad eyes the pitiful blood of their human victims?

5. *The White-skinned Conqueror*

A shuddering, white-faced dawn crept over the black hills to shiver above the red shambles that had been the village of Bogonda. The huts stood intact, except for the one which had sunk to smoldering coals, but the thatches of many were torn. Dismembered bones, half or wholly stripped of flesh, lay in the streets, and some were splintered as though they had been dropped from a great height.

It was a realm of the dead where was but one sign of life. Solomon Kane leaned on his blood-clotted ax and gazed upon the scene with dull, mad eyes. He was grimed and clotted with half-dried blood from long gashes on chest, face and shoulders, but he paid no heed to his hurts.

The people of Bogonda had not died alone. Seventeen harpies lay among the bones. Six of these Kane had slain. The rest had fallen before the frantic dying desperation of the black people. But it was poor toll to take in return. Of the four hundred odd people of Upper Bogonda, not one had lived to see the dawn. And the harpies were gone—back to their caves in the black hills, gorged to repletion.

With slow, mechanical steps Kane went about gathering up his weapons. He found his sword, dirk, pistols and the ju-ju stave. He left the main village and went up the slope to the great hut of Goru. And there he halted, stung by a new horror. The ghastly humor of the harpies had prompted a delicious jest. Above the hut door stared the severed head of Goru. The fat cheeks were shrunken, the lips lolled in an aspect of horrified idiocy, and the eyes stared like a

45

hurt child. And in those dead eyes Kane saw wonder and reproach.

Kane looked at the shambles that had been Bogonda, and he looked at the death mask of Goru. And he lifted his clenched fists above his head, and with glaring eyes raised and writhing lips flecked with froth, he cursed the sky and the earth and the spheres above and below. He cursed the cold stars, the blazing sun, the mocking moon and the whisper of the wind. He cursed all fates and destinies, all that he had loved or hated, the silent cities beneath the seas, the past ages and the future eons. In one soul-shaking burst of blasphemy he cursed the gods and devils who make mankind their sport, and he cursed Man who lives blindly on and blindly offers his back to the iron-hoofed feet of his gods.

Then as breath failed he halted, panting. From the lower reaches sounded the deep roaring of a lion and into the eyes of Solomon Kane came a crafty gleam. He stood long, as one frozen, and out of his madness grew a desperate plan. And he silently recanted his blasphemy, for if the brazen-hoofed gods made Man for their sport and plaything, they also gave him a brain that holds craft and cruelty greater than any other living thing.

"There you shall bide," said Solomon Kane to the head of Goru. "The sun will wither you and the cold dews of night will shrivel you. But I will keep the kites from you and your eyes shall see the fall of your slayers. Aye, I could not save the people of Bogonda, but by the God of my race, I can avenge them. Man is the sport and sustenance of titanic beings of Night and Horror whose giant wings hover ever above him. But even evil things may come to an end—and watch ye, Goru."

In the days that followed Kane labored mightily, beginning with the first gray light of dawn and toiling on past sunset, into the white moonlight till he fell and slept the sleep of utter exhaustion. He snatched food as he worked and he gave his wounds absolutely no heed, scarcely being aware that they healed of themselves. He went down into the lower levels and cut bamboo, great stacks of long, tough stalks. He cut thick branches of trees, and tough vines to serve as ropes. And with this material he reinforced the walls and roof of Goru's hut. He set the bamboos deep in the earth, hard against the wall, and interwove and twined them, binding them fast with the vines that were pliant and tough as cords. The long branches he made fast along the thatch, binding them close together. When he had finished, an elephant could scarcely have burst through the walls.

The lions had come into the plateau in great quantities and the herds of little pigs dwindled fast. Those the lions spared, Kane slew, and tossed to the jackals. This racked Kane's heart, for he was a kindly man and this wholesale slaughter, even of pigs who would fall prey to hunting beasts anyhow, grieved him. But it was part of his plan of vengeance and he steeled his heart.

The days stretched into weeks. Kane toiled by day and by night, and between his stints he talked to the shriveled, mummied head of Goru, whose eyes, strangely enough, did not change in the blaze of the sun or the haunt of the moon, but retained their lifelike expression. When the memory of those lunacy-haunted days had become only a vague nightmare, Kane wondered if, as it had seemed to him, Goru's dried lips had moved in answer, speaking strange and mysterious things.

Kane saw the akaanas wheeling against the sky at a distance, but they did not come near, even when he slept in the great hut, pistols at hand. They feared his power to deal death with smoke and thunder. At first he noted that they flew sluggishly, gorged with the flesh they had eaten on that red night, and the bodies they had borne to their caves. But as the weeks passed they appeared leaner and leaner and ranged far afield in search of food. And Kane laughed, deeply and madly. This plan of his would never have worked before, but now there were no humans to fill the bellies of the harpy-folk. And there were no more pigs. In all the plateau there were no creatures for the bat-people to eat. Why they did not range east of the hills, Kane thought he knew. That must be a region of thick jungle like the country to the west. He saw them fly into the grassland for antelopes and he saw the lions take toll of them. After all, the akaanas were weak beings among the hunters, strong enough only to slay pigs and deer—and humans.

At last they began to soar close to him at night and he saw their greedy eyes glaring at him through the gloom. He judged the time was ripe. Huge buffaloes, too big and ferocious for the bat-people to slay, had strayed up into the plateau to ravage the deserted fields of the dead black people. Kane cut one of these out of the herd and drove him, with shouts and volleys of stones, to the hut of Goru. It was a tedious, dangerous task, and time and again Kane barely escaped the surly bull's sudden charges, but persevered and at last shot the beast before the hut.

A strong west wind was blowing and Kane flung handfuls of blood into the air for the scent to waft to the harpies in the hills. He cut the bull to pieces and carried its quarters into the hut, then managed to drag the huge trunk itself inside. Then he retired into the thick trees nearby and waited.

He had not long to wait. The morning air filled suddenly with the beat of many wings and a hideous flock alighted before the hut of Goru. All of the beasts—or men—seemed to be there, and Kane gazed in wonder at the tall, strange creatures, so like to humanity and yet so unlike—the veritable demons of priestly legend. They folded their wings like cloaks about them as they walked upright and they talked to one another in a strident crackling voice that had nothing of the human in it. No, these things were not men, Kane decided. They were the materialization of some ghastly jest of Nature—some travesty of the world's infancy when Creation was an experiment. Perhaps they were the offspring of a forbidden and obscene mating of man and beast; more likely they were a freakish offshoot on the branch of evolution—for Kane had long ago dimly sensed a truth in the heretical theories of the ancient philosophers, that Man is but a higher beast. And if Nature made many strange beasts in the past ages, why should she not have experimented with monstrous forms of mankind? Surely Man as Kane knew him was not the first of his breed to walk the earth, nor yet to be the last.

Now the harpies hesitated, with their natural distrust for a building, and some soared to the roof and tore at the thatch. But Kane had built well. They returned to earth and at last, driven beyond endurance by the smell of raw blood and the sight of the flesh within, one of them ventured inside. In an instant all were crowded into the great hut, tearing ravenously at the meat, and when the last one was within, Kane reached out a hand and jerked a long vine which tripped the catch that held the door he had built. It fell with a crash and the bar he had fashioned dropped into place. That door would hold against the charge of a wild bull.

Kane came from his covert and scanned the sky. Some hundred and forty harpies had entered the hut. He saw no more winging through the skies, and believed it safe to suppose he had the whole flock trapped. Then with a cruel, brooding smile, Kane struck flint and steel to a pile of dead leaves next the wall. Within sounded an uneasy mumbling as the creatures realized that they were prisoners. A thin wisp of smoke curled upward and a flicker of red followed it; the whole heap burst into flame and the dry bamboo caught.

A few moments later the whole side of the wall was ablaze. The fiends inside scented the smoke and grew restless. Kane heard them cackling wildly and clawing at the walls. He grinned savagely, bleakly and without mirth. Now a veer of the wind drove the flames around the wall and up over the thatch—with a roar the whole hut caught and leaped into flame. From within sounded a fearful pandemonium. Kane heard bodies crash against the walls, which shook to the impact but held. The horrid screams were music to his soul, and brandishing his arms, he answered them with screams of fearful, soul-shaking laughter. The cataclysm of horror rose unbearably, paling the tumult of the flames. Then it dwindled to a medley of strangled gibbering and gasps as the flames ate in and the smoke thickened. An intolerable scent of burning flesh pervaded the atmosphere, and had there been room in Kane's brain for aught else than insane triumph, he would have shuddered to realize that the scent was of that nauseating and indescribable odor that only human flesh emits when burning.

From the thick cloud of smoke Kane saw a mowing, gibbering thing emerge through the shredding roof and flap slowly and agonizingly upward on fearfully burned wings. Calmly he aimed and fired, and the scorched and blinded thing tumbled back into the flaming mass just as the walls crashed in. To Kane it seemed that Goru's crumbling face, vanishing in the smoke, split suddenly in a wide grin and a sudden shout of exultant human laughter mingled eerily in the roar of the flames. But the smoke and an insane brain plays queer tricks.

Kane stood with the ju-ju stave in one hand and the smoking pistol in the other, above the smoldering ruins that hid forever from the sight of man the last of those terrible, semi-human monsters whom another white-skinned hero had banished from Europe in an unknown age. Kane stood, an unconscious statue of triumph—the ancient empires fall, the dark-skinned peoples fade and even the demons of antiquity gasp their last, but over all stands the Aryan barbarian, white-skinned, cold-eyed, dominant, the supreme fighting man of the earth, whether he be clad in wolf-hide and horned helmet, or boots and doublet—whether he bear in his hand battle-ax or rapier—whether he be called Dorian, Saxon or Englishman—whether his name be Jason, Hengist or Solomon Kane.

Kane stood and the smoke curled upward into the morning sky, the roaring of foraging lions shook the plateau, and slowly, like light breaking through mists, sanity returned to him.

"The light of God's morning enters even into dark and lonesome lands," said Solomon Kane somberly. "Evil rules in the waste lands of the earth, but even evil may come to an end. Dawn follows midnight and even in this lost land the shadows shrink. Strange are Thy ways, oh God of my people, and who am I to question Thy wisdom? My feet have fallen in evil ways but Thou hast brought me forth scatheless and hast made me a scourge for the Powers of Evil. Over the souls of men spread the condor wings of colossal monsters and all manner of evil things prey upon the heart and soul and body of Man. Yet it may be in some far day the shadows shall fade and the Prince of Darkness be chained forever in his Hell. And till then mankind can but stand up stoutly to the monsters in his own heart and without, and with the aid of God he may yet triumph."

And Solomon Kane looked up into the silent hills and felt the silent call of the hills and the unguessed distances beyond; and Solomon Kane shifted his belt, took his staff firmly in his hand and turned his face eastward.

ARKHAM
Weird Tales, August 1932

———

Drowsy and dull with age the houses blink
*   On aimless streets the rat-gnawed years forget—*
But what inhuman figures leer and slink
*   Down the old alleys when the moon has set?*

AN OPEN WINDOW

Weird Tales, September 1932

Behind the Veil what gulfs of Time and Space?
　　What blinking mowing Shapes to blast the sight?
I shrink before a vague colossal Face
　　Born in the mad immensities of Night.

WORMS OF THE EARTH

Weird Tales, November 1932

———

"Strike in the nails, soldiers, and let our guest see the reality of our good Roman justice!"

The speaker wrapped his purple cloak closer about his powerful frame and settled back into his official chair, much as he might have settled back in his seat at the Circus Maximus to enjoy the clash of gladiatorial swords. Realization of power colored his every move. Whetted pride was necessary to Roman satisfaction, and Titus Sulla was justly proud; for he was military governor of Eboracum and answerable only to the emperor of Rome. He was a strongly built man of medium height, with the hawk-like features of the pure-bred Roman. Now a mocking smile curved his full lips, increasing the arrogance of his haughty aspect. Distinctly military in appearance, he wore the golden-scaled corselet and chased breastplate of his rank, with the short stabbing sword at his belt, and he held on his knee the silvered helmet with its plumed crest. Behind him stood a clump of impassive soldiers with shield and spear—blond titans from the Rhineland.

Before him was taking place the scene which apparently gave him so much real gratification—a scene common enough wherever stretched the far-flung boundaries of Rome. A rude cross lay flat upon the barren earth and on it was bound a man—half-naked, wild of aspect with his corded limbs, glaring eyes and shock of tangled hair. His executioners were Roman soldiers, and with heavy hammers they prepared to pin the victim's hands and feet to the wood with iron spikes.

Only a small group of men watched this ghastly scene, in the dread place of execution beyond the city walls: the governor and his watchful guards; a few young Roman officers; the man to whom Sulla had referred as "guest" and who stood like a bronze image, unspeaking. Beside the gleaming splendor of the Roman, the quiet garb of this man seemed drab, almost somber.

He was dark, but he did not resemble the Latins around him. There was about him none of the warm, almost Oriental sensuality of the Mediterranean which colored their features. The blond barbarians behind Sulla's chair were less unlike the man in facial outline than were the Romans. Not his were the full curving red lips, nor the rich waving locks suggestive of the Greek. Nor was his dark complexion the rich olive of the south; rather it was the bleak darkness of the north. The whole aspect of the man vaguely suggested the shadowed mists, the gloom, the cold and the icy winds of the naked northern lands. Even his black eyes were savagely cold, like black fires burning through fathoms of ice.

His height was only medium but there was something about him which transcended mere physical bulk—a certain fierce innate vitality, comparable only to that of a wolf or a panther. In every line of his supple, compact body, as well as in his coarse straight hair and thin lips, this was evident—in the hawk-like set of the head on the corded neck, in the broad square shoulders, in the deep chest, the lean loins, the narrow feet. Built with the savage economy of a panther, he was an image of dynamic potentialities, pent in with iron self-control.

At his feet crouched one like him in complexion—but there the resemblance ended. This other was a stunted giant, with gnarly limbs, thick body, a low sloping brow and an expression of dull ferocity, now clearly mixed with fear. If the man on the cross resembled, in a tribal way, the man Titus Sulla called guest, he far more resembled the stunted crouching giant.

"Well, Partha Mac Othna," said the governor with studied effrontery, "when you return to your tribe, you will have a tale to tell of the justice of Rome, who rules the south."

"I will have a tale," answered the other in a voice which betrayed no emotion, just as his dark face, schooled to immobility, showed no evidence of the maelstrom in his soul.

"Justice to all under the rule of Rome," said Sulla. "*Pax Romana!* Reward for virtue, punishment for wrong!" He laughed inwardly at his own black hypocrisy, then continued: "You see, emissary of Pictland, how swiftly Rome punishes the transgressor."

"I see," answered the Pict in a voice which strongly-curbed anger made deep with menace, "that the subject of a foreign king is dealt with as though he were a Roman slave."

"He has been tried and condemned in an unbiased court," retorted Sulla.

"Aye! And the accuser was a Roman, the witnesses Roman, the judge Roman! He committed murder? In a moment of fury he struck down a Roman merchant who cheated, tricked and robbed him, and to injury added insult—aye, and a blow! Is his king but a dog, that Rome crucifies his subjects at will, condemned by Roman courts? Is his king too weak or foolish to do justice, were he informed and formal charges brought against the offender?"

"Well," said Sulla cynically, "you may inform Bran Mak Morn yourself. Rome, my friend, makes no account of her actions to barbarian kings. When savages come among us, let them act with discretion or suffer the consequences."

The Pict shut his iron jaws with a snap that told Sulla further badgering would elicit no reply. The Roman made a gesture to the executioners. One of them seized a spike and placing it against the thick wrist of the victim, smote heavily. The iron point sank deep through the flesh, crunching against the bones. The lips of the man on the cross writhed, though no moan escaped him. As a trapped wolf fights against his cage, the bound victim instinctively wrenched and struggled. The veins swelled in his temples, sweat beaded his low forehead, the muscles in arms and legs writhed and knotted. The hammers fell in inexorable strokes, driving the cruel points deeper and deeper, through wrists and ankles; blood flowed in a black river over the hands that held the spikes, staining the wood of the cross, and the splintering of bones was distinctly heard. Yet the sufferer made no outcry, though his blackened lips writhed back until the gums were visible, and his shaggy head jerked involuntarily from side to side.

The man called Partha Mac Othna stood like an iron image, eyes burning from an inscrutable face, his whole body hard as iron from the tension of his control. At his feet crouched his misshapen servant, hiding his face from the grim sight, his arms locked about his master's knees. Those arms gripped like steel and under his breath the fellow mumbled ceaselessly as if in invocation.

The last stroke fell; the cords were cut from arm and leg, so that the man would hang supported by the nails alone. He had ceased his struggling that only twisted the spikes in his agonizing wounds. His bright black eyes, unglazed, had not left the face of the man called Partha Mac Othna; in them lingered a desperate shadow of hope. Now the soldiers lifted the cross and set the end of it in the hole prepared, stamped the dirt about it to hold it erect. The Pict hung in midair, suspended by the nails in his flesh, but still no sound escaped his lips. His eyes still hung on the somber face of the emissary, but the shadow of hope was fading.

"He'll live for days!" said Sulla cheerfully. "These Picts are harder than cats to kill! I'll keep a guard of ten soldiers watching night and day to see that no one takes him down before he dies. Ho, there, Valerius, in honor of our esteemed neighbor, King Bran Mak Morn, give him a cup of wine!"

With a laugh the young officer came forward, holding a brimming wine cup, and rising on his toes, lifted it to the parched lips of the sufferer. In the black eyes flared a red wave of unquenchable hatred; writhing his head aside to avoid even touching the cup, he spat full into the young Roman's eyes. With a curse Valerius dashed the cup to the ground, and before any could halt him, wrenched out his sword and sheathed it in the man's body.

Sulla rose with an imperious exclamation of anger; the man called Partha Mac Othna had started violently, but he bit his lip and said nothing. Valerius seemed somewhat surprized at him as he sullenly cleansed his sword. The act had been instinctive, following the insult to Roman pride, the one thing unbearable.

"Give up your sword, young sir!" exclaimed Sulla. "Centurion Publius, place him under arrest. A few days in a cell with stale bread and water will teach you to curb your patrician pride in matters dealing with the will of the empire. What, you young fool, do you not realize that you could not have made the dog a more kindly gift? Who would not rather desire a quick death on the sword than the slow agony on the cross? Take him away. And you, centurion, see that guards remain at the cross so that the body is not cut down until the ravens pick bare the bones. Partha Mac Othna, I go to a banquet at the house of Demetrius—will you not accompany me?"

The emissary shook his head, his eyes fixed on the limp form which sagged on the black-stained cross. He made no reply. Sulla smiled sardonically, then rose and strode away, followed by his secretary who bore the gilded chair ceremoniously, and by the stolid soldiers, with whom walked Valerius, head sunken.

The man called Partha Mac Othna flung a wide fold of his cloak about his shoulder, halted a moment to gaze at the grim cross with its burden, darkly etched against the crimson sky, where the clouds of night were gathering. Then he stalked away, followed by his silent servant.

2.

In an inner chamber of Eboracum, the man called Partha Mac Othna paced tigerishly to and fro. His sandaled feet made no sound on the marble tiles.

"Grom!" he turned to the gnarled servant. "Well I know why you held my knees so tightly—why you muttered aid of the Moon-Woman—you feared I would lose my self-control and make a mad attempt to succor that poor wretch. By the gods, I believe that was what the dog Roman wished—his iron-cased watchdogs watched me narrowly, I know, and his baiting was harder to bear than ordinarily.

"Gods black and white, dark and light!" He shook his clenched fists above his head in the black gust of his passion. "That I should stand by and see a man of mine butchered on a Roman cross—without justice and with no more trial than that farce! Black gods of R'lyeh, even you would I invoke to the ruin and destruction of those butchers! I swear by the Nameless Ones, men shall die howling for that deed, and Rome shall cry out as a woman in the dark who treads upon an adder!"

"He knew you, master," said Grom.

The other dropped his head and covered his eyes with a gesture of savage pain.

"His eyes will haunt me when I lie dying. Aye, he knew me, and almost until the last, I read in his eyes the hope that I might aid him. Gods and devils, is Rome to butcher my people beneath my very eyes? Then I am not king but dog!"

"Not so loud, in the name of all the gods!" exclaimed Grom in affright. "Did these Romans suspect you were Bran Mak Morn, they would nail you on a cross beside that other."

"They will know it ere long," grimly answered the king. "Too long I have lingered here in the guise of an emissary, spying upon mine enemies. They have thought to play with me, these Romans, masking their contempt and scorn only under polished satire. Rome is courteous to barbarian ambassadors, they give us fine houses to live in, offer us slaves, pander to our lusts with women and gold and wine and games, but all the while they laugh at us; their very courtesy is an insult, and sometimes—as today—their contempt discards all veneer. Bah! I've seen through their baitings—have remained imperturbably serene and swallowed their studied insults. But this—by the fiends of Hell, this is beyond human endurance! My people look to me; if I fail them—if I fail even one—even the lowest of my people, who will aid them? To whom shall they turn? By the gods, I'll answer the gibes of these Roman dogs with black shaft and trenchant steel!"

"And the chief with the plumes?" Grom meant the governor and his gutturals thrummed with the blood-lust. "He dies?" He flicked out a length of steel.

Bran scowled. "Easier said than done. He dies—but how may I reach him? By day his German guards keep at his back; by night they stand at door and window. He has many enemies, Romans as well as barbarians. Many a Briton would gladly slit his throat."

Grom seized Bran's garment, stammering as fierce eagerness broke the bonds of his inarticulate nature.

"Let me go, master! My life is worth nothing. I will cut him down in the midst of his warriors!"

Bran smiled fiercely and clapped his hand on the stunted giant's shoulder with a force that would have felled a lesser man.

"Nay, old war-dog, I have too much need of thee! You shall not throw your life away uselessly. Sulla would read the intent in your eyes, besides, and the javelins of his Teutons would be through you ere you could reach him. Not by the dagger in the dark will we strike this Roman, not by the venom in the cup nor the shaft from the ambush."

The king turned and paced the floor a moment, his head bent in thought. Slowly his eyes grew murky with a thought so fearful he did not speak it aloud to the waiting warrior.

"I have become somewhat familiar with the maze of Roman politics during my stay in this accursed waste of mud and marble," said he. "During a war on the Wall, Titus Sulla, as governor of this province, is supposed to hasten thither with his centuries. But this Sulla does not do; he is no coward, but the bravest avoid certain things—to each man, however bold, his own particular fear. So he sends in his place Caius Camillus, who in times of peace patrols the fens of the west, lest the Britons break over the border. And Sulla takes his place in the Tower of Trajan. Ha!"

He whirled and gripped Grom with steely fingers.

"Grom, take the red stallion and ride north! Let no grass grow under the stallion's hoofs! Ride to Cormac na Connacht and tell him to sweep the frontier with sword and torch! Let his wild Gaels feast their fill of slaughter. After a time I will be with him. But for a time I have affairs in the west."

Grom's black eyes gleamed and he made a passionate gesture with his crooked hand—an instinctive move of savagery.

Bran drew a heavy bronze seal from beneath his tunic.

"This is my safe-conduct as an emissary to Roman courts," he said grimly. "It will open all gates between this house and Baal-dor. If any official questions you too closely—here!"

Lifting the lid of an iron-bound chest, Bran took out a small, heavy leather bag which he gave into the hands of the warrior.

"When all keys fail at a gate," said he, "try a golden key. Go now!"

There were no ceremonious farewells between the barbarian king and his barbarian vassal. Grom flung up his arm in a gesture of salute; then turning, he hurried out.

Bran stepped to a barred window and gazed out into the moonlit streets.

"Wait until the moon sets," he muttered grimly. "Then I'll take the road to—Hell! But before I go I have a debt to pay."

The stealthy clink of a hoof on the flags reached him.

"With the safe-conduct and gold, not even Rome can hold a Pictish reaver," muttered the king. "Now I'll sleep until the moon sets."

With a snarl at the marble frieze-work and fluted columns, as symbols of Rome, he flung himself down on a couch, from which he had long since impatiently torn the cushions and silk stuffs, as too soft for his hard body. Hate and the black passion of vengeance seethed in him, yet he went instantly to sleep. The first lesson he had learned in his bitter hard life was to snatch sleep any time he could, like a wolf that snatches sleep on the hunting trail. Generally his slumber was as light and dreamless as a panther's, but tonight it was otherwise.

He sank into fleecy gray fathoms of slumber and in a timeless, misty realm of shadows he met the tall, lean, white-bearded figure of old Gonar, the priest of the Moon, high counselor to the king. And Bran stood aghast, for Gonar's face was white as driven snow and he shook as with ague. Well might Bran stand appalled, for in all the years of his life he had never before seen Gonar the Wise show any sign of fear.

"What now, old one?" asked the king. "Goes all well in Baal-dor?"

"All is well in Baal-dor where my body lies sleeping," answered old Gonar. "Across the void I have come to battle with you for your soul. King, are you mad, this thought you have thought in your brain?"

"Gonar," answered Bran somberly, "this day I stood still and watched a man of mine die on the cross of Rome. What his name or his rank, I do not know. I do not care. He might have been a faithful unknown warrior of mine, he might have been an outlaw. I only know that he was mine; the first scents he knew were the scents of the heather; the first light he saw was the sunrise on the Pictish hills. He belonged to me, not to Rome. If punishment was just, then none but me should have dealt it. If he were to be tried, none but me should have been his judge. The same blood flowed in our veins; the same fire maddened our brains; in infancy we listened to the same old tales, and in youth we sang the same old songs. He was bound to my heartstrings, as every man and every woman and every child of Pictland is bound. It was mine to protect him; now it is mine to avenge him."

"But in the name of the gods, Bran," expostulated the wizard, "take your vengeance in another way! Return to the heather—mass your warriors—join with Cormac and his Gaels, and spread a sea of blood and flame the length of the great Wall!"

"All that I will do," grimly answered Bran. "But now—

now—I will have a vengeance such as no Roman ever dreamed of! Ha, what do they know of the mysteries of this ancient isle, which sheltered strange life long before Rome rose from the marshes of the Tiber?"

"Bran, there are weapons too foul to use, even against Rome!"

Bran barked short and sharp as a jackal.

"Ha! There are no weapons I would not use against Rome! My back is at the wall. By the blood of the fiends, has Rome fought me fair? Bah! I am a barbarian king with a wolfskin mantle and an iron crown, fighting with my handful of bows and broken pikes against the queen of the world. What have I? The heather hills, the wattle huts, the spears of my shock-headed tribesmen! And I fight Rome—with her armored legions, her broad fertile plains and rich seas—her mountains and her rivers and her gleaming cities—her wealth, her steel, her gold, her mastery and her wrath. By steel and fire I will fight her—and by subtlety and treachery—by the thorn in the foot, the adder in the path, the venom in the cup, the dagger in the dark; aye," his voice sank somberly, "and by the worms of the earth!"

"But it is madness!" cried Gonar. "You will perish in the attempt you plan—you will go down to Hell and you will not return! What of your people then?"

"If I can not serve them I had better die," growled the king.

"But you can not even reach the beings you seek," cried Gonar. "For untold centuries they have dwelt *apart*. There is no door by which you can come to them. Long ago they severed the bonds that bound them to the world we know."

"Long ago," answered Bran somberly, "you told me that nothing in the universe was separated from the stream of Life—a saying the truth of which I have often seen evident. No race, no form of life but is close-knit somehow, by some manner, to the rest of Life and the world. Somewhere there is a thin link connecting *those* I seek to the world I know. Somewhere there is a Door: And somewhere among the bleak fens of the west I will find it."

Stark horror flooded Gonar's eyes and he gave back crying, "Woe! Woe! Woe! to Pictdom! Woe to the unborn kingdom! Woe, black woe to the sons of men! Woe, woe, woe, woe!"

Bran awoke to a shadowed room and the starlight on the window-bars. The moon had sunk from sight though its glow was still faint above the house tops. Memory of his dream shook him and he swore beneath his breath.

Rising, he flung off cloak and mantle, donning a light shirt of black mesh-mail, and girding on sword and dirk. Going again to the iron-bound chest he lifted several compact bags and emptied the clinking contents into the leathern pouch at his girdle. Then wrapping his wide cloak about him, he silently left the house. No servants there were to spy on him—he had impatiently refused the offer of slaves which it was Rome's policy to furnish her barbarian emissaries. Gnarled Grom had attended to all Bran's simple needs.

The stables fronted on the courtyard. A moment's groping in the dark and he placed his hand over a great stallion's nose, checking the nicker of recognition. Working without a light he swiftly bridled and saddled the great brute, and went through the courtyard into a shadowy side street, leading him. The moon was setting, the border of floating shadows widening along the western wall. Silence lay on the marble palaces and mud hovels of Eboracum under the cold stars.

Bran touched the pouch at his girdle, which was heavy with minted gold that bore the stamp of Rome. He had come to Eboracum posing as an emissary of Pictdom, to act the spy. But being a barbarian, he had not been able to play his part in aloof formality and sedate dignity. He retained a crowded memory of wild feasts where wine flowed in fountains; of white-bosomed Roman women, who, sated with civilized lovers, looked with something more than favor on a virile barbarian; of gladiatorial games; and of other games where dice clicked and spun and tall stacks of gold changed hands. He had drunk deeply and gambled recklessly, after the manner of barbarians, and he had had a remarkable run of luck, due possibly to the indifference with which he won or lost. Gold to the Pict was so much dust, flowing through his fingers. In his land there was no need of it. But he had learned its power in the boundaries of civilization.

Almost under the shadow of the northwestern wall he saw ahead of him loom the great watchtower which was connected with and reared above the outer wall. One corner of the castle-like fortress, farthest from the wall, served as a dungeon. Bran left his horse standing in a dark alley, with the reins hanging on the ground, and stole like a prowling wolf into the shadows of the fortress.

The young officer Valerius was awakened from a light, unquiet sleep by a stealthy sound at the barred window. He sat up, cursing softly under his breath as the faint starlight which etched the window-bars fell across the bare stone floor and reminded him of his disgrace. Well, in a few days, he ruminated, he'd be well out of it; Sulla would not be too harsh on a man with such high connections; then let any man or woman gibe at him! Damn that insolent Pict! But wait, he thought suddenly, remembering: what of the sound which had roused him?

"Hsssst!" it was a voice from the window.

Why so much secrecy? It could hardly be a foe—yet, why should it be a friend? Valerius rose and crossed his cell, coming close to the window. Outside all was dim in the starlight and he made out but a shadowy form close to the window.

"Who are you?" he leaned close against the bars, straining his eyes into the gloom.

His answer was a snarl of wolfish laughter, a long flicker of steel in the starlight. Valerius reeled away from the window and crashed to the floor, clutching his throat, gurgling horribly as he tried to scream. Blood gushed through his fingers, forming about his twitching body a pool that reflected the dim starlight dully and redly.

Outside Bran glided away like a shadow, without pausing to peer into the cell. In another minute the guards would round the corner on their regular routine. Even now he heard the measured tramp of their iron-clad feet. Before they came in sight he had vanished and they clumped stolidly by the cell-window with no intimation of the corpse that lay on the floor within.

Bran rode to the small gate in the western wall, unchallenged by the sleepy watch. What fear of foreign invasion in Eboracum?—and certain well organized thieves and women-stealers made it profitable for the watchmen not to be too vigilant. But the single guardsman at the western gate—his fellows lay drunk in a nearby brothel—lifted his spear and bawled for Bran to halt and give an account of himself. Silently the Pict reined closer. Masked in the dark cloak, he seemed dim and indistinct to the Roman, who was only aware of the glitter of his cold eyes in the gloom. But Bran held up his hand against the starlight and the soldier caught the gleam of gold; in the other hand he saw a long sheen of steel. The soldier understood, and he did not hesitate between the choice of a golden bribe or a battle to the death with this unknown rider who was apparently a barbarian of some sort. With a grunt he lowered his spear and swung the gate open. Bran rode through, casting a handful of coins to the Roman. They fell about his feet in a golden shower, clinking against the flags. He bent in greedy haste to retrieve them and Bran Mak Morn rode westward like a flying ghost in the night.

3.

Into the dim fens of the west came Bran Mak Morn. A cold wind breathed across the gloomy waste and against the gray sky a few herons flapped heavily. The long reeds and marsh-grass waved in broken undulations and out across the desolation of the wastes a few still meres reflected the dull light. Here and there rose curiously regular hillocks above the general levels, and gaunt against the somber sky Bran saw a marching line of upright monoliths—menhirs, reared by what nameless hands?

As a faint blue line to the west lay the foothills that beyond the horizon grew to the wild mountains of Wales where dwelt still wild Celtic tribes—fierce blue-eyed men that knew not the yoke of Rome. A row of well-garrisoned watchtowers held them in check. Even now, far away across the moors, Bran glimpsed the unassailable keep men called the Tower of Trajan.

These barren wastes seemed the dreary accomplishment of desolation, yet human life was not utterly lacking. Bran met the silent men of the fen, reticent, dark of eye and hair, speaking a strange mixed tongue whose long-blended elements had forgotten their pristine separate sources. Bran recognized a certain kinship in these people to himself, but he looked on them with the scorn of a pure-blooded patrician for men of mixed strains.

Not that the common people of Caledonia were altogether pure-blooded; they got their stocky bodies and massive limbs from a primitive Teutonic race which had found its way into the northern tip of the isle even before the Celtic conquest of Britain was completed, and had been absorbed by the Picts. But the chiefs of Bran's folk had kept their blood from foreign taint since the beginnings of time, and he himself was a pure-bred Pict of the Old Race. But these fenmen, overrun repeatedly by British, Gaelic and Roman conquerors, had assimilated blood of each, and in the process almost forgotten their original language and lineage.

For Bran came of a race that was very old, which had spread over western Europe in one vast Dark Empire, before the coming of the Aryans, when the ancestors of the Celts, the Hellenes and the Germans were one primal people, before the days of tribal splitting-off and westward drift.

Only in Caledonia, Bran brooded, had his people resisted

the flood of Aryan conquest. He had heard of a Pictish people called Basques, who in the crags of the Pyrenees called themselves an unconquered race; but he knew that they had paid tribute for centuries to the ancestors of the Gaels, before these Celtic conquerors abandoned their mountain-realm and set sail for Ireland. Only the Picts of Caledonia had remained free, and they had been scattered into small feuding tribes—he was the first acknowledged king in five hundred years—the beginning of a new dynasty—no, a revival of an ancient dynasty under a new name. In the very teeth of Rome he dreamed his dreams of empire.

He wandered through the fens, seeking a Door. Of his quest he said nothing to the dark-eyed fenmen. They told him news that drifted from mouth to mouth—a tale of war in the north, the skirl of war-pipes along the winding Wall, of gathering-fires in the heather, of flame and smoke and rapine and the glutting of Gaelic swords in the crimson sea of slaughter. The eagles of the legions were moving northward and the ancient road resounded to the measured tramp of the iron-clad feet. And Bran, in the fens of the west, laughed, well pleased.

In Eboracum, Titus Sulla gave secret word to seek out the Pictish emissary with the Gaelic name who had been under suspicion, and who had vanished the night young Valerius was found dead in his cell with his throat ripped out. Sulla felt that this sudden bursting flame of war on the Wall was connected closely with his execution of a condemned Pictish criminal, and he set his spy system to work, though he felt sure that Partha Mac Othna was by this time far beyond his reach. He prepared to march from Eboracum, but he did not accompany the considerable force of legionaries which he sent north. Sulla was a brave man, but each man has his own dread, and Sulla's was Cormac na Connacht, the black-haired prince of the Gaels, who had sworn to cut out the governor's heart and eat it raw. So Sulla rode with his ever-present body-guard, westward, where lay the Tower of Trajan with its war-like commander, Caius Camillus, who enjoyed nothing more than taking his superior's place when the red waves of war washed at the foot of the Wall. Devious politics, but the legate of Rome seldom visited this far isle, and what of his wealth and intrigues, Titus Sulla was the highest power in Britain.

And Bran, knowing all this, patiently waited his coming, in the deserted hut in which he had taken up his abode.

One gray evening he strode on foot across the moors, a stark figure, blackly etched against the dim crimson fire of the sunset. He felt the incredible antiquity of the slumbering land, as he walked like the last man on the day after the end of the world. Yet at last he saw a token of human life—a drab hut of wattle and mud, set in the reedy breast of the fen.

A woman greeted him from the open door and Bran's somber eyes narrowed with a dark suspicion. The woman was not old, yet the evil wisdom of ages was in her eyes; her garments were ragged and scanty, her black locks tangled and unkempt, lending her an aspect of wildness well in keeping with her grim surroundings. Her red lips laughed but there was no mirth in her laughter, only a hint of mockery, and under the lips her teeth showed sharp and pointed like fangs.

"Enter, master," said she, "if you do not fear to share the roof of the witch-woman of Dagon-moor!"

Bran entered silently and sat him down on a broken

bench while the woman busied herself with the scanty meal cooking over an open fire on the squalid hearth. He studied her lithe, almost serpentine motions, the ears which were almost pointed, the yellow eyes which slanted curiously.

"What do you seek in the fens, my lord?" she asked, turning toward him with a supple twist of her whole body.

"I seek a Door," he answered, chin resting on his fist. "I have a song to sing to the worms of the earth!"

She started upright, a jar falling from her hands to shatter on the hearth.

"This is an ill saying, even spoken in chance," she stammered.

"I speak not by chance but by intent," he answered.

She shook her head. "I know not what you mean."

"Well you know," he returned. "Aye, you know well! My race is very old—they reigned in Britain before the nations of the Celts and the Hellenes were born out of the womb of peoples. But my people were not first in Britain. By the mottles on your skin, by the slanting of your eyes, by the taint in your veins, I speak with full knowledge and meaning."

Awhile she stood silent, her lips smiling but her face inscrutable.

"Man, are you mad," she asked, "that in your madness you come seeking that from which strong men fled screaming in old times?"

"I seek a vengeance," he answered, "that can be accomplished only by Them I seek."

She shook her head.

"You have listened to a bird singing; you have dreamed empty dreams."

74

"I have heard a viper hiss," he growled, "and I do not dream. Enough of this weaving of words. I came seeking a link between two worlds; I have found it."

"I need lie to you no more, man of the North," answered the woman. "They you seek still dwell beneath the sleeping hills. They have drawn *apart*, farther and farther from the world you know."

"But they still steal forth in the night to grip women straying on the moors," said he, his gaze on her slanted eyes. She laughed wickedly.

"What would you of me?"

"That you bring me to Them."

She flung back her head with a scornful laugh. His left hand locked like iron in the breast of her scanty garment and his right closed on his hilt. She laughed in his face.

"Strike and be damned, my northern wolf! Do you think that such life as mine is so sweet that I would cling to it as a babe to the breast?"

His hand fell away.

"You are right. Threats are foolish. I will buy your aid."

"How?" the laughing voice hummed with mockery.

Bran opened his pouch and poured into his cupped palm a stream of gold.

"More wealth than the men of the fen ever dreamed of."

Again she laughed. "What is this rusty metal to me? Save it for some white-breasted Roman woman who will play the traitor for you!"

"Name me a price!" he urged. "The head of an enemy—"

"By the blood in my veins, with its heritage of ancient hate, who is mine enemy but thee?" she laughed and springing, struck catlike. But her dagger splintered on the mail beneath his cloak and he flung her off with a loathsome flit of his wrist which tossed her sprawling across her grass-strewn bunk. Lying there she laughed up at him.

"I will name you a price, then, my wolf, and it may be in days to come you will curse the armor that broke Atla's dagger!" She rose and came close to him, her disquietingly long hands fastened fiercely into his cloak. "I will tell you, Black Bran, king of Caledon! Oh, I knew you when you came into my hut with your black hair and your cold eyes! I will lead you to the doors of Hell if you wish—and the price shall be the kisses of a king!

"What of my blasted and bitter life, I, whom mortal men loathe and fear? I have not known the love of men, the clasp of a strong arm, the sting of human kisses, I, Atla, the were-woman of the moors! What have I known but the lone winds of the fens, the dreary fire of cold sunsets, the whispering of the marsh grasses?—the faces that blink up at me in the waters of the meres, the foot-pad of night—things in the gloom, the glimmer of red eyes, the grisly murmur of nameless beings in the night!

"I am half-human, at least! Have I not known sorrow and yearning and crying wistfulness, and the drear ache of loneliness? Give to me, king—give me your fierce kisses and your hurtful barbarian's embrace. Then in the long drear years to come I shall not utterly eat out my heart in vain envy of the white-bosomed women of men; for I shall have a memory few of them can boast—the kisses of a king! One night of love, oh king, and I will guide you to the gates of Hell!"

Bran eyed her somberly; he reached forth and gripped her

arm in his iron fingers. An involuntary shudder shook him at the feel of her sleek skin. He nodded slowly and drawing her close to him, forced his head down to meet her lifted lips.

4.

The cold gray mists of dawn wrapped King Bran like a clammy cloak. He turned to the woman whose slanted eyes gleamed in the gray gloom.

"Make good your part of the contract," he said roughly. "I sought a link between worlds, and in you I found it. I seek the one thing sacred to Them. It shall be the Key opening the Door that lies unseen between me and Them. Tell me how I can reach it."

"I will," the red lips smiled terribly. "Go to the mound men call Dagon's Barrow. Draw aside the stone that blocks the entrance and go under the dome of the mound. The floor of the chamber is made of seven great stones, six grouped about the seventh. Lift out the center stone—and you will see!"

"Will I find the Black Stone?" he asked.

"Dagon's Barrow is the Door to the Black Stone," she answered, "if you dare follow the Road."

"Will the symbol be well guarded?" He unconsciously loosened his blade in its sheath. The red lips curled mockingly.

"If you meet any on the Road you will die as no mortal man has died for long centuries. The Stone is not guarded, as men guard their treasures. Why should They guard what man has never sought? Perhaps They will be near, perhaps not. It is a chance you must take, if you wish the Stone. Beware, king of Pictdom! Remember it was your folk who, so long ago, cut the thread that bound Them to human life. They were almost human then—they overspread the land and knew the sunlight. Now they have drawn *apart*. They know not the sunlight and they shun the light of the moon. Even the starlight they hate. Far, far apart have they drawn, who might have been men in time, but for the spears of your ancestors."

The sky was overcast with misty gray, through which the sun shone coldly yellow when Bran came to Dagon's Barrow, a round hillock overgrown with rank grass of a curious fungoid appearance. On the eastern side of the mound showed the entrance of a crudely built stone tunnel which evidently penetrated the barrow. One great stone blocked the entrance to the tomb. Bran laid hold of the sharp edges and exerted all his strength. It held fast. He drew his sword and worked the blade between the blocking stone and the sill. Using the sword as a lever, he worked carefully, and managed to loosen the great stone and wrench it out. A foul charnel house scent flowed out of the aperture and the dim sunlight seemed less to illuminate the cavern-like opening than to be fouled by the rank darkness which clung there.

Sword in hand, ready for he knew not what, Bran groped his way into the tunnel, which was long and narrow, built up of heavy joined stones, and was too low for him to stand erect. Either his eyes became somewhat accustomed to the gloom, or the darkness was, after all, somewhat lightened by the sunlight filtering in through the entrance. At any rate he came into a round low chamber and was able to make out its general dome-like outline. Here, no doubt, in old times, had reposed the bones of him for whom the stones of the tomb had been joined and the earth heaped high above them; but now of those bones no vestige remained on the stone floor. And bending close and straining his eyes, Bran made out the strange, startlingly regular pattern of that floor: six well-cut slabs clustered about a seventh, six-sided stone.

He drove his sword-point into a crack and pried carefully. The edge of the central stone tilted slightly upward. A little work and he lifted it out and leaned it against the curving wall. Straining his eyes downward he saw only the gaping blackness of a dark well, with small, worn steps that led downward and out of sight. He did not hesitate. Though the skin between his shoulders crawled curiously, he swung himself into the abyss and felt the clinging blackness swallow him.

Groping downward, he felt his feet slip and stumble on steps too small for human feet. With one hand pressed hard against the side of the well he steadied himself, fearing a fall into unknown and unlighted depths. The steps were cut into solid rock, yet they were greatly worn away. The farther he progressed, the less like steps they became, mere bumps of worn stone. Then the direction of the shaft changed sharply. It still led down, but at a shallow slant down which he could walk, elbows braced against the hollowed sides, head bent low beneath the curved roof. The steps had ceased altogether and the stone felt slimy to the touch, like a serpent's lair. What beings, Bran wondered, had slithered up and down this slanting shaft, for how many centuries?

The tunnel narrowed until Bran found it rather difficult to shove through. He lay on his back and pushed himself along with his hands, feet first. Still he knew he was sinking deeper and deeper into the very guts of the earth; how far below the surface he was, he dared not contemplate. Then ahead a faint witch-fire gleam tinged the abysmal blackness. He grinned savagely and without mirth. If They he sought came suddenly upon him, how could he fight in that narrow shaft? But he had put the thought of personal fear behind him when he began this hellish quest. He crawled on, thoughtless of all else but his goal.

And he came at last into a vast space where he could stand upright. He could not see the roof of the place, but he got an impression of dizzying vastness. The blackness pressed in on all sides and behind him he could see the entrance to the shaft from which he had just emerged—a black well in the darkness. But in front of him a strange grisly radiance glowed about a grim altar built of human skulls. The source of that light he could not determine, but on the altar lay a sullen night-black object—the Black Stone!

Bran wasted no time in giving thanks that the guardians of the grim relic were nowhere near. He caught up the Stone, and gripping it under his left arm, crawled into the shaft. When a man turns his back on peril its clammy menace looms more grisly than when he advances upon it. So Bran, crawling back up the nighted shaft with his grisly prize, felt the darkness turn on him and slink behind him, grinning with dripping fangs. Clammy sweat beaded his flesh and he hastened to the best of his ability, ears strained for some stealthy sound to betray that fell shapes were at his heels. Strong shudders shook him, despite himself, and the short hair on his neck prickled as if a cold wind blew at his back.

When he reached the first of the tiny steps he felt as if he had attained to the outer boundaries of the mortal world. Up them he went, stumbling and slipping, and with a deep gasp of relief, came out into the tomb, whose spectral grayness seemed like the blaze of noon in comparison to the stygian depths he had just traversed. He replaced the central stone and strode into the light of the outer day, and never was the cold yellow light of the sun more grateful, as it dispelled the shadows of black-winged nightmares of fear and madness that seemed to have ridden him up out of the black deeps. He shoved the great blocking stone back into place, and picking up the cloak he had left at the mouth of the tomb, he wrapped it about the Black Stone and hurried away, a strong revulsion and loathing shaking his soul and lending wings to his strides.

A gray silence brooded over the land. It was desolate as the blind side of the moon, yet Bran felt the potentialities of life—under his feet, in the brown earth—sleeping, but how soon to waken, and in what horrific fashion?

He came through the tall masking reeds to the still deep men called Dagon's Mere. No slightest ripple ruffled the cold blue water to give evidence of the grisly monster legend said dwelt beneath. Bran closely scanned the breathless landscape. He saw no hint of life, human or unhuman. He sought the instincts of his savage soul to know if any unseen eyes fixed their lethal gaze upon him, and found no response. He was alone as if he were the last man alive on earth.

Swiftly he unwrapped the Black Stone, and as it lay in his hands like a solid sullen block of darkness, he did not seek to learn the secret of its material nor scan the cryptic characters carved thereon. Weighing it in his hands and calculating the distance, he flung it far out, so that it fell almost exactly in the middle of the lake. A sullen splash and the waters closed over it. There was a moment of shimmering flashes on the bosom of the lake; then the blue surface stretched placid and unrippled again.

5.

The were-woman turned swiftly as Bran approached her door. Her slant eyes widened.

"You! And alive! And sane!"

"I have been into Hell and I have returned," he growled. "What is more, I have that which I sought."

"The Black Stone?" she cried. "You really dared steal it? Where is it?"

"No matter; but last night my stallion screamed in his stall and I heard something crunch beneath his thundering hoofs which was not the wall of the stable—and there was blood on his hoofs when I came to see, and blood on the floor of the stall. And I have heard stealthy sounds in the night, and noises beneath my dirt floor, as if worms burrowed deep in the earth. They know I have stolen their Stone. Have you betrayed me?"

She shook her head.

"I keep your secret; they do not need my word to know you. The farther they have retreated from the world of men, the greater have grown their powers in other uncanny ways. Some dawn your hut will stand empty and if men dare investigate they will find nothing—except crumbling bits of earth on the dirt floor."

Bran smiled terribly.

"I have not planned and toiled thus far to fall prey to the talons of vermin. If They strike me down in the night, They will never know what became of their idol—or whatever it be to Them. I would speak with Them."

"Dare you come with me and meet them in the night?" she asked.

"Thunder of all gods!" he snarled. "Who are you to ask me if I dare? Lead me to Them and let me bargain for a vengeance this night. The hour of retribution draws nigh. This day I saw silvered helmets and bright shields gleam across the fens—the new commander has arrived at the Tower of Trajan and Caius Camillus has marched to the Wall."

That night the king went across the dark desolation of the moors with the silent were-woman. The night was thick and still as if the land lay in ancient slumber. The stars blinked vaguely, mere points of red struggling through the unbreathing gloom. Their gleam was dimmer than the glitter in the eyes of the woman who glided beside the king. Strange thoughts shook Bran, vague, titanic, primeval. To-night ancestral linkings with these slumbering fens stirred in his soul and troubled him with the phantasmal, eon-veiled shapes of monstrous dreams. The vast age of his race was borne upon him; where now he walked an outlaw and an alien, dark-eyed kings in whose mold he was cast had reigned in old times. The Celtic and Roman invaders were as strangers to this ancient isle beside his people. Yet his race likewise had been invaders, and there was an older race than his—a race whose beginnings lay lost and hidden back beyond the dark oblivion of antiquity.

Ahead of them loomed a low range of hills, which formed the easternmost extremity of those straying chains which far away climbed at last to the mountains of Wales. The woman led the way up what might have been a sheep-path, and halted before a wide black gaping cave.

"A door to those you seek, oh king!" her laughter rang hateful in the gloom. "Dare ye enter?"

His fingers closed in her tangled locks and he shook her viciously.

"Ask me but once more if I dare," he grated, "and your head and shoulders part company! Lead on."

Her laughter was like sweet deadly venom. They passed into the cave and Bran struck flint and steel. The flicker of the tinder showed him a wide dusty cavern, on the roof of which hung clusters of bats. Lighting a torch, he lifted it and scanned the shadowy recesses, seeing nothing but dust and emptiness.

"Where are They?" he growled.

She beckoned him to the back of the cave and leaned against the rough wall, as if casually. But the king's keen eyes caught the motion of her hand pressing hard against a projecting ledge. He recoiled as a round black well gaped suddenly at his feet. Again her laughter slashed him like a keen silver knife. He held the torch to the opening and again saw small worn steps leading down.

"They do not need those steps," said Atla. "Once they did, before your people drove them into the darkness. But you will need them."

She thrust the torch into a niche above the well; it shed a faint red light into the darkness below. She gestured into the well and Bran loosened his sword and stepped into the shaft. As he went down into the mystery of the darkness, the light was blotted out above him, and he thought for an instant Atla had covered the opening again. Then he realized that she was descending after him.

The descent was not a long one. Abruptly Bran felt his feet on a solid floor. Atla swung down beside him and stood in the dim circle of light that drifted down the shaft. Bran could not see the limits of the place into which he had come.

"Many caves in these hills," said Atla, her voice sounding small and strangely brittle in the vastness, "are but doors to greater caves which lie beneath, even as a man's words and deeds are but small indications of the dark caverns of murky thought lying behind and beneath."

And now Bran was aware of movement in the gloom. The darkness was filled with stealthy noises not like those made by any human foot. Abruptly sparks began to flash and float in the blackness, like flickering fireflies. Closer they came until they girdled him in a wide half-moon. And beyond the ring gleamed other sparks, a solid sea of them, fading away in the gloom until the farthest were mere tiny pin-points of light. And Bran knew they were the slanted eyes of the beings who had come upon him in such numbers that his brain reeled at the contemplation—and at the vastness of the cavern.

Now that he faced his ancient foes, Bran knew no fear. He felt the waves of terrible menace emanating from them, the grisly hate, the inhuman threat to body, mind and soul. More than a member of a less ancient race, he realized the horror of his position, but he did not fear, though he confronted the ultimate Horror of the dreams and legends of his race. His blood raced fiercely but it was with the hot excitement of the hazard, not the drive of terror.

"They know you have the Stone, oh king," said Atla, and though he knew she feared, though he felt her physical efforts to control her trembling limbs, there was no quiver of fright in her voice. "You are in deadly peril; they know your breed of old—oh, they remember the days when their ancestors were men! I can not save you; both of us will die as no human has died for ten centuries. Speak to them, if you will; they can understand your speech, though you may not understand theirs. But it will avail not—you are human— and a Pict."

Bran laughed and the closing ring of fire shrank back at the savagery in his laughter. Drawing his sword with a soul-chilling rasp of steel, he set his back against what he hoped was a solid stone wall. Facing the glittering eyes with his sword gripped in his right hand and his dirk in his left, he laughed as a blood-hungry wolf snarls.

"Aye," he growled, "I am a Pict, a son of those warriors who drove your brutish ancestors before them like chaff before the storm!—who flooded the land with your blood and heaped high your skulls for a sacrifice to the Moon-Woman! You who fled of old before my race, dare ye now snarl at your master? Roll on me like a flood now, if ye dare! Before your viper fangs drink my life I will reap your multitudes like ripened barley—of your severed heads will I build a tower and of your mangled corpses will I rear up a wall! Dogs of the dark, vermin of Hell, worms of the earth, rush in and try my steel! When Death finds me in this dark cavern, your living will howl for the scores of your dead and your Black Stone will be lost to you forever—for only I know where it is hidden and not all the tortures of all the Hells can wring the secret from my lips!"

Then followed a tense silence; Bran faced the fire-lit darkness, tensed like a wolf at bay, waiting the charge; at his side the woman cowered, her eyes ablaze. Then from the silent ring that hovered beyond the dim torchlight rose a vague abhorrent murmur. Bran, prepared as he was for anything, started. Gods, was *that* the speech of creatures which had once been called men?

Atla straightened, listening intently. From her lips came the same hideous soft sibilances, and Bran, though he had already known the grisly secret of her being, knew that never again could he touch her save with soul-shaken loathing.

She turned to him, a strange smile curving her red lips dimly in the ghostly light.

"They fear you, oh king! By the black secrets of R'lyeh, who are you that Hell itself quails before you? Not your steel, but the stark ferocity of your soul has driven unused fear into their strange minds. They will buy back the Black Stone at any price."

"Good," Bran sheathed his weapons. "They shall promise not to molest you because of your aid of me. And," his voice hummed like the purr of a hunting tiger, "they shall deliver into my hands Titus Sulla, governor of Eboracum, now commanding the Tower of Trajan. This They can do—how, I know not. But I know that in the old days, when my people warred with these Children of the Night, babes disappeared from guarded huts and none saw the stealers come or go. Do They understand?"

Again rose the low frightful sounds and Bran, who feared not their wrath, shuddered at their voices.

"They understand," said Atla. "Bring the Black Stone to Dagon's Ring tomorrow night when the earth is veiled with the blackness that foreruns the dawn. Lay the Stone on the altar. There They will bring Titus Sulla to you. Trust Them; They have not interfered in human affairs for many centuries, but They will keep their word."

Bran nodded and turning, climbed up the stair with Atla close behind him. At the top he turned and looked down once more. As far as he could see floated a glittering ocean of slanted yellow eyes upturned. But the owners of those eyes kept carefully beyond the dim circle of torchlight and of their bodies he could see nothing. Their low hissing speech floated up to him and he shuddered as his imagination visualized, not a throng of biped creatures, but a swarming, swaying myriad of serpents, gazing up at him with their glittering unwinking eyes.

He swung into the upper cave and Atla thrust the blocking stone back in place. It fitted into the entrance of the well with uncanny precision; Bran was unable to discern any crack in the apparently solid floor of the cavern. Atla made a motion to extinguish the torch, but the king stayed her.

"Keep it so until we are out of the cave," he grunted. "We might tread on an adder in the dark."

Atla's sweetly hateful laughter rose maddeningly in the flickering gloom.

6.

It was not long before sunset when Bran came again to the reed-grown marge of Dagon's Mere. Casting cloak and sword-belt on the ground, he stripped himself of his short leathern breeches. Then gripping his naked dirk in his teeth, he went into the water with the smooth ease of a diving seal. Swimming strongly, he gained the center of the small lake, and turning, drove himself downward.

The mere was deeper than he had thought. It seemed he would never reach the bottom, and when he did, his groping hands failed to find what he sought. A roaring in his ears warned him and he swam to the surface.

Gulping deep of the refreshing air, he dived again, and again his quest was fruitless. A third time he sought the depth, and this time his groping hands met a familiar object in the silt of the bottom. Grasping it, he swam up to the surface.

The Stone was not particularly bulky, but it was heavy. He swam leisurely, and suddenly was aware of a curious stir in the waters about him which was not caused by his own exertions. Thrusting his face below the surface, he tried to pierce the blue depths with his eyes and thought to see a dim gigantic shadow hovering there.

He swam faster, not frightened, but wary. His feet struck the shallows and he waded up on the shelving shore. Looking back he saw the waters swirl and subside. He shook his head, swearing. He had discounted the ancient legend which made Dagon's Mere the lair of a nameless water-monster, but now he had a feeling as if his escape had been narrow. The time-worn myths of the ancient land were taking form and coming to life before his eyes. What primeval shape lurked below the surface of that treacherous mere, Bran could not guess, but he felt that the fenmen had good reason for shunning the spot, after all.

Bran donned his garments, mounted the black stallion and rode across the fens in the desolate crimson of the sunset's afterglow, with the Black Stone wrapped in his cloak. He rode, not to his hut, but to the west, in the direction of the Tower of Trajan and the Ring of Dagon. As he covered the miles that lay between, the red stars winked out. Midnight passed him in the moonless night and still Bran rode on. His heart was hot for his meeting with Titus Sulla. Atla had gloated over the anticipation of watching the Roman writhe under torture, but no such thought was in the Pict's mind. The governor should have his chance with weapons—with Bran's own sword he should face the Pictish king's dirk, and live or die according to his prowess. And though Sulla was famed throughout the provinces as a swordsman, Bran felt no doubt as to the outcome.

Dagon's Ring lay some distance from the Tower—a sullen circle of tall gaunt stones planted upright, with a rough-hewn stone altar in the center. The Romans looked on these menhirs with aversion; they thought the Druids had reared them; but the Celts supposed Bran's people, the Picts, had planted them—and Bran well knew what hands reared those grim monoliths in lost ages, though for what reasons, he but dimly guessed.

The king did not ride straight to the Ring. He was consumed with curiosity as to how his grim allies intended carrying out their promise. That They could snatch Titus Sulla from the very midst of his men, he felt sure, and he believed he knew how They would do it. He felt the gnawings of a strange misgiving, as if he had tampered with powers of unknown breadth and depth, and had loosed forces which he could not control. Each time he remembered that reptilian murmur, those slanted eyes of the night before, a cold breath passed over him. They had been abhorrent enough when his people drove Them into the caverns under the hills, ages ago; what had long centuries of retrogression made of them? In their nighted, subterranean life, had They retained any of the attributes of humanity at all?

Some instinct prompted him to ride toward the Tower. He knew he was near; but for the thick darkness he could have plainly seen its stark outline tusking the horizon. Even now he should be able to make it out dimly. An obscure, shuddersome premonition shook him and he spurred the stallion into swift canter.

And suddenly Bran staggered in his saddle as from a physical impact, so stunning was the surprize of what met his gaze. The impregnable Tower of Trajan was no more! Bran's astounded gaze rested on a gigantic pile of ruins—of shattered stone and crumbled granite, from which jutted the jagged and splintered ends of broken beams. At one corner of the tumbled heap one tower rose out of the waste of crumpled masonry, and it leaned drunkenly as if its foundations had been half-cut away.

Bran dismounted and walked forward, dazed by bewilderment. The moat was filled in places by fallen stones and broken pieces of mortared wall. He crossed over and came among the ruins. Where, he knew, only a few hours before the flags had resounded to the martial tramp of iron-clad feet, and the walls had echoed to the clang of shields and the blast of the loud-throated trumpets, a horrific silence reigned.

Almost under Bran's feet, a broken shape writhed and groaned. The king bent down to the legionary who lay in a sticky red pool of his own blood. A single glance showed the Pict that the man, horribly crushed and shattered, was dying.

Lifting the bloody head, Bran placed his flask to the pulped lips and the Roman instinctively drank deep, gulping through splintered teeth. In the dim starlight Bran saw his glazed eyes roll.

"The walls fell," muttered the dying man. "They crashed down like the skies falling on the day of doom. Ah Jove, the skies rained shards of granite and hailstones of marble!"

"I have felt no earthquake shock," Bran scowled, puzzled.

"It was no earthquake," muttered the Roman. "Before last dawn it began, the faint dim scratching and clawing far below the earth. We of the guard heard it—like rats burrowing, or like worms hollowing out the earth. Titus laughed at us, but all day long we heard it. Then at midnight the Tower quivered and seemed to settle—as if the foundations were being dug away—"

A shudder shook Bran Mak Morn. The worms of the earth! Thousands of vermin digging like moles far below the castle, burrowing away the foundations—gods, the land must be honeycombed with tunnels and caverns—these creatures were even less human than he had thought—what ghastly shapes of darkness had he invoked to his aid?

"What of Titus Sulla?" he asked, again holding the flask to the legionary's lips; in that moment the dying Roman seemed to him almost like a brother.

"Even as the Tower shuddered we heard a fearful scream from the governor's chamber," muttered the soldier. "We rushed there—as we broke down the door we heard his shrieks—they seemed to recede—*into the bowels of the earth!* We rushed in; the chamber was empty. His blood-stained sword lay on the floor; in the stone flags of the floor a black hole gaped. Then—the—towers—reeled—the—roof—broke;—through—a—storm—of—crashing—walls—I—crawled—"

A strong convulsion shook the broken figure.

"Lay me down, friend," whispered the Roman. "I die."

He had ceased to breathe before Bran could comply. The Pict rose, mechanically cleansing his hands. He hastened from the spot, and as he galloped over the darkened fens, the weight of the accursed Black Stone under his cloak was as the weight of a foul nightmare on a mortal breast.

As he approached the Ring, he saw an eery glow within, so that the gaunt stones stood etched like the ribs of a skeleton in which a witch-fire burns. The stallion snorted and reared as Bran tied him to one of the menhirs. Carrying the Stone he strode into the grisly circle and saw Atla standing beside the altar, one hand on her hip, her sinuous body swaying in a serpentine manner. The altar glowed all over with ghastly light and Bran knew someone, probably Atla, had rubbed it with phosphorus from some dank swamp or quagmire.

He strode forward and whipping his cloak from about the Stone, flung the accursed thing on to the altar.

"I have fulfilled my part of the contract," he growled.

"And They, theirs," she retorted. "Look!—They come!"

He wheeled, his hand instinctively dropping to his sword. Outside the Ring the great stallion screamed savagely and reared against his tether. The night wind moaned through the waving grass and an abhorrent soft hissing mingled with it. Between the menhirs flowed a dark tide of shadows, unstable and chaotic. The Ring filled with glittering eyes which hovered beyond the dim illusive circle of illumination cast by the phosphorescent altar. Somewhere in the darkness a human voice tittered and gibbered idiotically. Bran stiffened, the shadows of a horror clawing at his soul.

He strained his eyes, trying to make out the shapes of those who ringed him. But he glimpsed only billowing masses of shadow which heaved and writhed and squirmed with almost fluid consistency.

"Let them make good their bargain!" he exclaimed angrily.

"Then see, oh king!" cried Atla in a voice of piercing mockery.

There was a stir, a seething in the writhing shadows, and from the darkness crept, like a four-legged animal, a human shape that fell down and groveled at Bran's feet and writhed and mowed, and lifting a death's-head, howled like a dying dog. In the ghastly light, Bran, soul-shaken, saw the blank glassy eyes, the bloodless features, the loose, writhing, froth-covered lips of sheer lunacy—gods, was this Titus Sulla, the proud lord of life and death in Eboracum's proud city?

Bran bared his sword.

"I had thought to give this stroke in vengeance," he said somberly. "I give it in mercy—*Vale Cæsar!*"

The steel flashed in the eery light and Sulla's head rolled to the foot of the glowing altar, where it lay staring up at the shadowed sky.

"They harmed him not!" Atla's hateful laugh slashed the sick silence. "It was what he saw and came to know that broke his brain! Like all his heavy-footed race, he knew nothing of the secrets of this ancient land. This night he has been dragged through the deepest pits of Hell, where even you might have blenched!"

"Well for the Romans that they know not the secrets of this accursed land!" Bran roared, maddened, "with its monster-haunted meres, its foul witch-women, and its lost caverns and subterranean realms where spawn in the darkness shapes of Hell!"

"Are they more foul than a mortal who seeks their aid?" cried Atla with a shriek of fearful mirth. "Give them their Black Stone!"

A cataclysmic loathing shook Bran's soul with red fury.

"Aye, take your cursed Stone!" he roared, snatching it from the altar and dashing it among the shadows with such savagery that bones snapped under its impact. A hurried babel of grisly tongues rose and the shadows heaved in turmoil. One segment of the mass detached itself for an instant and Bran cried out in fierce revulsion, though he caught only a fleeting glimpse of the thing, had only a brief impression of a broad strangely flattened head, pendulous writhing lips that bared curved pointed fangs, and a hideously misshapen, dwarfish body that seemed—*mottled*—all set off by those unwinking reptilian eyes. Gods!—the myths had prepared him for horror in human aspect, horror induced by bestial visage and stunted deformity—but this was the horror of nightmare and the night.

"Go back to Hell and take your idol with you!" he yelled, brandishing his clenched fists to the skies, as the thick shadows receded, flowing back and away from him like the foul waters of some black flood. "Your ancestors were men, though strange and monstrous—but gods, ye have become in ghastly fact what my people called ye in scorn! Worms of the earth, back into your holes and burrows! Ye foul the air and leave on the clean earth the slime of the serpents ye have become! Gonar was right—there are shapes too foul to use even against Rome!"

He sprang from the Ring as a man flees the touch of a coiling snake, and tore the stallion free. At his elbow Atla was shrieking with fearful laughter, all human attributes dropped from her like a cloak in the night.

"King of Pictland!" she cried, "King of fools! Do you blench at so small a thing? Stay and let me show you real fruits of the pits! Ha! ha! ha! Run, fool, run! But you are stained with the taint—you have called them forth and they will remember! And in their own time they will come to you again!"

He yelled a wordless curse and struck her savagely in the mouth with his open hand. She staggered, blood starting from her lips, but her fiendish laughter only rose higher.

Bran leaped into the saddle, wild for the clean heather and the cold blue hills of the north where he could plunge his sword into clean slaughter and his sickened soul into the red maelstrom of battle, and forget the horror which lurked below the fens of the west. He gave the frantic stallion the rein, and rode through the night like a hunted ghost, until the hellish laughter of the howling were-woman died out in the darkness behind.

THE PHOENIX ON THE SWORD

Weird Tales, December 1932

"Know, oh prince, that between the years when the oceans drank Atlantis and the gleaming cities, and the years of the rise of the Sons of Aryas, there was an Age undreamed of, when shining kingdoms lay spread across the world like blue mantles beneath the stars—Nemedia, Ophir, Brythunia, Hyperborea, Zamora with its dark-haired women and towers of spider-haunted mystery, Zingara with its chivalry, Koth that bordered on the pastoral lands of Shem, Stygia with its shadow-guarded tombs, Hyrkania whose riders wore steel and silk and gold. But the proudest kingdom of the world was Aquilonia, reigning supreme in the dreaming west. Hither came Conan, the Cimmerian, black-haired, sullen-eyed, sword in hand, a thief, a reaver, a slayer, with gigantic melancholies and gigantic mirth, to tread the jeweled thrones of the Earth under his sandaled feet."

—The Nemedian Chronicles.

Over shadowy spires and gleaming towers lay the ghostly darkness and silence that runs before dawn. Into a dim alley, one of a veritable labyrinth of mysterious winding ways, four masked figures came hurriedly from a door which a dusky hand furtively opened. They spoke not but went swiftly into the gloom, cloaks wrapped closely about them;

as silently as the ghosts of murdered men they disappeared in the darkness. Behind them a sardonic countenance was framed in the partly opened door; a pair of evil eyes glittered malevolently in the gloom.

"Go into the night, creatures of the night," a voice mocked. "Oh, fools, your doom hounds your heels like a blind dog, and you know it not."

The speaker closed the door and bolted it, then turned and went up the corridor, candle in hand. He was a somber giant, whose dusky skin revealed his Stygian blood. He came into an inner chamber, where a tall, lean man in worn velvet lounged like a great lazy cat on a silken couch, sipping wine from a huge golden goblet.

"Well, Ascalante," said the Stygian, setting down the candle, "your dupes have slunk into the streets like rats from their burrows. You work with strange tools."

"Tools?" replied Ascalante. "Why, they consider *me* that. For months now, ever since the Rebel Four summoned me from the southern desert, I have been living in the very heart of my enemies, hiding by day in this obscure house, skulking through dark alleys and darker corridors at night. And I have accomplished what those rebellious nobles could not. Working through them, and through other agents, many of whom have never seen my face, I have honeycombed the empire with sedition and unrest. In short I, working in the shadows, have paved the downfall of the king who sits throned in the sun. By Mitra, I was a statesman before I was an outlaw."

"And these dupes who deem themselves your masters?"

"They will continue to think that I serve them, until

our present task is completed. Who are they to match wits with Ascalante? Volmana, the dwarfish count of Karaban; Gromel, the giant commander of the Black Legion; Dion, the fat baron of Attalus; Rinaldo, the hare-brained minstrel. I am the force which has welded together the steel in each, and by the clay in each, I will crush them when the time comes. But that lies in the future; tonight the king dies."

"Days ago I saw the imperial squadrons ride from the city," said the Stygian.

"They rode to the frontier which the heathen Picts assail—thanks to the strong liquor which I've smuggled over the borders to madden them. Dion's great wealth made *that* possible. And Volmana made it possible to dispose of the rest of the imperial troops which remained in the city. Through his princely kin in Nemedia, it was easy to persuade King Numa to request the presence of Count Trocero of Poitain, seneschal of Aquilonia; and of course, to do him honor, he'll be accompanied by an imperial escort, as well as his own troops, and Prospero, King Conan's right-hand man. That leaves only the king's personal bodyguard in the city— besides the Black Legion. Through Gromel I've corrupted a spendthrift officer of that guard, and bribed him to lead his men away from the king's door at midnight.

"Then, with sixteen desperate rogues of mine, we enter the palace by a secret tunnel. After the deed is done, even if the people do not rise to welcome us, Gromel's Black Legion will be sufficient to hold the city and the crown."

"And Dion thinks that crown will be given to him?"

"Yes. The fat fool claims it by reason of a trace of royal blood. Conan makes a bad mistake in letting men live who still boast descent from the old dynasty, from which he tore the crown of Aquilonia.

"Volmana wishes to be reinstated in royal favor as he was under the old regime, so that he may lift his poverty-ridden estates to their former grandeur. Gromel hates Pallantides, commander of the Black Dragons, and desires the command of the whole army, with all the stubbornness of the Bossonian. Alone of us all, Rinaldo has no personal ambition. He sees in Conan a red-handed, rough-footed barbarian who came out of the north to plunder a civilized land. He idealizes the king whom Conan killed to get the crown, remembering only that he occasionally patronized the arts, and forgetting the evils of his reign, and he is making the people forget. Already they openly sing *The Lament for the King* in which Rinaldo lauds the sainted villain and denounces Conan as 'that black-hearted savage from the abyss.' Conan laughs, but the people snarl."

"Why does he hate Conan?"

"Poets always hate those in power. To them perfection is always just behind the last corner, or beyond the next. They escape the present in dreams of the past and future. Rinaldo is a flaming torch of idealism, rising, as he thinks, to overthrow a tyrant and liberate the people. As for me—well, a few months ago I had lost all ambition but to raid the caravans for the rest of my life; now old dreams stir. Conan will die; Dion will mount the throne. Then he, too, will die. One by one, all who oppose me will die—by fire, or steel, or those deadly wines you know so well how to brew. Ascalante, king of Aquilonia! How like you the sound of it?"

The Stygian shrugged his broad shoulders.

"There was a time," he said with unconcealed bitterness, "when I, too, had my ambitions, beside which yours seem tawdry and childish. To what a state I have fallen! My old-time peers and rivals would stare indeed could they see Thoth-Amon of the Ring serving as the slave of an outlander, and an outlaw at that; and aiding in the petty ambitions of barons and kings!"

"You laid your trust in magic and mummery," answered Ascalante carelessly. "I trust my wits and my sword."

"Wits and swords are as straws against the wisdom of the Darkness," growled the Stygian, his dark eyes flickering with menacing lights and shadows. "Had I not lost the Ring, our positions might be reversed."

"Nevertheless," answered the outlaw impatiently, "you wear the stripes of my whip on your back, and are likely to continue to wear them."

"Be not so sure!" The fiendish hatred of the Stygian glittered for an instant redly in his eyes. "Someday, somehow, I will find the Ring again, and when I do, by the serpent-fangs of Set, you shall pay—"

The hot-tempered Aquilonian started up and struck him heavily across the mouth. Thoth reeled back, blood starting from his lips.

"You grow over-bold, dog," growled the outlaw. "Have a care; I am still your master who knows your dark secret. Go upon the housetops and shout that Ascalante is in the city plotting against the king—if you dare."

"I dare not," muttered the Stygian, wiping the blood from his lips.

"No, you do not dare," Ascalante grinned bleakly. "For

if I die by your stealth or treachery, a hermit priest in the southern desert will know of it, and will break the seal of a manuscript I left in his hands. And having read, a word will be whispered in Stygia, and a wind will creep up from the south by midnight. And where will you hide your head, Thoth-Amon?"

The slave shuddered and his dusky face went ashen.

"Enough!" Ascalante changed his tone peremptorily. "I have work for you. I do not trust Dion. I bade him ride to his country estate and remain there until the work tonight is done. The fat fool could never conceal his nervousness before the king today. Ride after him, and if you do not overtake him on the road, proceed to his estate and remain with him until we send for him. Don't let him out of your sight. He is mazed with fear, and might bolt—might even rush to Conan in a panic, and reveal the whole plot, hoping thus to save his own hide. Go!"

The slave bowed, hiding the hate in his eyes, and did as he was bidden. Ascalante turned again to his wine. Over the jeweled spires was rising a dawn crimson as blood.

2.

When I was a fighting-man, the kettle-drums they beat,
The people scattered gold-dust before my horse's feet;
But now I am a great king, the people hound my track
With poison in my wine-cup, and daggers at my back.
                              —The Road of Kings.

The room was large and ornate, with rich tapestries on the polished-paneled walls, deep rugs on the ivory floor, and with the lofty ceiling adorned with intricate carvings and silver scrollwork. Behind an ivory, gold-inlaid writing-table sat a man whose broad shoulders and sun-browned skin seemed out of place among those luxuriant surroundings. He seemed more a part of the sun and winds and high places of the outlands. His slightest movement spoke of steel-spring muscles knit to a keen brain with the coordination of a born fighting-man. There was nothing deliberate or measured about his actions. Either he was perfectly at rest—still as a bronze statue—or else he was in motion, not with the jerky quickness of over-tense nerves, but with a catlike speed that blurred the sight which tried to follow him.

His garments were of rich fabric, but simply made. He wore no ring or ornaments, and his square-cut black mane was confined merely by a cloth-of-silver band about his head.

Now he laid down the golden stylus with which he had been laboriously scrawling on waxed papyrus, rested his chin on his fist, and fixed his smoldering blue eyes enviously on the man who stood before him. This person was occupied in his own affairs at the moment, for he was taking up the laces of his gold-chased armor, and abstractedly whistling— a rather unconventional performance, considering that he was in the presence of a king.

"Prospero," said the man at the table, "these matters of statecraft weary me as all the fighting I have done never did."

"All part of the game, Conan," answered the dark-eyed Poitainian. "You are king—you must play the part."

"I wish I might ride with you to Nemedia," said Conan

enviously. "It seems ages since I had a horse between my knees—but Publius says that affairs in the city require my presence. Curse him!

"When I overthrew the old dynasty," he continued, speaking with the easy familiarity which existed only between the Poitainian and himself, "it was easy enough, though it seemed bitter hard at the time. Looking back now over the wild path I followed, all those days of toil, intrigue, slaughter and tribulation seem like a dream.

"I did not dream far enough, Prospero. When King Numedides lay dead at my feet and I tore the crown from his gory head and set it on my own, I had reached the ultimate border of my dreams. I had prepared myself to take the crown, not to hold it. In the old free days all I wanted was a sharp sword and a straight path to my enemies. Now no paths are straight and my sword is useless.

"When I overthrew Numedides, *then* I was the Liberator—now they spit at my shadow. They have put a statue of that swine in the temple of Mitra, and people go and wail before it, hailing it as the holy effigy of a saintly monarch who was done to death by a red-handed barbarian. When I led her armies to victory as a mercenary, Aquilonia overlooked the fact that I was a foreigner, but now she can not forgive me.

"Now in Mitra's temple there come to burn incense to Numedides' memory, men whom his hangmen maimed and blinded, men whose sons died in his dungeons, whose wives and daughters were dragged into his seraglio. The fickle fools!"

"Rinaldo is largely responsible," answered Prospero,

drawing up his sword-belt another notch. "He sings songs that make men mad. Hang him in his jester's garb to the highest tower in the city. Let him make rhymes for the vultures."

Conan shook his lion head. "No, Prospero, he's beyond my reach. A great poet is greater than any king. His songs are mightier than my scepter; for he has near ripped the heart from my breast when he chose to sing for me. I shall die and be forgotten, but Rinaldo's songs will live forever.

"No, Prospero," the king continued, a somber look of doubt shadowing his eyes, "there is something hidden, some undercurrent of which we are not aware. I sense it as in my youth I sensed the tiger hidden in the tall grass. There is a nameless unrest throughout the kingdom. I am like a hunter who crouches by his small fire amid the forest, and hears stealthy feet padding in the darkness, and almost sees the glimmer of burning eyes. If I could but come to grips with something tangible, that I could cleave with my sword! I tell you, it's not by chance that the Picts have of late so fiercely assailed the frontiers, so that the Bossonians have called for aid to beat them back. I should have ridden with the troops."

"Publius feared a plot to trap and slay you beyond the frontier," replied Prospero, smoothing his silken surcoat over his shining mail, and admiring his tall lithe figure in a silver mirror. "That's why he urged you to remain in the city. These doubts are born of your barbarian instincts. Let the people snarl! The mercenaries are ours, and the Black Dragons, and every rogue in Poitain swears by you. Your only danger is assassination, and that's impossible, with men of the imperial troops guarding you day and night. What are you working at there?"

"A map," Conan answered with pride. "The maps of the court show well the countries of south, east and west, but in the north they are vague and faulty. I am adding the northern lands myself. Here is Cimmeria, where I was born. And—"

"Asgard and Vanaheim," Prospero scanned the map. "By Mitra, I had almost believed those countries to have been fabulous."

Conan grinned savagely, involuntarily touching the scars on his dark face. "You had known otherwise, had you spent your youth on the northern frontiers of Cimmeria! Asgard lies to the north, and Vanaheim to the northwest of Cimmeria, and there is continual war along the borders."

"What manner of men are these northern folk?" asked Prospero.

"Tall and fair and blue-eyed. Their god is Ymir, the frost-giant, and each tribe has its own king. They are wayward and fierce. They fight all day and drink ale and roar their wild songs all night."

"Then I think you are like them," laughed Prospero. "You laugh greatly, drink deep and bellow good songs; though I never saw another Cimmerian who drank aught but water, or who ever laughed, or ever sang save to chant dismal dirges."

"Perhaps it's the land they live in," answered the king. "A gloomier land never was—all of hills, darkly wooded, under skies nearly always gray, with winds moaning drearily down the valleys."

"Little wonder men grow moody there," quoth Prospero with a shrug of his shoulders, thinking of the smiling sun-washed plains and blue lazy rivers of Poitain, Aquilonia's southernmost province.

"They have no hope here or hereafter," answered Conan. "Their gods are Crom and his dark race, who rule over a sunless place of everlasting mist, which is the world of the dead. Mitra! The ways of the Æsir were more to my liking."

"Well," grinned Prospero, "the dark hills of Cimmeria are far behind you. And now I go. I'll quaff a goblet of white Nemedian wine for you at Numa's court."

"Good," grunted the king, "but kiss Numa's dancing-girls for yourself only, lest you involve the states!"

His gusty laughter followed Prospero out of the chamber.

3.

Under the caverned pyramids great Set coils asleep;
Among the shadows of the tombs his dusky people creep.
I speak the Word from the hidden gulfs
     that never knew the sun—
Send me a servant for my hate, oh scaled and shining One!

The sun was setting, etching the green and hazy blue of the forest in brief gold. The waning beams glinted on the thick golden chain which Dion of Attalus twisted continually in his pudgy hand as he sat in the flaming riot of blossoms and flower-trees which was his garden. He shifted his fat body on his marble seat and glanced furtively about, as if in quest of a lurking enemy. He sat within a circular grove of slender trees, whose interlapping branches cast a thick shade over him. Near at hand a fountain tinkled silverly, and other unseen fountains in various parts of the great garden whispered an everlasting symphony.

Dion was alone except for the great dusky figure which lounged on a marble bench close at hand, watching the baron with deep somber eyes. Dion gave little thought to Thoth-Amon. He vaguely knew that he was a slave in whom Ascalante reposed much trust, but like so many rich men, Dion paid scant heed to men below his own station in life.

"You need not be so nervous," said Thoth. "The plot can not fail."

"Ascalante can make mistakes as well as another," snapped Dion, sweating at the mere thought of failure.

"Not he," grinned the Stygian savagely, "else I had not been his slave, but his master."

"What talk is this?" peevishly returned Dion, with only half a mind on the conversation.

Thoth-Amon's eyes narrowed. For all his iron self-control, he was near bursting with long pent-up shame, hate and rage, ready to take any sort of a desperate chance. What he did not reckon on was the fact that Dion saw him, not as a human being with a brain and a wit, but simply a slave, and as such, a creature beneath notice.

"Listen to me," said Thoth. "You will be king. But you little know the mind of Ascalante. You can not trust him, once Conan is slain. I can help you. If you will protect me when you come to power, I will aid you.

"Listen, my lord. I was a great sorcerer in the south. Men spoke of Thoth-Amon as they spoke of Rammon. King

Ctesphon of Stygia gave me great honor, casting down the magicians from the high places to exalt me above them. They hated me, but they feared me, for I controlled beings from *outside* which came at my call and did my bidding. By Set, mine enemy knew not the hour when he might awake at midnight to feel the taloned fingers of a nameless horror at his throat! I did dark and terrible magic with the Serpent Ring of Set, which I found in a nighted tomb a league beneath the earth, forgotten before the first man crawled out of the slimy sea.

"But a thief stole the Ring and my power was broken. The magicians rose up to slay me, and I fled. Disguised as a camel-driver, I was traveling in a caravan in the land of Koth, when Ascalante's reavers fell upon us. All in the caravan were slain except myself; I saved my life by revealing my identity to Ascalante and swearing to serve him. Bitter has been that bondage!

"To hold me fast, he wrote of me in a manuscript, and sealed it and gave it into the hands of a hermit who dwells on the southern borders of Koth. I dare not strike a dagger into him while he sleeps, or betray him to his enemies, for then the hermit would open the manuscript and read—thus Ascalante instructed him. And he would speak a word in Stygia—"

Again Thoth shuddered and an ashen hue tinged his dusky skin.

"Men knew me not in Aquilonia," he said. "But should my enemies in Stygia learn my whereabouts, not the width of half a world between us would suffice to save me from such a doom as would blast the soul of a bronze statue. Only a king with castles and hosts of swordsmen could protect me. So I have told you my secret, and urge that you make a pact with me. I can aid you with my wisdom, and you can protect me. And some day I will find the Ring—"

"Ring? Ring?" Thoth had underestimated the man's utter egoism. Dion had not even been listening to the slave's words, so completely engrossed was he in his own thoughts, but the final word stirred a ripple in his self-centeredness.

"Ring?" he repeated. "That makes me remember—my ring of good fortune. I had it from a Shemitish thief who swore he stole it from a wizard far to the south, and that it would bring me luck. I paid him enough, Mitra knows. By the gods, I need all the luck I can have, what with Volmana and Ascalante dragging me into their bloody plots—I'll see to the ring."

Thoth sprang up, blood mounting darkly to his face, while his eyes flamed with the stunned fury of a man who suddenly realizes the full depths of a fool's swinish stupidity. Dion never heeded him. Lifting a secret lid in the marble seat, he fumbled for a moment among a heap of gewgaws of various kinds—barbaric charms, bits of bones, pieces of tawdry jewelry—luck-pieces and conjures which the man's superstitious nature had prompted him to collect.

"Ah, here it is!" He triumphantly lifted a ring of curious make. It was of a metal like copper, and was made in the form of a scaled serpent, coiled in three loops, with its tail in its mouth. Its eyes were yellow gems which glittered balefully. Thoth-Amon cried out as if he had been struck, and Dion wheeled and gaped, his face suddenly bloodless. The slave's eyes were blazing, his mouth wide, his huge dusky hands outstretched like talons.

"The Ring! By Set! The Ring!" he shrieked. "My Ring—stolen from me—"

Steel glittered in the Stygian's hand and with a heave of his great dusky shoulders he drove the dagger into the baron's fat body. Dion's high thin squeal broke in a strangled gurgle and his whole flabby frame collapsed like melted butter. A fool to the end, he died in mad terror, not knowing why. Flinging aside the crumpled corpse, already forgetful of it, Thoth grasped the ring in both hands, his dark eyes blazing with a fearful avidness.

"My Ring!" he whispered in terrible exultation. "My power!"

How long he crouched over the baleful thing, motionless as a statue, drinking the evil aura of it into his dark soul, not even the Stygian knew. When he shook himself from his revelry and drew back his mind from the nighted abysses where it had been questing, the moon was rising, casting long shadows across the smooth marble back of the garden-seat, at the foot of which sprawled the darker shadow which had been the lord of Attalus.

"No more, Ascalante, no more!" whispered the Stygian, and his eyes burned red as a vampire's in the gloom. Stooping, he cupped a handful of congealing blood from the sluggish pool in which his victim sprawled, and rubbed it in the copper serpent's eyes until the yellow sparks were covered by a crimson mask.

"Blind your eyes, mystic serpent," he chanted in a blood-freezing whisper. "Blind your eyes to the moonlight and open them on darker gulfs! What do you see, oh serpent of Set? Whom do you call from the gulfs of the Night? Whose shadow falls on the waning Light? Call him to me, oh serpent of Set!"

Stroking the scales with a peculiar circular motion of his fingers, a motion which always carried the fingers back to their starting place, his voice sank still lower as he whispered dark names and grisly incantations forgotten the world over save in the grim hinterlands of dark Stygia, where monstrous shapes move in the dusk of the tombs.

There was a movement in the air about him, such a swirl as is made in water when some creature rises to the surface. A nameless, freezing wind blew on him briefly, as if from an opened Door. Thoth felt a presence at his back, but he did not look about. He kept his eyes fixed on the moonlit space of marble, on which a tenuous shadow hovered. As he continued his whispered incantations, this shadow grew in size and clarity, until it stood out distinct and horrific. Its outline was not unlike that of a gigantic baboon, but no such baboon ever walked the earth, not even in Stygia. Still Thoth did not look, but drawing from his girdle a sandal of his master—always carried in the dim hope that he might be able to put it to such use—he cast it behind him.

"Know it well, slave of the Ring!" he exclaimed. "Find him who wore it and destroy him! Look into his eyes and blast his soul, before you tear out his throat! Kill him! Aye," in a blind burst of passion, "and all with him!"

Etched on the moonlit wall Thoth saw the horror lower its misshapen head and take the scent like some hideous hound. Then the grisly head was thrown back and the thing wheeled and was gone like a wind through the trees. The Stygian flung up his arms in maddened exultation, and his teeth and eyes gleamed in the moonlight.

A soldier on guard without the walls yelled in startled horror as a great loping black shadow with flaming eyes cleared the wall and swept by him with a swirling rush of wind. But it was gone so swiftly that the bewildered warrior was left wondering whether it had been a dream or a hallucination.

4.

When the world was young and men were weak,
and the fiends of the night walked free,
I strove with Set by fire and steel
and the juice of the upas-tree;
Now that I sleep in the mount's black heart,
and the ages take their toll,
Forget ye him who fought with the Snake
to save the human soul?

Alone in the great sleeping-chamber with its high golden dome King Conan slumbered and dreamed. Through swirling gray mists he heard a curious call, faint and far, and though he did not understand it, it seemed not within his power to ignore it. Sword in hand he went through the gray mist, as a man might walk through clouds, and the voice grew more distinct as he proceeded until he understood the word it spoke—it was his own name that was being called across the gulfs of Space or Time.

Now the mists grew lighter and he saw that he was in a great dark corridor that seemed to be cut in solid black stone. It was unlighted, but by some magic he could see plainly. The floor, ceiling and walls were highly polished and gleamed dully, and they were carved with the figures of ancient heroes and half-forgotten gods. He shuddered to see the vast shadowy outlines of the Nameless Old Ones, and he knew somehow that mortal feet had not traversed the corridor for centuries.

He came upon a wide stair carved in the solid rock, and the sides of the shaft were adorned with esoteric symbols so ancient and horrific that King Conan's skin crawled. The steps were carven each with the abhorrent figure of the Old Serpent, Set, so that at each step he planted his heel on the head of the Snake, as it was intended from old times. But he was none the less at ease for all that.

But the voice called him on, and at last, in darkness that would have been impenetrable to his material eyes, he came into a strange crypt, and saw a vague white-bearded figure sitting on a tomb. Conan's hair rose up and he grasped his sword, but the figure spoke in sepulchral tones.

"Oh man, do you know me?"

"Not I, by Crom!" swore the king.

"Man," said the ancient, "I am Epemitreus."

"But Epemitreus the Sage has been dead for fifteen hundred years!" stammered Conan.

"Harken!" spoke the other commandingly. "As a pebble cast into a dark lake sends ripples to the further shores, happenings in the Unseen World have broken like waves on my slumber. I have marked you well, Conan of Cimmeria, and the stamp of mighty happenings and great deeds is upon you. But dooms are loose in the land, against which your sword can not aid you."

"You speak in riddles," said Conan uneasily. "Let me see my foe and I'll cleave his skull to the teeth."

"Loose your barbarian fury against your foes of flesh

and blood," answered the ancient. "It is not against men I must shield you. There are dark worlds barely guessed by man, wherein formless monsters stalk—fiends which may be drawn from the Outer Voids to take material shape and rend and devour at the bidding of evil magicians. There is a serpent in your house, oh king—an adder in your kingdom, come up from Stygia, with the dark wisdom of the shadows in his murky soul. As a sleeping man dreams of the serpent which crawls near him, I have felt the foul presence of Set's neophyte. He is drunk with terrible power, and the blows he strikes at his enemy may well bring down the kingdom. I have called you to me, to give you a weapon against him and his hell-hound pack."

"But why?" bewilderedly asked Conan. "Men say you sleep in the black heart of Golamira, whence you send forth your ghost on unseen wings to aid Aquilonia in times of need, but I—I am an outlander and a barbarian."

"Peace!" the ghostly tones reverberated through the great shadowy cavern. "Your destiny is one with Aquilonia. Gigantic happenings are forming in the web and the womb of Fate, and a blood-mad sorcerer shall not stand in the path of imperial destiny. Ages ago Set coiled about the world like a python about its prey. All my life, which was as the lives of three common men, I fought him. I drove him into the shadows of the mysterious south, but in dark Stygia men still worship him who to us is the arch-demon. As I fought Set, I fight his worshippers and his votaries and his acolytes. Hold out your sword."

Wondering, Conan did so, and on the great blade, close to the heavy silver guard, the ancient traced with a bony finger a strange symbol that glowed like white fire in the shadows. And on the instant crypt, tomb and ancient vanished, and Conan, bewildered, sprang from his couch in the great golden-domed chamber. And as he stood, bewildered at the strangeness of his dream, he realized that he was gripping his sword in his hand. And his hair prickled at the nape of his neck, for on the broad blade was carven a symbol—the outline of a phoenix. And he remembered that on the tomb in the crypt he had seen what he had thought to be a similar figure, carven of stone. Now he wondered if it had been but a stone figure, and his skin crawled at the strangeness of it all.

Then as he stood, a stealthy sound in the corridor outside brought him to life, and without stopping to investigate, he began to don his armor; again he was the barbarian, suspicious and alert as a gray wolf at bay.

5.

What do I know of cultured ways, the gilt,
    the craft and the lie?
I, who was born in a naked land
    and bred in the open sky.
The subtle tongue, the sophist guile,
    they fail when the broadswords sing;
Rush in and die, dogs—I was a man before I was a king.
                —The Road of Kings.

Through the silence which shrouded the corridor of the royal palace stole twenty furtive figures. Their stealthy feet, bare or cased in soft leather, made no sound either on thick carpet or bare marble tile. The torches which stood in niches along the halls gleamed red on dagger, sword and keen-edged ax.

"Easy all!" hissed Ascalante. "Stop that cursed loud breathing, whoever it is! The officer of the night-guard has removed most of the sentries from these halls and made the rest drunk, but we must be careful, just the same. Back! Here come the guard!"

They crowded back behind a cluster of carven pillars, and almost immediately ten giants in black armor swung by at a measured pace. Their faces showed doubt as they glanced at the officer who was leading them away from their post of duty. This officer was rather pale; as the guard passed the hiding-places of the conspirators, he was seen to wipe the sweat from his brow with a shaky hand. He was young, and this betrayal of a king did not come easy to him. He mentally cursed the vain-glorious extravagance which had put him in debt to the money-lenders and made him a pawn of scheming politicians.

The guardsmen clanked by and disappeared up the corridor.

"Good!" grinned Ascalante. "Conan sleeps unguarded. Haste! If they catch us killing him, we're undone—but few men will espouse the cause of a dead king."

"Aye, haste!" cried Rinaldo, his blue eyes matching the gleam of the sword he swung above his head. "My blade is thirsty! I hear the gathering of the vultures! On!"

They hurried down the corridor with reckless speed and stopped before a gilded door which bore the royal dragon symbol of Aquilonia.

"Gromel!" snapped Ascalante. "Break me this door open!"

The giant drew a deep breath and launched his mighty frame against the panels, which groaned and bent at the impact. Again he crouched and plunged. With a snapping of bolts and a rending crash of wood, the door splintered and burst inward.

"In!" roared Ascalante, on fire with the spirit of the deed.

"In!" yelled Rinaldo. "Death to the tyrant!"

They stopped short. Conan faced them, not a naked man roused mazed and unarmed out of deep sleep to be butchered like a sheep, but a barbarian wide-awake and at bay, partly armored, and with his long sword in his hand.

For an instant the tableau held—the four rebel noblemen in the broken door, and the horde of wild hairy faces crowding behind them—all held momentarily frozen by the sight of the blazing-eyed giant standing sword in hand in the middle of the candle-lighted chamber. In that instant Ascalante beheld, on a small table near the royal couch, the silver scepter and the slender gold circlet which was the crown of Aquilonia, and the sight maddened him with desire.

"In, rogues!" yelled the outlaw. "He is one to twenty and he has no helmet!"

True; there had been lack of time to don the heavy plumed casque, or to lace in place the side-plates of the cuirass, nor was there now time to snatch the great shield from the wall. Still, Conan was better protected than any of his foes except Volmana and Gromel, who were in full armor.

The king glared, puzzled as to their identity. Ascalante he did not know; he could not see through the closed vizors of the armored conspirators, and Rinaldo had pulled his slouch cap down above his eyes. But there was no time for surmise. With a yell that rang to the roof, the killers flooded into the room, Gromel first. He came like a charging bull, head down, sword low for the disemboweling thrust. Conan sprang to meet him, and all his tigerish strength went into the arm that swung the sword. In a whistling arc the great blade flashed through the air and crashed on the Bossonian's helmet. Blade and casque shivered together and Gromel rolled lifeless on the floor. Conan bounded back, still gripping the broken hilt.

"Gromel!" he spat, his eyes blazing in amazement, as the shattered helmet disclosed the shattered head; then the rest of the pack were upon him. A dagger point raked along his ribs between breastplate and backplate, a sword-edge flashed before his eyes. He flung aside the dagger-wielder with his left arm, and smashed his broken hilt like a cestus into the swordsman's temple. The man's brains spattered in his face.

"Watch the door, five of you!" screamed Ascalante, dancing about the edge of the singing steel whirlpool, for he feared that Conan might smash through their midst and escape. The rogues drew back momentarily, as their leader seized several and thrust them toward the single door, and in that brief respite Conan leaped to the wall and tore therefrom an ancient battle-ax which, untouched by time, had hung there for half a century.

With his back to the wall he faced the closing ring for a flashing instant, then leaped into the thick of them. He was no defensive fighter; even in the teeth of overwhelming odds he always carried the war to the enemy. Any other man would have already died there, and Conan himself did not hope to survive, but he did ferociously wish to inflict as much damage as he could before he fell. His barbaric soul was ablaze, and the chants of old heroes were singing in his ears.

As he sprang from the wall his ax dropped an outlaw with a severed shoulder, and the terrible back-hand return crushed the skull of another. Swords whined venomously about him, but death passed him by breathless margins. The Cimmerian moved in a blur of blinding speed. He was like a tiger among baboons as he leaped, side-stepped and spun, offering an ever-moving target, while his ax wove a shining wheel of death about him.

For a brief space the assassins crowded him fiercely, raining blows blindly and hampered by their own numbers; then they gave back suddenly—two corpses on the floor gave mute evidence of the king's fury, though Conan himself was bleeding from wounds on arm, neck and legs.

"Knaves!" screamed Rinaldo, dashing off his feathered cap, his wild eyes glaring. "Do ye shrink from the combat? Shall the despot live? Out on it!"

He rushed in, hacking madly, but Conan, recognizing him, shattered his sword with a short terrific chop and with a powerful push of his open hand sent him reeling to the floor. The king took Ascalante's point in his left arm, and the outlaw barely saved his life by ducking and springing backward from the swinging ax. Again the wolves swirled in and Conan's ax sang and crushed. A hairy rascal stooped beneath its stroke and dived at the king's legs, but after wrestling for a brief instant at what seemed a solid iron tower, glanced up in time to see the ax falling, but not in time to avoid it. In the interim one of his comrades lifted a broadsword with both hands and hewed through the king's left shoulder-plate, wounding the shoulder beneath. In an instant Conan's cuirass was full of blood.

Volmana, flinging the attackers right and left in his savage impatience, came plowing through and hacked murderously at Conan's unprotected head. The king ducked deeply and the sword shaved off a lock of his black hair as it whistled above him. Conan pivoted on his heel and struck in from the side. The ax crunched through the steel cuirass and Volmana crumpled with his whole left side caved in.

"Volmana!" gasped Conan breathlessly. "I'll know that dwarf in Hell—"

He straightened to meet the maddened rush of Rinaldo, who charged in wild and wide open, armed only with a dagger. Conan leaped back, lifting his ax.

"Rinaldo!" his voice was strident with desperate urgency. "Back! I would not slay you—"

"Die, tyrant!" screamed the mad minstrel, hurling himself headlong on the king. Conan delayed the blow he was loath to deliver, until it was too late. Only when he felt the bite of the steel in his unprotected side did he strike, in a frenzy of blind desperation.

Rinaldo dropped with his skull shattered, and Conan reeled back against the wall, blood spurting from between the fingers which gripped his wound.

"In, now, and slay him!" yelled Ascalante.

Conan put his back against the wall and lifted his ax. He stood like an image of the unconquerable primordial—legs braced far apart, head thrust forward, one hand clutching the wall for support, the other gripping the ax on high, with the great corded muscles standing out in iron ridges, and his features frozen in a death snarl of fury—his eyes blazing terribly through the mist of blood which veiled them. The men faltered—wild, criminal and dissolute though they were, yet they came of a breed men called civilized, with a civilized background; here was the barbarian—the natural killer. They shrank back—the dying tiger could still deal death.

Conan sensed their uncertainty and grinned mirthlessly and ferociously.

"Who dies first?" he mumbled through smashed and bloody lips.

Ascalante leaped like a wolf, halted almost in midair with incredible quickness and fell prostrate to avoid the death which was hissing toward him. He frantically whirled his feet out of the way and rolled clear as Conan recovered from his missed blow and struck again. This time the ax sank inches deep into the polished floor close to Ascalante's revolving legs.

Another misguided desperado chose this instant to charge, followed half-heartedly by his fellows. He intended killing Conan before the Cimmerian could wrench his ax from the floor, but his judgment was faulty. The red ax lurched up and crashed down and a crimson caricature of a man catapulted back against the legs of the attackers.

At that instant a fearful scream burst from the rogues at the door as a black misshapen shadow fell across the wall. All but Ascalante wheeled at that cry, and then, howling like dogs, they burst blindly through the door in a raving, blaspheming mob, and scattered through the corridors in screaming flight.

Ascalante did not look toward the door; he had eyes only for the wounded king. He supposed that the noise of the fray had at last roused the palace, and that the loyal guards were upon him, though even in that moment it seemed strange that his hardened rogues should scream so terribly in their flight. Conan did not look toward the door because he was watching the outlaw with the burning eyes of a dying wolf. In this extremity Ascalante's cynical philosophy did not desert him.

"All seems to be lost, particularly honor," he murmured. "However, the king is dying on his feet—and—" Whatever other cogitation might have passed through his mind is not to be known; for, leaving the sentence uncompleted, he ran lightly at Conan just as the Cimmerian was perforce employing his ax-arm to wipe the blood from his blinded eyes.

But even as he began his charge, there was a strange rushing in the air and a heavy weight struck terrifically between his shoulders. He was dashed headlong and great talons sank agonizingly in his flesh. Writhing desperately beneath his attacker, he twisted his head about and stared into the face of Nightmare and lunacy. Upon him crouched a great black thing which he knew was born in no sane or human world. Its slavering black fangs were near his throat and the glare of its yellow eyes shriveled his limbs as a killing wind shrivels young corn.

The hideousness of its face transcended mere bestiality. It might have been the face of an ancient, evil mummy, quickened with demoniac life. In those abhorrent features the outlaw's dilated eyes seemed to see, like a shadow in the madness that enveloped him, a faint and terrible resemblance to the slave Thoth-Amon. Then Ascalante's cynical and all-sufficient philosophy deserted him, and with a ghastly cry he gave up the ghost before those slavering fangs touched him.

Conan, shaking the blood-drops from his eyes, stared frozen. At first he thought it was a great black hound which stood above Ascalante's distorted body; then as his sight cleared he saw that it was neither a hound nor a baboon.

With a cry that was like an echo of Ascalante's death-shriek, he reeled away from the wall and met the leaping horror with a cast of his ax that had behind it all the desperate power of his electrified nerves. The flying weapon glanced singing from the slanting skull it should have crushed, and the king was hurled halfway across the chamber by the impact of the giant body.

The slavering jaws closed on the arm Conan flung up to guard his throat, but the monster made no effort to secure a death-grip. Over his mangled arm it glared fiendishly into the king's eyes, in which there began to be mirrored a likeness of the horror which stared from the dead eyes of Ascalante. Conan felt his soul shrivel and begin to be drawn out of his body, to drown in the yellow wells of cosmic horror which glimmered spectrally in the formless chaos that was growing about him and engulfing all life and sanity. Those eyes grew and became gigantic, and in them the Cimmerian glimpsed the reality of all the abysmal and blasphemous horrors that lurk in the outer darkness of formless voids and nighted gulfs. He opened his bloody lips to shriek his hate and loathing, but only a dry rattle burst from his throat.

But the horror that paralyzed and destroyed Ascalante roused in the Cimmerian a frenzied fury akin to madness.

With a volcanic wrench of his whole body he plunged backward, heedless of the agony of his torn arm, dragging the monster bodily with him. And his outflung hand struck something his dazed fighting-brain recognized as the hilt of his broken sword. Instinctively he gripped it and struck with all the power of nerve and thew, as a man stabs with a dagger. The broken blade sank deep and Conan's arm was released as the abhorrent mouth gaped as in agony. The king was hurled violently aside, and lifting himself on one hand he saw, as one mazed, the terrible convulsions of the monster from which thick blood was gushing through the great wound his broken blade had torn. And as he watched, its struggles ceased and it lay jerking spasmodically, staring upward with its grisly dead eyes. Conan blinked and shook the blood from his own eyes; it seemed to him that the thing was melting and disintegrating into a slimy unstable mass.

Then a medley of voices reached his ears, and the room was thronged with the finally roused people of the court—knights, peers, ladies, men-at-arms, councilors—all babbling and shouting and getting in one another's way. The Black Dragons were on hand, wild with rage, swearing and ruffling, with their hands on their hilts and foreign oaths in their teeth. Of the young officer of the door-guard nothing was seen, nor was he found then or later, though earnestly sought after.

"Gromel! Volmana! Rinaldo!" exclaimed Publius, the high councilor, wringing his fat hands among the corpses. "Black treachery! Some one shall dance for this! Call the guard."

"The guard is here, you old fool!" cavalierly snapped Pallantides, commander of the Black Dragons, forgetting

Publius' rank in the stress of the moment. "Best stop your caterwauling and aid us to bind the king's wounds. He's like to bleed to death."

"Yes, yes!" cried Publius, who was a man of plans rather than action. "We must bind his wounds. Send for every leech of the court! Oh, my lord, what a black shame on the city! Are you entirely slain?"

"Wine!" gasped the king from the couch where they had laid him. They put a goblet to his bloody lips and he drank like a man half-dead of thirst.

"Good!" he grunted, falling back. "Slaying is cursed dry work."

They had stanched the flow of blood, and the innate vitality of the barbarian was asserting itself.

"See first to the dagger-wound in my side," he bade the court physicians. "Rinaldo wrote me a deathly song there, and keen was the stylus."

"We should have hanged him long ago," gibbered Publius. "No good can come of poets—who is this?"

He nervously touched Ascalante's body with his sandaled toe.

"By Mitra!" ejaculated the commander. "It is Ascalante, once count of Thune! What devil's work brought *him* up from his desert haunts?"

"But why does he stare so?" whispered Publius, drawing away, his own eyes wide and a peculiar prickling among the short hairs at the back of his fat neck. The others fell silent as they gazed at the dead outlaw.

"Had you seen what he and I saw," growled the king, sitting up despite the protests of the leeches, "you had not wondered. Blast your own gaze by looking at—" He stopped short, his mouth gaping, his finger pointing fruitlessly. Where the monster had died, only the bare floor met his eyes.

"Crom!" he swore. "The thing's melted back into the foulness which bore it!"

"The king is delirious," whispered a noble. Conan heard and swore with barbaric oaths.

"By Badb, Morrigan, Macha and Nemain!" he concluded wrathfully. "I am sane! It was like a cross between a Stygian mummy and a baboon. It came through the door, and Ascalante's rogues fled before it. It slew Ascalante, who was about to run me through. Then it came upon me and I slew it—how I know not, for my ax glanced from it as from a rock. But I think that the Sage Epemitreus had a hand in it—"

"Hark how he names Epemitreus, dead for fifteen hundred years!" they whispered to each other.

"By Ymir!" thundered the king. "This night I talked with Epemitreus! He called to me in my dreams, and I walked down a black stone corridor carved with old gods, to a stone stair on the steps of which were the outlines of Set, until I came to a crypt, and a tomb with a phoenix carved on it—"

"In Mitra's name, lord king, be silent!" It was the high-priest of Mitra who cried out, and his countenance was ashen.

Conan threw up his head like a lion tossing back its mane, and his voice was thick with the growl of the angry lion.

"Am I a slave, to shut my mouth at your command?"

"Nay, nay, my lord!" The high-priest was trembling, but not through fear of the royal wrath. "I meant no offense." He bent his head close to the king and spoke in a whisper that carried only to Conan's ears.

"My lord, this is a matter beyond human understanding. Only the inner circle of the priestcraft know of the black stone corridor carved in the black heart of Mount Golamira, by unknown hands, or of the phœnix-guarded tomb where Epemitreus was laid to rest fifteen hundred years ago. And since that time no living man has entered it, for his chosen priests, after placing the Sage in the crypt, blocked up the outer entrance of the corridor so that no man could find it, and today not even the high-priests know where it is. Only by word of mouth, handed down by the high-priests to the chosen few, and jealously guarded, does the inner circle of Mitra's acolytes know of the resting-place of Epemitreus in the black heart of Golamira. It is one of the Mysteries, on which Mitra's cult stands."

"I can not say by what magic Epemitreus brought me to him," answered Conan. "But I talked with him, and he made a mark on my sword. Why that mark made it deadly to demons, or what magic lay behind the mark, I know not; but though the blade broke on Gromel's helmet, yet the fragment was long enough to kill the horror."

"Let me see your sword," whispered the high-priest from a throat gone suddenly dry.

Conan held out the broken weapon and the high-priest cried out and fell to his knees.

"Mitra guard us against the powers of darkness!" he gasped. "The king has indeed talked with Epemitreus this night! There on the sword—it is the secret sign none might make but him—the emblem of the immortal phœnix which broods forever over his tomb! A candle, quick! Look again at the spot where the king said the goblin died!"

It lay in the shade of a broken screen. They threw the screen aside and bathed the floor in a flood of candlelight. And a shuddering silence fell over the people as they looked. Then some fell on their knees calling on Mitra, and some fled screaming from the chamber.

There on the floor where the monster had died, there lay, like a tangible shadow, a broad dark stain that could not be washed out; the thing had left its outline clearly etched in its blood, and that outline was of no being of a sane and normal world. Grim and horrific it brooded there, like the shadow cast by one of the apish gods that squat on the shadowy altars of dim temples in the dark land of Stygia.

THE SCARLET CITADEL

Weird Tales, January 1933

———

They trapped the Lion on Shamu's plain;
They weighted his limbs with an iron chain;
They cried loud in the trumpet-blast,
They cried, "The Lion is caged at last!"
Woe to the cities of river and plain
If ever the Lion stalks again!

—Old Ballad.

The roar of battle had died away; the shout of victory mingled with the cries of the dying. Like gay-hued leaves after an autumn storm, the fallen littered the plain; the sinking sun shimmered on burnished helmets, gilt-worked mail, silver breastplates, broken swords, and the heavy regal folds of silken standards, overthrown in pools of curdling crimson. In silent heaps lay war-horses and their steel-clad riders, flowing manes and blowing plumes stained alike in the red tide. About them and among them, like the drift of a storm, were strewn slashed and trampled bodies in steel caps and leather jerkins—archers and pikemen.

The oliphants sounded a fanfare of triumph all over the plain, and the hoofs of the victors crunched in the breasts of the vanquished as all the straggling, shining lines converged inward like the spokes of a glittering wheel, to the spot where the last survivor still waged unequal strife.

That day Conan, king of Aquilonia, had seen the pick of his chivalry cut to pieces, smashed and hammered to bits, and swept into eternity. With five thousand knights he had crossed the southeastern border of Aquilonia and ridden into the grassy meadowlands of Ophir, to find his former ally, King Amalrus of Ophir, drawn up against him with the hosts of Strabonus, king of Koth. Too late he had seen the trap. All that a man might do he had done with his five thousand cavalrymen against the thirty thousand knights, archers and spearmen of the conspirators.

Without bowmen or infantry, he had hurled his armored horsemen against the oncoming host, had seen the knights of his foes in their shining mail go down before his lances, had torn the opposing center to bits, driving the riven ranks headlong before him, only to find himself caught in a vise as the untouched wings closed in. Strabonus' Shemitish bowmen had wrought havoc among his knights, feathering them with shafts that found every crevice in their armor, shooting down the horses, the Kothian pikemen rushing in to spear the fallen riders. The mailed lancers of the routed center had reformed, reinforced by the riders from the wings, and had charged again and again, sweeping the field by sheer weight of numbers.

The Aquilonians had not fled; they had died on the field, and of the five thousand knights who had followed Conan southward, not one left the plain of Shamu alive. And now the king himself stood at bay among the slashed bodies of his house-troops, his back against a heap of dead horses and men. Ophirean knights in gilded mail leaped their horses over mounds of corpses to slash at the solitary figure; squat Shemites with blue-black beards, and dark-faced Kothian knights ringed him on foot. The clangor of steel rose deafeningly; the black-mailed figure of the western king loomed among his swarming foes, dealing blows like a butcher wielding a great cleaver. Riderless horses raced down the field; about his iron-clad feet grew a ring of mangled corpses. His attackers drew back from his desperate savagery, panting and livid.

Now through the yelling, cursing lines rode the lords of the conquerors—Strabonus, with his broad dark face and crafty eyes; Amalrus, slender, fastidious, treacherous, dangerous as a cobra; and the lean vulture Tsotha-lanti, clad only in silken robes, his great black eyes glittering from a face that was like that of a bird of prey. Of this Kothian wizard dark tales were told; tousle-headed women in northern and western villages frightened children with his name, and rebellious slaves were brought to abased submission quicker than by the lash, with the threat of being sold to him. Men said that he had a whole library of dark works bound in skin flayed from living human victims, and that in nameless pits below the hill whereon his palace sat, he trafficked with the powers of darkness, trading screaming girl slaves for unholy secrets. He was the real ruler of Koth.

Now he grinned bleakly as the kings reined back a safe distance from the grim iron-clad figure looming among the dead. Before the savage blue eyes blazing murderously from beneath the crested, dented helmet, the boldest shrank.

Conan's dark scarred face was darker yet with passion; his black armor was hacked to tatters and splashed with blood; his great sword red to the crosspiece. In this stress all the veneer of civilization had faded; it was a barbarian who faced his conquerors. Conan was a Cimmerian by birth, one of those fierce moody hillmen who dwelt in their gloomy, cloudy land in the north. His saga, which had led him to the throne of Aquilonia, was the basis of a whole cycle of hero-tales.

So now the kings kept their distance, and Strabonus called on his Shemitish archers to loose their arrows at his foe from a distance; his captains had fallen like ripe grain before the Cimmerian's broadsword, and Strabonus, penurious of his knights as of his coins, was frothing with fury. But Tsotha shook his head.

"Take him alive."

"Easy to say!" snarled Strabonus, uneasy lest in some way the black-mailed giant might hew a path to them through the spears. "Who can take a man-eating tiger alive? By Ishtar, his heel is on the necks of my finest swordsmen! It took seven years and stacks of gold to train each, and there they lie, so much kite's meat. Arrows, I say!"

"Again, nay!" snapped Tsotha, swinging down from his horse. He laughed coldly. "Have you not learned by this time that my brain is mightier than any sword?"

He passed through the lines of the pikemen, and the giants in their steel caps and mail brigandines shrank back fearfully, lest they so much as touch the skirts of his robe. Nor were the plumed knights slower in making room for him. He stepped over the corpses and came face to face with the grim king. The hosts watched in tense silence, holding their breath. The black-armored figure loomed in terrible menace over the lean, silk-robed shape, the notched, dripping sword hovering on high.

"I offer you life, Conan," said Tsotha, a cruel mirth bubbling at the back of his voice.

"I give you death, wizard," snarled the king, and backed by iron muscles and ferocious hate the great sword swung in a stroke meant to shear Tsotha's lean torso in half. But even as the host cried out, the wizard stepped in, too quick for the eye to follow, and apparently merely laid an open hand on Conan's left forearm, from the rigid muscles of which the mail had been hacked away. The whistling blade veered from its arc and the mailed giant crashed heavily to earth, to lie motionless. Tsotha laughed silently.

"Take him up and fear not; the lion's fangs are drawn."

The kings reined in and gazed in awe at the fallen lion. Conan lay stiffly, like a dead man, but his eyes glared up at them, wide open, and blazing with helpless fury.

"What have you done to him?" asked Amalrus uneasily.

Tsotha displayed a broad ring of curious design on his finger. He pressed his fingers together and on the inner side of the ring a tiny steel fang darted out like a snake's tongue.

"It is steeped in the juice of the purple lotus which grows in the ghost-haunted swamps of southern Stygia," said the magician. "Its touch produces temporary paralysis. Put him in chains and lay him in a chariot. The sun sets and it is time we were on the road for Khorshemish."

Strabonus turned to his general Arbanus.

"We return to Khorshemish with the wounded. Only a troop of the royal cavalry will accompany us. Your orders are to march at dawn to the Aquilonian border, and invest the city of Shamar. The Ophireans will supply you with food along the march. We will rejoin you as soon as possible, with reinforcements."

So the host, with its steel-sheathed knights, its pikemen and archers and camp-servants, went into camp in the meadowlands near the battlefield. And through the starry night the two kings and the sorcerer who was greater than any king rode to the capital of Strabonus, in the midst of the glittering palace troop, and accompanied by a long line of chariots, loaded with the wounded. In one of these chariots lay Conan, king of Aquilonia, weighted with chains, the tang of defeat in his mouth, the blind fury of a trapped tiger in his soul.

The poison which had frozen his mighty limbs to helplessness had not paralyzed his brain. As the chariot in which he lay rumbled over the meadowlands, his mind revolved maddeningly about his defeat. Amalrus had sent an emissary imploring aid against Strabonus, who, he said, was ravaging his western domain, which lay like a tapering wedge between the border of Aquilonia and the vast southern kingdom of Koth. He asked only a thousand horsemen and the presence of Conan, to hearten his demoralized subjects. Conan now blasphemed mentally. In his generosity he had come with five times the number the treacherous monarch had asked. In good faith he had ridden into Ophir, and had been confronted by the supposed rivals allied against him. It spoke significantly of his prowess that they had brought up a whole host to trap him and his five thousand.

A red cloud veiled his vision; his veins swelled with fury and in his temples a pulse throbbed maddeningly. In all his life he had never known greater and more helpless wrath. In swift-moving scenes the pageant of his life passed fleetingly before his mental eye—a panorama wherein moved shadowy figures which were himself, in many guises and conditions—a skin-clad barbarian; a mercenary swordsman in horned helmet and scale-mail corselet; a corsair in a dragon-prowed galley that trailed a crimson wake of blood and pillage along southern coasts; a captain of hosts in burnished steel, on a rearing black charger; a king on a golden throne with the lion banner flowing above, and throngs of gay-hued courtiers and ladies on their knees. But always the jouncing and rumbling of the chariot brought his thoughts back to revolve with maddening monotony about the treachery of Amalrus and the sorcery of Tsotha. The veins nearly burst in his temples and the cries of the wounded in the chariots filled him with ferocious satisfaction.

Before midnight they crossed the Ophirean border and at dawn the spires of Khorshemish stood up gleaming and rose-tinted on the southeastern horizon, the slim towers overawed by the grim scarlet citadel that at a distance was like a splash of bright blood in the sky. That was the castle of Tsotha. Only one narrow street, paved with marble and guarded by heavy iron gates, led up to it, where it crowned the hill dominating the city. The sides of that hill were too sheer to be climbed elsewhere. From the walls of the citadel one could look down on the broad white streets of the city, on minaretted mosques, shops, temples, mansions, and markets. One could look down, too, on the palaces of the king, set in broad gardens, high-walled, luxurious riots of fruit trees and blossoms, through which artificial streams murmured, and silvery fountains rippled incessantly. Over all brooded the citadel, like a condor stooping above its prey, intent on its own dark meditations.

The mighty gates between the huge towers of the outer wall clanged open, and the king rode into his capital between lines of glittering spearmen, while fifty trumpets pealed salute. But no throngs swarmed the white-paved streets to fling roses before the conqueror's hoofs. Strabonus had raced ahead of news of the battle, and the people, just rousing to the occupations of the day, gaped to see their king returning with a small retinue, and were in doubt as to whether it portended victory or defeat.

Conan, life sluggishly moving in his veins again, craned his neck from the chariot floor to view the wonders of this city which men called the Queen of the South. He had thought to ride some day through these golden-chased gates at the head of his steel-clad squadrons, with the great lion banner flowing over his helmeted head. Instead he entered in chains, stripped of his armor, and thrown like a captive slave on the bronze floor of his conqueror's chariot. A wayward devilish mirth of mockery rose above his fury, but to the nervous soldiers who drove the chariot his laughter sounded like the muttering of a rousing lion.

2.

Gleaming shell of an outworn lie; fable of Right divine—
You gained your crowns by heritage,
*   but Blood was the price of mine.*
The throne that I won by blood and sweat,
*   by Crom, I will not sell*
For promise of valleys filled with gold,
*   or threat of the Halls of Hell!*

—The Road of Kings.

In the citadel, in a chamber with a domed ceiling of carven jet, and the fretted arches of doorways glimmering with strange dark jewels, a strange conclave came to pass. Conan of Aquilonia, blood from unbandaged wounds caking his huge limbs, faced his captors. On either side of him stood a dozen black giants, grasping their long-shafted axes. In front of him stood Tsotha, and on divans lounged Strabonus and Amalrus in their silks and gold, gleaming with jewels, naked slave-boys beside them pouring wine into cups carved of a single sapphire. In strong contrast stood Conan, grim, bloodstained, naked but for a loincloth, shackles on his mighty limbs, his blue eyes blazing beneath the tangled black mane that fell over his low broad forehead. He dominated the scene, turning to tinsel the pomp of the conquerors by the sheer vitality of his elemental personality, and the kings in their pride and splendor were aware of it each in his secret heart, and were not at ease. Only Tsotha was not disturbed.

"Our desires are quickly spoken, king of Aquilonia," said Tsotha. "It is our wish to extend our empire."

"And so you want to swine my kingdom," rasped Conan.

"What are you but an adventurer, seizing a crown to which you had no more claim than any other wandering barbarian?" parried Amalrus. "We are prepared to offer you suitable compensation—"

"Compensation?" It was a gust of deep laughter from Conan's mighty chest. "The price of infamy and treachery! I am a barbarian, so I shall sell my kingdom and its people for life and your filthy gold? Ha! How did you come to your crown, you and that black-faced pig beside you? Your fathers did the fighting and the suffering, and handed their crowns to you on golden platters. What you inherited without lifting a finger—except to poison a few brothers—I fought for.

"You sit on satin and guzzle wine the people sweat for, and talk of divine rights of sovereignty—bah! I climbed out of the abyss of naked barbarism to the throne and in that climb I spilt my blood as freely as I spilt that of others. If either of us has the right to rule men, by Crom, it is I! How have you proved yourself my superior?

"I found Aquilonia in the grip of a pig like you—one who traced his genealogy for a thousand years. The land was torn with the wars of the barons, and the people cried out under suppression and taxation. Today no Aquilonian noble dares maltreat the humblest of my subjects, and the taxes of the people are lighter than anywhere else in the world.

"What of you? Your brother, Amalrus, holds the eastern half of your kingdom and defies you. And you, Strabonus, your soldiers are even now besieging castles of a dozen or more rebellious barons. The people of both your kingdoms are crushed into the earth by tyrannous taxes and levies.

And you would loot mine—ha! Free my hands and I'll varnish this floor with your brains!"

Tsotha grinned bleakly to see the rage of his kingly companions.

"All this, truthful though it be, is beside the point. Our plans are no concern of yours. Your responsibility is at an end when you sign this parchment, which is an abdication in favor of Prince Arpello of Pellia. We will give you arms and horse, and five thousand golden lunas, and escort you to the eastern frontiers."

"Setting me adrift where I was when I rode into Aquilonia to take service in her armies, except with the added burden of a traitor's name!" Conan's laugh was like the deep short bark of a timber wolf. "Arpello, eh? I've had suspicions of that butcher of Pellia. Can you not even steal and pillage frankly and honestly, but you must have an excuse, however thin? Arpello claims a trace of royal blood; so you use him as an excuse for theft, and a satrap to rule through! I'll see you in Hell first."

"You're a fool!" exclaimed Amalrus. "You are in our hands, and we can take both crown and life at our pleasure!"

Conan's answer was neither kingly nor dignified, but characteristically instinctive in the man, whose barbaric nature had never been submerged in his adopted culture. He spat full in Amalrus' eyes. The king of Ophir leaped up with a scream of outraged fury, groping for his slender sword. Drawing it, he rushed at the Cimmerian, but Tsotha intervened.

"Wait, your majesty; this man is *my* prisoner."

"Aside, wizard!" shrieked Amalrus, maddened by the glare in the Cimmerian's blue eyes.

"Back, I say!" roared Tsotha, roused to awesome wrath. His lean hand came from his sleeve and cast a shower of dust into the Ophirean's contorted face. Amalrus cried out and staggered back, clutching at his eyes, the sword falling from his hand. He dropped limply on the divan, while the Kothian guards looked on stolidly and King Strabonus hurriedly gulped another goblet of wine, holding it with hands that trembled. Amalrus lowered his hands and shook his head violently, intelligence slowly sifting back into his gray eyes.

"I went blind," he growled. "What did you do to me, wizard?"

"Merely a gesture to convince you who was the real master," snapped Tsotha, the mask of his formal pretense dropped, revealing the naked evil personality of the man. "Strabonus has learned his lesson—let you learn yours. It was but a dust I found in a Stygian tomb which I flung into your eyes—if I brush out their sight again, I will leave you to grope in darkness for the rest of your life."

Amalrus shrugged his shoulders, smiled whimsically and reached for a goblet, dissembling his fear and fury. A polished diplomat, he was quick to regain his poise. Tsotha turned to Conan, who had stood imperturbably during the episode. At the wizard's gesture, the blacks laid hold of their prisoner and marched him behind Tsotha, who led the way out of the chamber through an arched doorway into a winding corridor, whose floor was of many-hued mosaics, whose walls were inlaid with gold tissue and silver chasing, and from whose fretted arched ceiling swung golden censers, filling the corridor with dreamy perfumed clouds. They turned down a smaller corridor, done in jet and black jade, gloomy and awful, which ended at a brass door, over whose arch a human skull grinned horrifically. At this door stood a fat repellent figure, dangling a bunch of keys—Tsotha's chief eunuch, Shukeli, of whom grisly tales were whispered—a man with whom a bestial lust for torture took the place of normal human passions.

The brass door let onto a narrow stair that seemed to wind down into the very bowels of the hill on which the citadel stood. Down these stairs went the band, to halt at last at an iron door, the strength of which seemed unnecessary. Evidently it did not open on outer air, yet it was built as if to withstand the battering of mangonels and rams. Shukeli opened it, and as he swung back the ponderous portal, Conan noted the evident uneasiness among the black giants who guarded him; nor did Shukeli seem altogether devoid of nervousness as he peered into the darkness beyond. Inside the great door there was a second barrier, composed of great steel bars. It was fastened by an ingenious bolt which had no lock and could be worked only from the outside; this bolt shot back, the grille slid into the wall. They passed through, into a broad corridor, the floor, walls and arched ceiling of which seemed to be cut out of solid stone. Conan knew he was far underground, even below the hill itself. The darkness pressed in on the guardsmen's torches like a sentient, animate thing.

They made the king fast to a ring in the stone wall. Above his head in a niche in the wall they placed a torch, so that he stood in a dim semicircle of light. The blacks were anxious to be gone; they muttered among themselves, and cast fearful glances at the darkness. Tsotha motioned them out, and they filed through the door in stumbling haste, as if fearing the darkness might take tangible form and spring upon their backs. Tsotha turned toward Conan, and the king noticed uneasily that the wizard's eyes shone in the semi-darkness, and that his teeth much resembled the fangs of a wolf, gleaming whitely in the shadows.

"And so, farewell, barbarian," mocked the sorcerer. "I must ride to Shamar, and the siege. In ten days I will be in your palace in Tamar, with my warriors. What word from you shall I say to your women, before I flay their dainty skins for scrolls whereon to chronicle the triumphs of Tsotha-lanti?"

Conan answered with a searing Cimmerian curse that would have burst the very eardrums of an ordinary man, and Tsotha laughed thinly and withdrew. Conan had a glimpse of his vulture-like figure through the thick-set bars, as he slid home the grate; then the heavy outer door clanged, and silence fell like a pall.

3.

The Lion strode through the halls of Hell;
Across his path grim shadows fell
Of many a mowing, nameless shape—
Monsters with dripping jaws agape.
The darkness shuddered with scream and yell
When the Lion stalked through the halls of Hell.
                                        —Old Ballad.

King Conan tested the ring in the wall and the chain that bound him. His limbs were free, but he knew that his shackles were beyond even his iron strength. The links of the chain were as thick as his thumb, and were fastened to a band of steel about his waist, a band broad as his hand and half an inch thick. The sheer weight of his shackles would have slain a lesser man with exhaustion. The locks that held band and chain were massive affairs that a sledge-hammer could hardly have dinted. As for the ring, evidently it went clear through the wall and was clinched on the other side.

Conan cursed and panic surged through him as he glared into the darkness that pressed against the half-circle of light. All the superstitious dread of the barbarian slept in his soul, untouched by civilized logic. His primitive imagination peopled the subterranean darkness with grisly shapes. Besides, his reason told him that he had not been placed there merely for confinement. His captors had no reason to spare him. He had been placed in these pits for a definite doom. He cursed himself for his refusal of their offer, even while his stubborn manhood revolted at the thought, and he knew that were he taken forth and given another chance, his reply would be the same. He would not sell his subjects to the butcher. And yet it had been with no thought of anyone's gain but his own that he had seized the kingdom originally. Thus subtly does the instinct of sovereign responsibility enter even a red-handed plunderer sometimes.

Conan thought of Tsotha's last abominable threat, and groaned in sick fury, knowing it was no idle boast. Men and women were to the wizard no more than the writhing insect is to the scientist. Soft white hands that had caressed him, red lips that had been pressed to his, dainty white bosoms that had quivered to his hot fierce kisses, to be stripped of their delicate skin, white as ivory and pink as young petals—from Conan's lips burst a yell so frightful and inhuman in its mad fury that a listener would have started in horror to know that it came from a human throat.

The shuddering echoes made him start and brought back his own situation vividly to the king. He glared fearsomely at the outer gloom, and thought of all the grisly tales he had heard of Tsotha's necromantic cruelty, and it was with an icy sensation down his spine that he realized that these must be the very Halls of Horror named in shuddering legendry, the tunnels and dungeons wherein Tsotha performed horrible experiments with beings human, bestial, and, it was whispered, demoniac, tampering blasphemously with the naked basic elements of life itself. Rumor said that the mad poet Rinaldo had visited these pits, and been shown horrors by the wizard, and that the nameless monstrosities of which he hinted in his awful poem, *The Song of the Pit*, were no mere fantasies of a disordered brain. That brain had crashed to dust beneath Conan's battle-ax on the night the king had fought for his life with the assassins the mad rhymer had led into the betrayed palace, but the shuddersome words of that grisly song still rang in the king's ears as he stood there in his chains.

Even with the thought the Cimmerian was frozen by a soft rustling sound, blood-freezing in its implication. He tensed in an attitude of listening, painful in its intensity. An icy hand stroked his spine. It was the unmistakable sound of pliant scales slithering softly over stone. Cold sweat beaded his skin, as beyond the ring of dim light he saw a vague and colossal form, awful even in its indistinctness. It reared upright, swaying slightly, and yellow eyes burned icily on him from the shadows. Slowly a huge, hideous, wedge-shaped head took form before his dilated eyes, and from the darkness oozed, in flowing scaly coils, the ultimate horror of reptilian development.

It was a snake that dwarfed all Conan's previous ideas of snakes. Eighty feet it stretched from its pointed tail to its triangular head, which was bigger than that of a horse. In the dim light its scales glistened coldly, white as hoar-frost. Surely this reptile was one born and grown in darkness, yet its eyes were full of evil and sure sight. It looped its titan coils in front of the captive, and the great head on the arching neck swayed a matter of inches from his face. Its forked tongue almost brushed his lips as it darted in and out, and its fetid odor made his senses reel with nausea. The great yellow eyes burned into his, and Conan gave back the stare of a trapped wolf. He fought frenziedly against the mad impulse to grasp the great arching neck in his tearing hands. Strong beyond the comprehension of civilized man, he had broken the neck of a python in a fiendish battle on the Stygian coast, in his corsair days. But this reptile was venomous; he saw the great fangs, a foot long, curved like scimitars. From them dripped a colorless liquid that he instinctively knew was death. He might conceivably crush that wedge-shaped skull with a desperate clenched fist, but he knew that at his first hint of movement, the monster would strike like lightning.

It was not because of any logical reasoning process that Conan remained motionless, since reason might have told him—since he was doomed anyway—to goad the snake into striking and get it over with; it was the blind black instinct of self-preservation that held him rigid as a statue blasted out of iron. Now the great barrel reared up and the head was poised high above his own, as the monster investigated the torch. A drop of venom fell on his naked thigh, and the feel of it was like a white-hot dagger driven into his flesh. Red jets of agony shot through Conan's brain, yet he held himself immovable; not by the twitching of a muscle or the flicker of an eyelash did he betray the pain of the hurt that left a scar he bore to the day of his death.

The serpent swayed above him, as if seeking to ascertain whether there were in truth life in this figure which stood so death-like still. Then suddenly, unexpectedly, the outer door, all but invisible in the shadows, clanged stridently. The serpent, suspicious as all its kind, whipped about with a quickness incredible for its bulk, and vanished with a long-drawn slithering down the corridor. The door swung open and remained open. The grille was withdrawn and a huge dark figure was framed in the glow of torches outside. The figure glided in, pulling the grille partly to behind it, leaving the bolt poised. As it moved into the light of the torch over Conan's head, the king saw that it was a gigantic black man, stark naked, bearing in one hand a huge sword and in the other a bunch of keys. The black spoke in a sea-coast dialect, and Conan replied; he had learned the jargon while a corsair on the coasts of Cush.

"Long have I wished to meet you, Amra." The black gave Conan the name by which the Cimmerian had been known to the Cushites in his piratical days—Amra, the Lion. The slave's woolly skull split in an animal-like grin, showing white tusks, but his eyes glinted redly in the torchlight. "I have dared much for this meeting. Look! The keys to your chains! I stole them from Shukeli. What will you give me for them?"

He dangled the keys in front of Conan's eyes.

"Ten thousand golden lunas," answered the king quickly, new hope surging fiercely in his breast.

"Not enough!" cried the black, a ferocious exultation shining on his ebon countenance. "Not enough for the risks I take. Tsotha's pets might come out of the dark and eat me, and if Shukeli finds out I stole his keys, he'll hang me up by my—well, what will you give me?"

"Fifteen thousand lunas and a palace in Poitain," offered the king.

The black yelled and stamped in a frenzy of barbaric gratification.

"More!" he cried. "Offer me more! What will you give me?"

"You black dog!" A red mist of fury swept across Conan's eyes. "Were I free I'd give you a broken back! Did Shukeli send you here to mock me?"

"Shukeli knows nothing of my coming, white man," answered the black, craning his thick neck to peer into Conan's savage eyes. "I know you from of old, since the days when I was a chief among a free people, before the Stygians took me and sold me into the north. Do you not remember the sack of Abombi, when your sea-wolves swarmed in? Before the palace of King Ajaga you slew a chief and a chief fled from you. It was my brother who died; it was I who fled. I demand of you a blood-price, Amra!"

"Free me and I'll pay you your weight in gold pieces," growled Conan.

The red eyes glittered, the white teeth flashed wolfishly in the torchlight.

"Aye, you white dog, you are like all your race; but to a black man gold can never pay for blood. The price I ask is—your head!"

The word was a maniacal shriek that sent the echoes shivering. Conan tensed, unconsciously straining against his shackles in his abhorrence of dying like a sheep; then he was frozen by a greater horror. Over the black's shoulder he saw a vague horrific form swaying in the darkness.

"Tsotha will never know!" laughed the black fiendishly, too engrossed in his gloating triumph to take heed of anything else, too drunk with hate to know that Death swayed behind his shoulder. "He will not come into the vaults until the demons have torn your bones from their chains. I will have your head, Amra!"

He braced his knotted legs like ebon columns and swung up the massive sword in both hands, his great black muscles rolling and cracking in the torchlight. And at that instant the titanic shadow behind him darted down and out, and the wedge-shaped head smote with an impact that re-echoed down the tunnels. Not a sound came from the thick blubbery lips that flew wide in fleeting agony. With the thud of the stroke, Conan saw the life go out of the wide black eyes with the suddenness of a candle blown out. The blow knocked the great black body clear across the corridor, and horribly the gigantic sinuous shape whipped around it in glistening coils that hid it from view, and the snap and splintering of bones came plainly to Conan's ears. Then something made his heart leap madly. The sword and the keys had flown from the black's hands to crash and jangle on the stone—and the keys lay almost at the king's feet.

He tried to bend to them, but the chain was too short; almost suffocated by the mad pounding of his heart, he slipped one foot from its sandal, and gripped them with his toes; drawing his foot up, he grasped them fiercely, barely stifling the yell of ferocious exultation that rose instinctively to his lips.

An instant's fumbling with the huge locks and he was free. He caught up the fallen sword and glared about. Only empty darkness met his eyes, into which the serpent had dragged a mangled, tattered object that only faintly resembled a human body. Conan turned to the open door. A few quick strides brought him to the threshold—a squeal of high-pitched laughter shrilled through the vaults, and the grille shot home under his very fingers, the bolt crashed down. Through the bars peered a face like a fiendishly mocking carven gargoyle—Shukeli the eunuch, who had followed his stolen keys. Surely he did not, in his gloating, see the sword in the prisoner's hand. With a terrible curse Conan struck as a cobra strikes; the great blade hissed between the bars and Shukeli's laughter broke in a death-scream. The fat eunuch bent at the middle, as if bowing to his killer, and crumpled like tallow, his pudgy hands clutching vainly at his spilling entrails.

Conan snarled in savage satisfaction; but he was still a prisoner. His keys were futile against the bolt which could be worked only from the outside. His experienced touch told him the bars were hard as the sword; an attempt to hew his way to freedom would only splinter his one weapon. Yet he found dents on those adamantine bars, like the marks of incredible fangs, and wondered with an involuntary shudder what nameless monster had assailed the barriers so terribly. Regardless, there was but one thing for him to do, and that was to seek some other outlet. Taking the torch from the niche, he set off down the corridor, sword in hand. He saw no sign of the serpent or its victim, only a great smear of blood on the stone floor.

Darkness stalked on noiseless feet about him, scarcely driven back by his flickering torch. On either hand he saw dark openings, but he kept to the main corridor, watching the floor ahead of him carefully, lest he fall into some pit. And suddenly he heard the sound of a woman, weeping piteously. Another of Tsotha's victims, he thought, cursing the wizard anew, and turning aside, followed the sound down a smaller tunnel, dank and damp.

The weeping grew nearer as he advanced, and lifting his torch, he made out a vague shape in the shadows. Stepping closer, he halted in sudden horror at the anthropomorphic bulk which sprawled before him. Its unstable outlines somewhat suggested at octopus, but its malformed tentacles were too short for its size, and its substance was a quaking, jelly-like stuff which made him physically sick to look at. From among this loathsome gelid mass reared up a frog-like head, and he was frozen with nauseated horror to realize that the sound of weeping was coming from those obscene blubbery lips. The noise changed to an abominable high-pitched tittering as the great unstable eyes of the monstrosity rested on him, and it hitched its quaking bulk toward him. He backed away and fled up the tunnel, not trusting his sword. The creature might be composed of terrestrial matter, but it shook his very soul to look upon it, and he doubted the power of man-made weapons to harm it. For a short distance he heard it flopping and floundering after him, screaming with horrible laughter. The unmistakably human note in its mirth almost staggered his reason. It was exactly such laughter as he had heard bubble obscenely from the fat lips of the salacious women of Shadizar, City of Wickedness, when captive girls were stripped naked on the public auction block. By what hellish arts had Tsotha brought this unnatural being into life? Conan felt vaguely that he had looked on blasphemy against the eternal laws of nature.

He ran toward the main corridor, but before he reached it he crossed a sort of small square chamber, where two tunnels crossed. As he reached this chamber, he was flashingly aware of some small squat bulk on the floor ahead of him; then before he could check his flight or swerve aside, his foot struck something yielding that squalled shrilly, and he was precipitated headlong, the torch flying from his hand and being extinguished as it struck the stone floor. Half-stunned by his fall, Conan rose and groped in the darkness. His sense of direction was confused, and he was unable to decide in which direction lay the main corridor. He did not look for the torch, as he had no means of rekindling it. His groping hands found the openings of the tunnels, and he chose one at random. How long he traversed it in utter darkness, he never knew, but suddenly his barbarian's instinct of near peril halted him short.

He had the same feeling he had had when standing on the brink of great precipices in the darkness. Dropping to all fours, he edged forward, and presently his outflung hand encountered the edge of a well, into which the tunnel floor apparently dropped abruptly. As far down as he could reach the sides fell away sheerly, dank and slimy to his touch. He stretched out an arm in the darkness and could barely touch the opposite edge with the point of his sword. He could leap across it then, but there was no point in that. He had taken the wrong tunnel and the main corridor lay somewhere behind him.

Even as he thought this, he felt a faint movement of air; a shadowy wind, rising from the well, stirred his black mane. Conan's skin crawled. He tried to tell himself that this well connected somehow with the outer world, but his instincts told him it was a thing unnatural. He was not merely inside the hill; he was below it, far below the level of the city streets. How then could an outer wind find its way into the pits and blow up from *below*? A faint throbbing pulsed on that ghostly wind, like drums beating far, far below. A strong shudder shook the king of Aquilonia.

He rose to his feet and backed away, and as he did *something* floated up out of the well. What it was, Conan did not know. He could see nothing in the darkness, but he distinctly felt a presence—an invisible, intangible intelligence which hovered malignly near him. Turning, he fled the way he had come. Far ahead he saw a tiny red spark. He headed for it, and long before he thought to have reached it, he caromed headlong into a solid wall and saw the spark at his feet. It was his torch, the same extinguished, but the end a glowing coal. Carefully he took it up and blew upon it, fanning it into flame again. He gave a sigh as the tiny blaze leaped up.

He was back in the chamber where the tunnels crossed, and his sense of direction came back.

He located the tunnel by which he had left the main corridor, and even as he started toward it, his torch-flame flickered wildly as if blown upon by unseen lips. Again he felt a presence, and he lifted his torch, glaring about.

He saw nothing; yet he sensed, somehow, an invisible, bodiless thing that hovered in the air, dripping slimily and mouthing obscenities that he could not hear but was in some instinctive way aware of. He swung viciously with his sword and it felt as if he were cleaving cobwebs. A cold horror shook him then, and he fled down the tunnel, feeling a foul burning breath on his naked back as he ran.

But when he came out into the broad corridor, he was no longer aware of any presence, visible or invisible. Down it he went, momentarily expecting fanged and taloned fiends to leap at him from the darkness. The tunnels were not silent. From the bowels of the earth in all directions came sounds that did not belong in a sane world. There were titterings, squeals of demoniac mirth, long shuddering howls, and once the unmistakable squalling laughter of a hyena ended awfully in human words of shrieking blasphemy. He heard the pad of stealthy feet, and in the mouths of the tunnels caught glimpses of shadowy forms, monstrous and abnormal in outline.

It was as if he had wandered into Hell—a hell of Tsotha-lanti's making. But the shadowy things did not come into the great corridor, though he distinctly heard the greedy sucking-in of slavering lips, and felt the burning glare of hungry eyes. And presently he knew why. A slithering sound behind him electrified him, and he leaped to the darkness of a nearby tunnel, shaking out his torch. Down the corridor he heard the great serpent crawling, sluggish from its most grisly meal. From his very side something whimpered in fear and shrunk away in the darkness. Evidently the main corridor was the great snake's hunting-ground, and the other monsters gave it room.

To Conan the serpent was the least horror of them; he at least felt a kinship with it when he remembered the weeping, tittering obscenity, and the dripping, mouthing thing that came out of the well. At least it was of earthly matter; it was a crawling death, but it threatened only physical extinction, whereas these other horrors menaced mind and soul as well.

After it had passed on down the corridor, he followed, at what he hoped was a safe distance, blowing his torch into flame again. He had not gone far when he heard a low moan that seemed to emanate from the black entrance of a tunnel nearby. Caution warned him on, but curiosity drove him to the tunnel, holding high the torch that was now little more than a stump. He was braced for the sight of anything, yet what he saw was what he had least expected. He was looking into a broad cell, and a space of this was caged off with closely set bars extending from floor to ceiling, set firmly in the stone. Within these bars lay a figure, which, as he approached, he saw was either a man, or the exact likeness of a man, twined and bound about with the tendrils of a thick vine which seemed to grow through the solid stone of the floor. It was covered with strangely pointed leaves and crimson blossoms—not the satiny red of natural petals, but a livid, unnatural crimson, like a perversity of flower-life.

Its clinging, pliant branches wound about the man's naked body and limbs, seeming to caress his shrinking flesh with lustful avid kisses. One great blossom hovered exactly over his mouth. A low bestial moaning drooled from the loose lips; the head rolled as if in unbearable agony, and the eyes looked full at Conan. But there was no light of intelligence in them; they were blank, glassy, the eyes of an idiot.

Now the great crimson blossom dipped and pressed its petals over the writhing lips. The limbs of the wretch twisted in anguish; the tendrils of the plant quivered as if in ecstasy, vibrating their full snaky lengths. Waves of changing hues surged over them; their color grew deeper, more venomous.

Conan did not understand what he saw, but he knew that he looked on Horror of some kind. Man or demon, the suffering of the captive touched Conan's wayward and impulsive heart. He sought for entrance and found a grille-like door in the bars, fastened with a heavy lock, for which he found a key among the keys he carried, and entered. Instantly the petals of the livid blossoms spread like the hood of a cobra, the tendrils reared menacingly and the whole plant shook and swayed toward him. Here was no blind growth of natural vegetation. Conan sensed a strange, malignant intelligence; the plant could see him, and he felt its hate emanate from it in almost tangible waves. Stepping warily nearer, he marked the root-stem, a repulsively supple stalk thicker than his thigh, and even as the long tendrils arched toward him with a rattle of leaves and hiss, he swung his sword and cut through the stem with a single stroke.

Instantly the wretch in its clutches was thrown violently aside as the great vine lashed and knotted like a beheaded serpent, rolling into a huge irregular ball. The tendrils thrashed and writhed, the leaves shook and rattled like castanets, and petals opened and closed convulsively; then the whole length straightened out limply, the vivid colors paled and dimmed, a reeking white liquid oozed from the severed stump.

Conan stared, spellbound; then a sound brought him round, sword lifted. The freed man was on his feet, surveying him. Conan gaped in wonder. No longer were the eyes in the worn face expressionless. Dark and meditative, they were alive with intelligence, and the expression of imbecility had dropped from the face like a mask. The head was narrow and well-formed, with a high splendid forehead. The whole build of the man was aristocratic, evident no less in his tall slender frame than in his small trim feet and hands. His first words were strange and startling.

"What year is this?" he asked, speaking in Kothian.

"Today is the tenth day of the month Yuluk, of the year of the Gazelle," answered Conan.

"Yagkoolan Ishtar!" murmured the stranger. "Ten years!" he drew a hand across his brow, shaking his head as if to clear his brain from cobwebs. "All is dim yet. After a ten-year emptiness, the mind can not be expected to begin functioning clearly at once. Who are you?"

"Conan, once of Cimmeria, now king of Aquilonia."

The other's eyes showed surprize.

"Indeed? And Numedides?"

"I strangled him on his throne the night I took the royal city," answered Conan.

A certain naivete in the king's reply twitched the stranger's lips.

"Pardon, your majesty. I should have thanked you for the service you have done me. I am like a man woken suddenly from sleep deeper than death and shot with nightmares of agony more fierce than Hell, but I understand that you delivered me. Tell me—why did you cut the stem of the plant Yothga instead of tearing it up by the roots?"

"I learned long ago to avoid touching with my flesh that which I do not understand," answered the Cimmerian.

"Well for you," said the stranger. "Had you been able to tear it up, you might have found things clinging to the roots against which not even your sword would prevail. Yothga's roots are set in Hell."

"But who are you?" demanded Conan.

"Men called me Pelias."

"What!" cried the king. "Pelias the sorcerer, Tsotha-lanti's rival, who vanished from the Earth ten years ago?"

"Not entirely from the Earth," answered Pelias with a wry smile. "Tsotha preferred to keep me alive, in shackles more grim than rusted iron. He pent me in here with this devil-flower whose seeds drifted down through the black cosmos from Yag the Accursed, and found fertile field only in the maggot-writhing corruption that seethes on the floors of Hell.

"I could not remember my sorcery and the words and symbols of my power, with that cursed thing gripping me and drinking my soul with its loathsome caresses. It sucked the contents of my mind day and night, leaving my brain as empty as a broken wine-jug. Ten years! Ishtar preserve us!"

Conan found no reply, but stood holding the stump of the torch, and trailing his great sword. Surely the man was mad—yet there was no madness in the strange dark eyes that rested so calmly on him.

"Tell me, is the black wizard in Khorshemish? But no— you need not reply. My powers begin to wake, and I sense in your mind a great battle and a king trapped by treachery. And I see Tsotha-lanti riding hard for the Tybor with Strabonus and the king of Ophir. So much the better. My art is too frail from the long slumber to face Tsotha yet. I need time to recruit my strength, to assemble my powers. Let us go forth from these pits."

Conan jangled his keys discouragedly.

"The grille to the outer door is made fast by a bolt which can only he worked from outside. Is there no other exit from these tunnels?"

"Only one which neither of us would care to use, seeing that it goes down and not up," laughed Pelias. "But no matter. Let us see to the grille."

He moved toward the corridor with uncertain steps, as of long-unused limbs, which gradually became more sure. As he followed, Conan said uneasily, "There is a cursed big snake creeping about this tunnel. Let us be wary lest we step into his mouth."

"I remember him of old," answered Pelias grimly, "the more as I was forced to watch while ten of my acolytes were fed to him. He is Satha, the Old One, chiefest of Tsotha's pets."

"Did Tsotha dig these pits for no other reason than to house his cursed monstrosities?" asked Conan.

"He did not dig them. When the city was founded three thousand years ago there were ruins of an earlier city on and about this hill. King Khossus V, the founder, built his palace on the hill, and digging cellars beneath it, came upon a walled-up doorway, which he broke into and discovered the pits, which were about as we see them now. But his grand vizier came to such a grisly end in them that Khossus in a fright walled up the entrance again. He said the vizier fell into a well—but he had the cellars filled in, and later abandoned the palace itself and built himself another in the suburbs, from which he fled in panic on discovering some black mold scattered on the marble floor of his chamber one morning.

"He then departed with his whole court to the eastern corner of the kingdom and built a new city. The palace on the hill was not used and fell into ruins. When Akkutho I revived the lost glories of Khorshemish, he built a fortress there. It remained for Tsotha-lanti to rear the scarlet citadel and open the way to the pits again. Whatever fate overtook the grand vizier of Khossus, Tsotha avoided it. He fell into no well, though he did descend into a well he found, and came out with a strange expression which has not since left his eyes.

"I have seen that well, but I do not care to seek in it for wisdom. I am a sorcerer, and older than men reckon, but I am human. As for Tsotha—men say that a dancing-girl of Shadizar slept too near the pre-human ruins on Dagoth Hill and woke in the grip of a black demon; from that unholy ruin was spawned an accursed hybrid men call Tsotha-lanti—"

Conan cried out sharply and recoiled, thrusting his companion back. Before them rose the great shimmering white form of Satha, an ageless hate in its eyes. Conan tensed himself for one mad berserker onslaught—to thrust the glowing fagot into that fiendish countenance and throw his life into the ripping sword-stroke. But the snake was not looking at him. It was glaring over his shoulder at the man called Pelias, who stood with his arms folded, smiling. And in the great cold yellow eyes slowly the hate died out in a glitter of pure fear—the only time Conan ever saw such an expression in a reptile's eyes. With a swirling rush like the sweep of a strong wind, the great snake was gone.

"What did he see to frighten him?" asked Conan, eyeing his companion uneasily.

"The scaled people see what escapes the mortal eye," answered Pelias cryptically. "You see my fleshly guise; he saw my naked soul."

An icy trickle disturbed Conan's spine, and he wondered if, after all, Pelias were a man, or merely another demon of the pits in a mask of humanity. He contemplated the advisability of driving his sword through his companion's back without further hesitation. But while he pondered, they came to the steel grille, etched blackly in the torches beyond, and the body of Shukeli, still slumped against the bars in a curdled welter of crimson.

Pelias laughed, and his laugh was not pleasant to hear.

"By the ivory hips of Ishtar, who is our doorman? Lo, it is no less than the noble Shukeli himself, who hanged my young men by their feet and skinned them with squeals of laughter! Do you sleep, Shukeli? Why do you lie so stiffly, with your fat belly sunk in like a dressed pig's?"

"He is dead," muttered Conan, ill at ease to hear these wild words.

"Dead or alive," laughed Pelias, "he shall open the door for us."

He clapped his hands sharply and cried, "Rise, Shukeli! Rise from Hell and rise from the bloody floor and open the door for your masters! Rise, I say!"

An awful groan reverberated through the vaults. Conan's hair stood on end and he felt clammy sweat bead his hide. For the body of Shukeli stirred and moved, with infantile gropings of the fat hands. The laughter of Pelias was merciless as a flint hatchet, as the form of the eunuch reeled upright, clutching at the bars of the grille. Conan, glaring at him, felt his blood turn to ice, and the marrow of his bones to water; for Shukeli's wide-open eyes were glassy and empty, and from the great gash in his belly his entrails hung limply to the floor. The eunuch's feet stumbled among his entrails as he worked the bolt, moving like a brainless automaton. When he had first stirred, Conan had thought that by some incredible chance the eunuch was alive; but the man was dead—had been dead for hours.

Pelias sauntered through the opened grille, and Conan crowded through behind him, sweat pouring from his body, shrinking away from the awful shape that slumped on sagging legs against the grate it held open. Pelias passed on without a backward glance, and Conan followed him, in the grip of nightmare and nausea. He had not taken half a dozen strides when a sodden thud brought him round. Shukeli's corpse lay limply at the foot of the grille.

"His task is done, and Hell gapes for him again," remarked Pelias pleasantly, politely affecting not to notice the strong shudder which shook Conan's mighty frame.

He led the way up the long stair, and through the brass skull-crowned door at the top. Conan gripped his sword, expecting a rush of slaves, but silence gripped the citadel. They passed through the black corridor and came into that in which the censers swung, billowing forth their everlasting incense. Still they saw no one.

"The slaves and soldiers are quartered in another part of the citadel," remarked Pelias. "Tonight, their master being away, they doubtless lie drunk on wine or lotus-juice."

Conan glanced through an arched, golden-silled window that let out upon a broad balcony, and swore in surprize to see the dark-blue star-flecked sky. It had been shortly after sunrise when be was thrown into the pits. Now it was past midnight. He could scarcely realize he had been so long underground. He was suddenly aware of thirst and a ravenous appetite. Pelias led the way into a golden-domed chamber, floored with silver, its lapis lazuli walls pierced by the fretted arches of many doors.

With a sigh Pelias sank onto a silken divan.

"Silks and gold again," he sighed. "Tsotha affects to be above the pleasures of the flesh, but he is half-devil. I am human, despite my black arts. I love ease and good cheer—that's how Tsotha trapped me. He caught me helpless with drink. Wine is a curse—by the ivory bosom of Ishtar, even as I speak of it, the traitor is here! Friend, please pour me a goblet—hold! I forgot you are a king. I will pour."

"The devil with that," growled Conan, filling a crystal goblet and proffering it to Pelias. Then, lifting the jug, be drank deeply from the mouth, echoing Pelias' sigh of satisfaction.

"The dog knows good wine," said Conan, wiping his mouth with the back of his hand. "But by Crom, Pelias, are we to sit here until his soldiers awake and cut our throats?"

"No fear," answered Pelias. "Would you like to see how fortune holds with Strabonus?"

Blue fire burned in Conan's eyes and he gripped his sword until his knuckles showed blue. "Oh, to be at sword-points with him!" he rumbled.

Pelias lifted a great shimmering globe from an ebony table.

"Tsotha's crystal. A childish toy, but useful when there is lack of time for higher science. Look in, your majesty."

He laid it on the table before Conan's eyes. The king looked into cloudy depths which deepened and expanded. Slowly images crystallized out of mist and shadows. He was looking on a familiar landscape. Broad plains ran to a wide winding river, beyond which the level lands ran up quickly into a maze of low hills. On the northern bank of the river stood a walled town, guarded by a moat connected at each end with the river.

"By Crom!" ejaculated Conan. "It's Shamar! The dogs besiege it!"

The invaders had crossed the river; their pavilions stood in the narrow plain between the city and the hills. Their warriors swarmed about the walls, their mail gleaming palely under the moon. Arrows and stones rained on them from the towers and they staggered back, but came on again.

Even as Conan cursed, the scene changed. Tall spires and gleaming domes stood up in the mist, and he looked on his own capital of Tamar, where all was confusion. He saw the steel-clad knights of Poitain, his staunchest supporters, whom he had left in charge of the city, riding out of the gate, hooted and hissed by the multitude which swarmed the streets. He saw looting and rioting, and men-at-arms whose shields bore the insignia of Pellia, manning the towers and swaggering through the markets. Over all, like a phantasmal picture, he saw the dark, triumphant face of Prince Arpello of Pellia. The images faded.

"So! " cursed Conan. "My people turn on me the moment my back is turned—"

"Not entirely," broke in Pelias. "They have heard that you are dead. There is no one to protect them from outer enemies and civil war, they think. Naturally, they turn to the strongest noble, to avoid the horrors of anarchy. They do not trust the Poitanians, remembering former wars. But Arpello is on hand, and the strongest prince of the central realm."

"When I come to Aquilonia again he will be but a headless corpse rotting on Traitor's Common," Conan ground his teeth.

"Yet before you can reach your capital," reminded Pelias, "Strabonus may be before you. At least his riders will be ravaging your kingdom."

"True!" Conan paced the chamber liked a caged lion. "With the fastest horse I could not reach Shamar before midday. Even there I could do no good except to die with the people, when the town falls—as fall it will in a few days at most. From Shamar to Tamar is five days' ride, even if you kill your horses on the road. Before I could reach my capital and raise an army, Strabonus would he hammering at the gates; because raising an army is going to be hell—all my damnable nobles will have scattered to their own cursed fiefs at the word of my death. And since the people have driven out Trocero of Poitain, there's none to keep Arpello's greedy hands off the crown—and the crown-treasure. He'll hand the country over to Strabonus, in return for a mock-throne—and as soon as Strabonus' back is turned, he'll stir up revolt. But the nobles won't support him, and it will only give Strabonus excuse for annexing the kingdom openly. Oh Crom, Ymir, and Set! If I had but wings to fly like lightning to Tamar!"

Pelias, who sat tapping the jade tabletop with his finger-nails, halted suddenly, and rose as with a definite purpose, beckoning Conan to follow. The king complied, sunk in moody thoughts, and Pelias led the way out of the chamber and up a flight of marble, gold-worked stairs that let out on the pinnacle of the citadel, the roof of the tallest tower. It was night, and a strong wind was blowing through the star-filled skies, stirring Conan's black mane. Far below them twinkled the lights of Khorshemish, seemingly farther away than the stars above them. Pelias seemed withdrawn and aloof here, one in cold inhuman greatness with the company of the stars.

"There are creatures," said Pelias, "not alone of earth and sea, but of air and the far reaches of the skies as well, dwell-ing apart, unguessed of men. Yet to him who holds the Mas-ter-words and Signs and the Knowledge underlying all, they are not malignant nor inaccessible. Watch, and fear not."

He lifted his hands to the skies and sounded a long weird call that seemed to shudder endlessly out into space, dwin-dling and fading, yet never dying out, only receding farther and farther into some unreckoned cosmos. In the silence that followed, Conan heard a sudden beat of wings in the stars, and recoiled as a huge bat-like creature alighted beside him. He saw its great calm eyes regarding him in the star-light; he saw the forty-foot spread of its giant wings. And he saw it was neither bat nor bird.

"Mount and ride," said Pelias. "By dawn it will bring you to Tamar."

"By Crom!" muttered Conan. "Is this all nightmare from which I shall presently awaken in my palace in Tamar? What of you? I would not leave you alone among your enemies."

"Be at ease regarding me," answered Pelias. "At dawn the people of Khorshemish will know they have a new master. Doubt not what the gods have sent you. I will meet you in the plain by Shamar."

Doubtfully Conan clambered upon the ridged back, gripping the arched neck, still convinced that he was in the grasp of a fantastic nightmare. With a great rush and thunder of titan wings, the creature took the air, and the king grew dizzy as he saw the lights of the city dwindle far below him.

4.

"The sword that slays the king cuts the cords of the empire."

—Aquilonian proverb.

The streets of Tamar swarmed with howling mobs, shaking fists and rusty pikes. It was the hour before dawn of the second day after the battle of Shamar, and events had occurred so swiftly as to daze the mind. By means known only to Tsotha-lanti, word had reached Tamar of the king's death within half a dozen hours after the battle. Chaos had resulted. The barons had deserted the royal capital, galloping away to secure their castles against marauding neighbors. The well-knit kingdom Conan had built up seemed tottering on the edge of dissolution, and commoners and merchants trembled at the imminence of a return of the feudalistic regime. The people howled for a king to protect them against their own aristocracy no less than foreign foes. Count Trocero, left by Conan in charge of the city, tried to reassure them, but in their unreasoning terror they remembered old civil wars, and how this same count had besieged Tamar fifteen years before. It was shouted in the streets that Trocero had betrayed the king; that he planned to plunder the city. The mercenaries began looting the quarters, dragging forth screaming merchants and terrified women.

Trocero swept down on the looters, littered the streets with their corpses, drove them back into their quarter in confusion, and arrested their leaders. Still the people rushed wildly about, with brainless squawks, screaming that the count had incited the riot for his own purposes.

Prince Arpello came before the distracted council and announced himself ready to take over the government of the city until a king could be decided upon, Conan having no son. While they debated, his agents stole subtly among the people, who snatched at a shred of royalty. The council heard the storm outside the palace windows, where the multitude roared for Arpello the Rescuer. The council surrendered.

Trocero at first refused the order to give up his baton of authority, but the people swarmed about him, hissing and howling, hurling stones and offal at his knights. Seeing the futility of a pitched battle in the streets with Arpello's retainers, under such conditions, Trocero hurled the baton in his rival's face, hanged the leaders of the mercenaries in the market-square as his last official act, and rode out of the southern gate at the head of his fifteen hundred steel-clad knights. The gates slammed behind him and Arpello's suave mask fell away to reveal the grim visage of the hungry wolf.

With the mercenaries cut to pieces or hiding in their barracks, his were the only soldiers in Tamar. Sitting his war-horse in the great square, Arpello proclaimed himself king of Aquilonia, amid the clamor of the deluded multitude.

Publius the Chancellor, who opposed this move, was thrown into prison. The merchants, who had greeted the proclamation of a king with relief, now found with consternation that the new monarch's first act was to levy a staggering tax on them. Six rich merchants, sent as a delegation of protest, were seized and their heads slashed off without ceremony. A shocked and stunned silence followed this execution. The merchants, as is the habit of merchants when confronted by a power they can not control with money, fell on their fat bellies and licked their oppressor's boots.

The common people were not perturbed at the fate of the merchants, but they began to murmur when they found that the swaggering Pellian soldiery, pretending to maintain order, were as bad as Turanian bandits. Complaints of extortion, murder and rape poured in to Arpello, who had taken up his quarters in Publius' palace, because the desperate councilors, doomed by his order, were holding the royal palace against his soldiers. He had taken possession of the pleasure-palace, however, and Conan's girls were dragged to his quarters. The people muttered at the sight of the royal

beauties writhing in the brutal bands of the iron-clad retainers—dark-eyed damsels of Poitain, slim black-haired
wenches from Zamora, Zingara and Hyrkania, Brythunian
girls with tousled yellow heads, all weeping with fright and
shame, unused to brutality.

Night fell on a city of bewilderment and turmoil, and
before midnight word spread mysteriously in the street
that the Kothians had followed up their victory and were
hammering at the walls of Shamar. Somebody in Tsotha's
mysterious secret-service had babbled. Fear shook the people
like an earthquake, and they did not even pause to wonder
at the witchcraft by which the news had been so swiftly
transmitted. They stormed at Arpello's doors, demanding
that he march southward and drive the enemy back over the
Tybor. He might have subtly pointed out that his force was
not sufficient, and that he could not raise an army until the
barons recognized his claim to the crown. But be was drunk
with power, and laughed in their faces.

A young student, Athemides, mounted a column in
the market, and with burning words accused Arpello of
being a cats-paw for Strabonus, painting a vivid picture
of existence under Kothian rule, with Arpello as satrap.
Before he finished, the multitude was screaming with fear
and howling with rage. Arpello sent his soldiers to arrest
the youth, but the people caught him up and fled with him,
deluging the pursuing retainers with stones and dead cats.
A volley of crossbow quarrels routed the mob, and a charge
of horsemen littered the market with bodies, but Athemides
was smuggled out of the city to plead with Trocero to retake
Tamar, and march to aid Shamar.

Athemides found Trocero breaking his camp outside the walls, ready to march to Poitain, in the far southwestern corner of the kingdom. To the youth's urgent pleas he answered that he had neither the force necessary to storm Tamar, even with the aid of the mob inside, nor to face Strabonus. Besides, avaricious nobles would plunder Poitain behind his back, while he was fighting the Kothians. With the king dead, each man must protect his own. He was riding to Poitain, there to defend it as best he might against Arpello and his foreign allies.

While Athemides pleaded with Trocero, the mob still raved in the city with helpless fury. Under the great tower beside the royal palace the people swirled and milled, screaming their hate at Arpello, who stood on the turrets and laughed down at them while his archers ranged the parapets, bolts drawn and fingers on the triggers of their arbalests.

The prince of Pellia was a broad-built man of medium height, with a dark stern face. He was an intriguer, but he was also a fighter. Under his silken jupon with its gilt-braided skirts and jagged sleeves, glimmered burnished steel. His long black hair was curled and scented, and bound back with a cloth-of-silver band, but at his hip hung a broadsword, the jeweled hilt of which was worn with battles and campaigns.

"Fools! Howl as you will! Conan is dead and Arpello is king!"

What if all Aquilonia were leagued against him? He had men enough to hold the mighty walls until Strabonus came up. But Aquilonia was divided against itself. Already the barons were girding themselves each to seize his neighbor's treasure. Arpello had only the helpless mob to deal with. Strabonus would carve through the loose lines of the warring barons as a galley-ram through foam, and until his coming, Arpello had only to hold the royal capital.

"Fools! Arpello is king!"

The sun was rising over the eastern towers. Out of the crimson dawn came a flying speck that grew to a bat, then to an eagle. Then all who saw screamed in amazement, for over the walls of Tamar swooped a shape such as men knew only in half-forgotten legends, and from between its titan-wings sprang a human form as it roared over the great tower. Then with a deafening thunder of wings it was gone, and the folk blinked, wondering if they dreamed. But on the turret stood a wild barbaric figure, half-naked, bloodstained, brandishing a great sword. And from the multitude rose a roar that rocked the very towers, "The king! It is the king!"

Arpello stood transfixed; then with a cry he drew and leaped at Conan. With a lion-like roar the Cimmerian parried the whistling blade, then dropped his own sword, gripped the prince and heaved him high above his head by crotch and neck.

"Take your plots to Hell with you!" he roared, and like a sack of salt, he hurled the prince of Pellia far out, to fall through empty space for a hundred and fifty feet. The people gave back as the body came hurtling down, to smash on the marble pave, spattering blood and brains, and lie crushed in its splintered armor, like a mangled beetle.

The archers on the tower shrank back, their nerve broken. They fled, and the beleaguered councilmen sallied from the palace and hewed into them with joyous abandon. Pellian knights and men-at-arms sought safety in the streets, and the crowd tore them to pieces. In the streets the fighting milled and eddied, plumed helmets and steel caps tossed among the tousled heads and then vanished; swords hacked madly in a heaving forest of pikes, and over all rose the roar of the mob, shouts of acclaim mingling with screams of blood-lust and howls of agony. And high above all, the naked figure of the king rocked and swayed on the dizzy battlements, mighty arms brandished, roaring with gargantuan laughter that mocked all mobs and princes, even himself.

5.

A long bow and a strong bow, and let the sky grow dark!
The cord to the nock, the shaft to the ear,
and the king of Koth for a mark!
—Song of the Bossonian Archers.

The midafternoon sun glinted on the placid waters of the Tybor, washing the southern bastions of Shamar. The haggard defenders knew that few of them would see that sun rise again. The pavilions of the besiegers dotted the plain. The people of Shamar had not been able successfully to dispute the crossing of the river, outnumbered as they were. Barges, chained together, made a bridge over which the invader poured his hordes. Strabonus had not dared march on into Aquilonia with Shamar, unsubdued, at his back. He had sent his light riders, his spahis, inland to ravage the country, and had reared up his siege engines in the plain. He had anchored a flotilla of boats, furnished him by Amalrus, in the middle of the stream, over against the river-wall.

Some of these boats had been sunk by stones from the city's ballistas, which crashed through their decks and ripped out their planking, but the rest held their places and from their bows and mastheads, protected by mantlets, archers raked the riverward turrets. These were Shemites, born with bows in their hands, not to be matched by Aquilonian bowmen.

On the landward side mangonels rained boulders and tree trunks among the defenders, shattering through roofs and crushing humans like beetles; rams pounded incessantly at the stones; sappers burrowed like moles in the earth, sinking their mines beneath the towers. The moat had been dammed at the upper end, and emptied of its water, had been filled up with boulders, earth and dead horses and men. Under the walls the mailed figures swarmed, battering at the gates, rearing up scaling-ladders, pushing storming-towers, thronged with spearmen, against the turrets.

Hope had been abandoned in the city, where a bare fifteen hundred men resisted forty thousand warriors. No word had come from the kingdom whose outpost the city was. Conan was dead, so the invaders shouted exultantly. Only the strong walls and the desperate courage of the defenders had kept them so long at bay, and that could not suffice forever. The western wall was a mass of rubbish on which the defenders stumbled in hand-to-hand conflict with the invaders. The other walls were buckling from the mines beneath them, the towers leaning drunkenly.

Now the attackers were massing for a storm. The oliphants sounded, the steel-clad ranks drew up on the plain. The storming-towers, covered with raw bull-hides, rumbled forward. The people of Shamar saw the banners of Koth and Ophir, flying side by side, in the center, and made out, among their gleaming knights, the slim lethal figure of the golden-mailed Amalrus, and the squat black-armored form of Strabonus. And between them was a shape that made the bravest blanch with horror—a lean vulture figure in a filmy robe. The pikemen moved forward, flowing over the ground like the glinting waves of a river of molten steel; the knights cantered forward, lances lifted, guidons streaming. The warriors on the wall drew a long breath, consigned their souls to Mitra, and gripped their notched and red-stained weapons.

Then without warning, a bugle-call cut the din. A drum of hoofs rose above the rumble of the approaching host. North of the plain across which the army moved, rose ranges of low hills, mounting northward and westward like giant stair-steps. Now down out of these hills, like spume blown before a storm, shot the spahis who had been laying waste the countryside, riding low and spurring hard, and behind them the sun shimmering on moving ranks of steel. They moved into full view, out of the defiles—

Strabonus, frantically shouting orders, with Arbanus, that would wheel around the ponderous lines to meet this unexpected menace, grunted, "We still outnumber them, unless they have reserves hidden in the hills. The men on the battle-towers can mask any sorties from the city. These are Poitanians—we might have guessed Trocero would try some such mad gallantry."

Amalrus cried out in unbelief.

"I see Trocero and his captain Prospero—*but who rides between them*?"

"Ishtar preserve us!" shrieked Strabonus, paling. "It is King Conan!"

"You are mad!" squalled Tsotha, starting convulsively. "Conan has been in Satha's belly for days!" He stopped short, glaring wildly at the host which was dropping down, file by file, into the plain. He could not mistake the giant figure in black, gild-worked armor on the great black stallion, riding beneath the billowing silken folds of the great banner. A scream of feline fury burst from Tsotha's lips, flecking his beard with foam. For the first time in his life, Strabonus saw the wizard completely upset, and shrank from the sight.

"Here is sorcery!" screamed Tsotha, clawing madly at his beard. "How could he have escaped and reached his kingdom in time to return with an army so quickly? This is the work of Pelias, curse him! I feel his hand in this! May I be cursed for not killing him when I had the power!"

The kings gaped at the mention of a man they believed ten years dead, and panic, emanating from the leaders, shook the host. All recognized the rider on the black stallion. Tsotha felt the superstitious dread of his men, and fury made a hellish mask of his face.

"Strike home!" he screamed, brandishing his lean arm madly. "We are still the stronger! Charge and crush these dogs! We shall yet feast in the ruins of Shamar tonight! Oh Set!"—he lifted his hands and invoked the serpent-god to even Strabonus' horror—"grant us victory and I swear I will offer up to thee five hundred virgins of Shamar, writhing in their blood!"

Meanwhile the opposing host had debouched onto the plain. With the knights came what seemed a second, irregular army on tough swift ponies. These dismounted and formed their ranks on foot—stolid Bossonian archers, and keen pikemen from Gunderland, their tawny locks blowing from under their steel caps.

It was a motley army Conan had assembled, in the wild hours following his return to his capital. He had beaten the frothing mob away from the Pellian soldiers who held the outer walls of Tamar, and impressed them into his service. He had sent a swift rider after Trocero to bring him back. With these as a nucleus of an army he had raced southward, sweeping the surrounding countryside for recruits and for mounts. Nobles of Tamar and the surrounding countryside had augmented his forces, and he had levied recruits from every village and castle along his road. Yet it was but a paltry force he had gathered to dash against the invading hosts, though of the quality of tempered steel.

Nineteen hundred armored horsemen followed him, the main bulk of which consisted of the Poitanian knights. The remnants of the mercenaries and professional soldiers in the trains of loyal noblemen made up his infantry—five thousand archers and four thousand pikemen. This host now came on in good order—first the archers, then the pikemen, behind them the knights, moving at a walk.

Over against them Arbanus ordered his lines, and the allied army moved forward like a shimmering ocean of steel. The watchers on the city walls shook to see that vast host, which overshadowed the power of the rescuers. First marched the Shemitish archers, then the Kothian spearmen, then the mailed knights of Strabonus and Amalrus. Arbanus' intent was obvious—to employ his footmen to sweep away the infantry of Conan, and open the way for an overpowering charge of his heavy cavalry.

The Shemites opened fire at five hundred yards, and arrows flew like hail between the hosts, darkening the sun. The western archers, trained by a thousand years of merciless warfare with the Pictish savages, came stolidly on, closing their ranks as their comrades fell. They were far outnumbered, and the Shemitish bow had the longer range, but in accuracy the Bossonians were equal to their foes, and they balanced sheer skill in archery by superiority in morale, and in excellence of armor. Within good range they loosed, and the Shemites went down by whole ranks. The blue-bearded warriors in their light mail shirts could not endure punishment as could the heavier-armored Bossonians. They broke, throwing away their bows, and their flight disordered the ranks of the Kothian spearmen behind them.

Without the support of the archers, these men-at-arms fell by the hundreds before the shafts of the Bossonians, and charging in madly to close quarters, they were met by the spears of the pikemen. No infantry was a match for the wild Gundermen, whose homeland, the northernmost province of Aquilonia, was but a day's ride across the Bossonian marches from the borders of Cimmeria, and who, born and bred to battle, were the purest blood of all the Hyborian peoples. The Kothian spearmen, dazed by their losses from arrows, were cut to pieces and fell back in disorder.

Strabonus roared in fury as he saw his infantry repulsed, and shouted for a general charge. Arbanus demurred, pointing out the Bossonians reforming in good order before the Aquilonian knights, who had sat their steeds motionless during the melee. The general advised a temporary retirement, to draw the western knights out of the cover of the bows, but Strabonus was mad with rage. He looked at the long shimmering ranks of his knights, he glared at the handful of mailed figures over against him, and he commanded Arbanus to give the order to charge.

The general commended his soul to Ishtar and sounded the golden oliphant. With a thunderous roar the forest of lances dipped, and the great host rolled across the plain, gaining momentum as it came. The whole plain shook to the rumbling avalanche of hoofs, and the shimmer of gold and steel dazzled the watchers on the towers of Shamar.

The squadrons clave the loose ranks of the spearmen, riding down friend and foe alike, and rushed into the teeth of a blast of arrows from the Bossonians. Across the plain they thundered, grimly riding the storm that scattered their way with gleaming knights like autumn leaves. Another hundred paces and they would ride among the Bossonians and cut them down like corn; but flesh and blood could not endure the rain of death that now ripped and howled among them. Shoulder to shoulder, feet braced wide, stood the archers, drawing shaft to ear and loosing as one man, with deep short shouts.

The whole front rank of the knights melted away, and over the pin-cushioned corpses of horses and riders, their comrades stumbled and fell headlong. Arbanus was down, an arrow through his throat, his skull smashed by the hoofs of his dying war-horse, and confusion ran through the disordered host. Strabonus was screaming an order, Amalrus another, and through all ran the superstitious dread the sight of Conan had awakened.

And while the gleaming ranks milled in confusion, the trumpets of Conan sounded, and through the opening ranks of the archers crashed home the terrible charge of the Aquilonian knights.

The hosts met with a shock like that of an earthquake, that shook the tottering towers of Shamar. The disordered squadrons of the invaders could not withstand the solid steel wedge, bristling with spears, that rushed like a thunderbolt against them. The long lances of the attackers ripped their ranks to pieces, and into the heart of their host rode the knights of Poitain, swinging their terrible two-handed swords.

The clash and clangor of steel was as that of a million sledges on as many anvils. The watchers on the walls were stunned and deafened by the thunder as they gripped the battlements and watched the steel maelstrom swirl and eddy, where plumes tossed high among the flashing swords, and standards dipped and reeled.

Amalrus went down, dying beneath the trampling hoofs, his shoulder-bone hewn in twain by Prospero's two-handed sword. The invaders' numbers had engulfed the nineteen hundred knights of Conan, but about this compact wedge, which hewed deeper and deeper into the looser formation of their foes, the knights of Koth and Ophir swirled and smote in vain. They could not break the wedge.

Archer and pikemen, having disposed of the Kothian infantry which was strewn in disorderly flight across the plain, came to the edges of the fight, loosing their arrows point-blank, running in to slash at girths and horses' bellies with their knives, thrusting upward to spit the riders on their long pikes.

At the tip of the steel wedge Conan roared his heathen battle-cry and swung his great sword in glittering arcs of death that made naught of steel burganet or mail haburgeon. Straight through a thundering waste of steel-sheathed foes he rode, and the knights of Koth closed in behind him, cutting him off from his warriors. As a thunderbolt strikes, Conan struck, hurtling through the ranks by sheer power and velocity, until he came to Strabonus, livid, among his palace troops. Now here the battle hung in balance, for with his superior numbers, Strabonus still had opportunity to pluck victory from the knees of the gods.

But he screamed when he saw his arch-foe within arm's length at last, and lashed out wildly with his ax. It clanged on Conan's helmet, striking fire, and the Cimmerian reeled and struck back. The five-foot blade crushed Strabonus' casque and skull, and the king's charger reeled screaming, hurling a limp and sprawling corpse from the saddle. A great cry went up from the host, which faltered and gave back. Trocero and his house troops, hewing desperately, cut their way to Conan's side, and the great banner of Koth went down. Then behind the dazed and stricken invaders went up a mighty clamor and the blaze of a huge conflagration. The defenders of Shamar had made a desperate sortie, cut down the men masking the gates, and were raging among the tents of the besiegers, cutting down the camp followers, burning the pavilions, and destroying the siege engines. It was the last straw. The gleaming army melted away in flight and the furious conquerors cut them down as they ran.

The fugitives raced for the river, but the men on the flotilla, harried sorely by the stones and shafts of the revived citizens, cast loose and pulled for the southern shore, leaving their comrades to their fate. Of these many gained the shore, racing across the barges that served as a bridge, until the men of Shamar cut these adrift and severed them from the shore. Then the fight became a slaughter. Driven into the river to drown in their armor, or hacked down along the bank, the invaders perished by thousands. No quarter they had promised; no quarter they got.

From the foot of the low hills to the shores of the Tybor, the plain was littered with corpses, and the river whose tide ran red, floated thick with the dead. Of the nineteen hundred knights who had ridden south with Conan, scarcely five hundred lived to boast of their scars, and the slaughter among the archers and pikemen was ghastly. But the great and shining host of Strabonus and Amalrus was hacked out of existence, and those that fled were less than those that died.

While the slaughter yet went on along the river, the final act of a grim drama was being played out in the meadowland beyond. Among those who had crossed the barge-bridge before it was destroyed was Tsotha, riding like the wind on a gaunt weird-looking steed whose stride no natural horse could match. Ruthlessly riding down friend and foe, he gained the southern bank, and then a glance backward showed him a grim figure on a great black stallion in mad pursuit. The lashings had already been cut, and the barges were drifting apart, but Conan came recklessly on, leaping his steed from boat to boat as a man might leap from one cake of floating ice to another. Tsotha screamed a curse, but the great stallion took the last leap with a straining groan, and gained the southern bank. Then the wizard fled away into the empty meadowland, and on his trail came the king, riding madly and silently, swinging the great sword that spattered his trail with crimson drops.

On they fled, the hunted and the hunter, and not a foot could the black stallion gain, though he strained each nerve and thew. Through a sunset land of dim light and illusive shadows they fled, till sight and sound of the slaughter died out behind them. Then in the sky appeared a dot, that grew into a huge eagle as it approached. Swooping down from the sky, it drove at the head of Tsotha's steed, which screamed and reared, throwing his rider.

Old Tsotha rose and faced his pursuer, his eyes those of a maddened serpent, his face an inhuman mask of awful fury. In each hand he held something that shimmered, and Conan knew he held death there.

The king dismounted and strode toward his foe, his armor clanking, his great sword gripped high.

"Again we meet, wizard!" he grinned savagely.

"Keep off!" screamed Tsotha like a blood-mad jackal. "I'll blast the flesh from your bones! You can not conquer me—if you hack me in pieces, the bits of flesh and bone will reunite and haunt you to your doom! I see the hand of Pelias in this, but I defy ye both! I am Tsotha, son of—"

Conan rushed, sword gleaming, eyes slits of wariness. Tsotha's right hand came back and forward, and the king ducked quickly. Something passed by his helmeted head and exploded behind him, searing the very sands with a flash of hellish fire. Before Tsotha could toss the globe in his left hand, Conan's sword sheared through his lean neck. The wizard's head shot from his shoulders on an arching fount of blood, and the robed figure staggered and crumpled drunkenly. Yet the mad black eyes glared up at Conan with no dimming of their feral light, the lips writhed awfully, and the hands groped hideously, as if searching for the severed head. Then with a swift rush of wings, something swooped from the sky—the eagle which had attacked Tsotha's horse. In its mighty talons it snatched up the dripping head and soared skyward, and Conan stood struck dumb, for from the eagle's throat boomed human laughter, in the voice of Pelias the sorcerer.

Then a hideous thing came to pass, for the headless body reared up from the sand, and staggered away in awful flight on stiffening legs, hands outstretched blindly toward the dot speeding and dwindling in the dusky sky. Conan stood like one turned to stone, watching until the swift reeling figure faded in the dusk that purpled the meadows.

"Crom!" his mighty shoulders twitched. "A murrain on these wizardly feuds! Pelias has dealt well with me, but I care not if I see him no more. Give me a clean sword and a clean foe to flesh it in. Damnation! What would I not give for a flagon of wine!"

THE CAIRN ON THE HEADLAND
Weird Tales, January 1933

"And the next instant this great red loon was shaking me like a dog shaking a rat. 'Where is Meve McDonnal?' he was screaming. By the Saints, it's a grisly thing to hear a madman in a lonely place at midnight screaming the name of a woman dead three hundred years."

—The Longshoreman's Tale

"This is the cairn you seek," I said, laying my hand gingerly on one of the rough stones which composed the strangely symmetrical heap.

An avid interest burned in Ortali's dark eyes. His gaze swept the landscape and came back to rest on the great pile of massive weather-worn boulders.

"What a wild, weird, desolate place!" he said. "Who would have thought to find such a spot in this vicinity? Except for the smoke rising yonder, one would scarcely dream that beyond that headland lies a great city! Here there is scarcely even a fisherman's hut within sight."

"The people shun the cairn as they have shunned it for centuries," I replied.

"Why?"

"You've asked me that before," I replied impatiently. "I can only answer that they now avoid by habit what their ancestors avoided through knowledge."

"Knowledge!" he laughed derisively. "Superstition!"

I looked at him somberly with unveiled hate. Two men could scarcely have been of more opposite types. He was slender, self-possessed, unmistakably Latin with his dark eyes and sophisticated air. I am massive, clumsy and bear-like, with cold blue eyes and tousled red hair. We were countrymen in that we were born in the same land; but the homelands of our ancestors were as far apart as South from North.

"Nordic superstition," he repeated. "I cannot imagine a Latin people allowing such a mystery as this to go unexplored all these years. The Latins are too practical—too prosaic, if you will. Are you sure of the date of this pile?"

"I find no mention of it in any manuscript prior to 1014 A. D.," I growled, "and I've read all such manuscripts extant, in the original. MacLiag, King Brian Boru's poet, speaks of the rearing of the cairn immediately after the battle, and there can be little doubt but that this is the pile referred to. It is mentioned briefly in the later chronicles of the Four Masters, also in the Book of Leinster, compiled in the late 1150's, and again in the Book of Lecan, compiled by the MacFirbis about 1416. All connect it with the battle of Clontarf, without mentioning why it was built."

"Well, what is the mystery about it?" he queried. "What more natural than that the defeated Norseman should rear a cairn above the body of some great chief who had fallen in the battle?"

"In the first place," I answered, "there is a mystery concerning the existence of it. The building of cairns above the dead was a Norse, not an Irish, custom. Yet according to the chroniclers, it was not Norsemen who reared this heap. How could they have built it immediately after the battle, in which they had been cut to pieces and driven in headlong flight through the gates of Dublin? Their chieftains lay where they had fallen and the ravens picked their bones. It was Irish hands that heaped these stones."

"Well, was that so strange?" persisted Ortali. "In old times the Irish heaped up stones before they went into battle, each man putting a stone in place; after the battle the living removed their stones, leaving in that manner a simple tally of the slain for any who wished to count the remaining stones."

I shook my head.

"That was in more ancient times; not in the battle of Clontarf. In the first place, there were more than twenty thousand warriors, and four thousand fell here; this cairn is not large enough to have served as a tally of the men killed in battle. And it is too symmetrically built. Hardly a stone has fallen away in all these centuries. No, it was reared to cover something."

"Nordic superstitions!" the man sneered again.

"Aye, superstitions if you will!" fired by his scorn, I exclaimed so savagely that he involuntarily stepped back, his hand slipping inside his coat. "We of North Europe had gods and demons before which the pallid mythologies of the South fade to childishness. At a time when your ancestors were lolling on silken cushions among the crumbling marble pillars of a decaying civilization, my ancestors were building their own civilization in hardships and gigantic battles against foes human and inhuman.

"Here, on this very plain, the Dark Ages came to an end and the light of a new era dawned faintly on a world of hate and anarchy. Here, as even you know, in the year 1014, Brian Boru and his Dalcassian ax-wielders broke the power of the heathen Norsemen forever—those grim anarchistic plunderers who had held back the progress of civilization for centuries.

"It was more than a struggle between Gael and Dane for the crown of Ireland. It was a war between the White Christ and Odin, between Christian and pagan. It was the last stand of the heathen—of the people of the old, grim ways. For three hundred years the world had writhed beneath the heel of the Viking, and here on Clontarf that scourge was lifted forever.

"Then, as now, the importance of that battle was underestimated by polite Latin and Latinized writers and historians. The polished sophisticates of the civilized cities of the South were not interested in the battles of barbarians in the remote northwestern corner of the world—a place and peoples of whose very names they were.only vaguely aware. They only knew that suddenly the terrible raids of the sea kings ceased to sweep along their coasts, and in another century the wild age of plunder and slaughter had almost been forgotten—because a rude, half-civilized people who scantily covered their nakedness with wolf hides rose up against the conquerors.

"Here was Ragnarok, the fall of the Gods! Here in very truth Odin fell, for his religion was given its death blow. He was last of all the heathen gods to stand before Christianity, and it looked for a time as if his children might prevail and plunge the world back into darkness and savagery. Before Clontarf, legends say, he often appeared on earth to his worshipers, dimly seen in the smoke of the sacrifices where naked human victims died screaming, or riding the wind-torn clouds, his wild locks flying in the gale, or, appareled like a Norse warrior, dealing thunderous blows in the forefront of nameless battles. But after Clontarf he was seen no more; his worshipers called on him in vain with wild chants and grim sacrifices. They lost faith in him, who had failed them in their wildest hour; his altars crumbled, his priests turned gray and died, and men turned to his conqueror, the White Christ. The reign of blood and iron was forgotten; the age of the red-handed sea kings passed. The rising sun slowly, dimly, lighted the night of the Dark Ages, and men forgot Odin, who came no more on earth.

"Aye, laugh if you will! But who knows what shapes of horror have had birth in the darkness, the cold gloom, and the whistling black gulfs of the North? In the southern lands the sun shines and flowers grow; under the soft skies men laugh at demons. But in the North who can say what elemental spirits of evil dwell in the fierce storms and the darkness? Well may it be that from such fiends of the night men evolved the worship of the grim ones, Odin and Thor, and their terrible kin."

Ortali was silent for an instant, as if taken aback by my vehemence; then he laughed. "Well said, my Northern phi-losopher! We will argue these questions another time. I could hardly expect a descendant of Nordic barbarians to escape some trace of the dreams and mysticism of his race. But you cannot expect me to be moved by your imaginings, either. I still believe that this cairn covers no grimmer secret than a Norse chief who fell in the battle—and really your ravings concerning Nordic devils have no bearing on the matter. Will you help me tear into this cairn?"

"No," I answered shortly.

"A few hours' work will suffice to lay bare whatever it may hide," he continued as if he had not heard. "By the way, speaking of superstitions, is there not some wild tale concerning holly connected with this heap?"

"An old legend says that all trees bearing holly were cut down for a league in all directions, for some mysterious reason," I answered sullenly. "That's another mystery. Holly was an important part of Norse magic-making. The Four Masters tell of a Norseman—a white-bearded ancient of wild aspect, and apparently a priest of Odin—who was slain by the natives while attempting to lay a branch of holly on the cairn, a year after the battle."

"Well," he laughed, "I have procured a sprig of holly—see?—and shall wear it in my lapel; perhaps it will protect me against your Nordic devils. I feel more certain than ever that this cairn covers a sea king—and they were always laid to rest with all their riches: golden cups and jewel-set sword hilts and silver corselets. I feel that this cairn holds wealth, wealth over which clumsy-footed Irish peasants have been stumbling for centuries, living in want and dying in hunger. Bah! We shall return here at about midnight, when we may be fairly certain that we will not be interrupted—and you will aid me at the excavations."

The last sentence was rapped out in a tone that sent a red surge of blood-lust through my brain. Ortali turned and began examining the cairn as he spoke, and almost involuntarily my hand reached out stealthily and closed on a wicked bit of jagged stone that had become detached from one of the boulders. In that instant I was a potential murderer if ever one walked the earth. One blow, quick, silent and savage, and I would be free forever from a slavery bitter as my Celtic ancestors knew beneath the heels of the Vikings.

As if sensing my thoughts, Ortali wheeled to face me. I quickly slipped the stone into my pocket, not knowing whether he noted the action. But he must have seen the red killing instinct burning in my eyes, for again he recoiled and again his hand sought the hidden revolver.

But he only said: "I've changed my mind. We will not uncover the cairn tonight. Tomorrow night perhaps. We may be spied upon. Just now I am going back to the hotel."

I made no reply, but turned my back upon him, and stalked moodily away in the direction of the shore. He started up the slope of the headland beyond which lay the city, and when I turned to look at him, he was just crossing the ridge, etched clearly against the hazy sky. If hate could kill, he would have dropped dead. I saw him in a red-tinged haze, and the pulses in my temples throbbed like hammers.

I turned back toward the shore, and stopped suddenly. Engrossed with my own dark thoughts, I had approached within a few feet of a woman before seeing her. She was tall and strongly made, with a strong stern face, deeply lined and weather-worn as the hills. She was dressed in a manner strange to me, but I thought little of it, knowing the curious styles of clothing worn by certain backward types of our people.

"What would you be doing at the cairn?" she asked in a

deep, powerful voice. I looked at her in surprise; she spoke in Gaelic, which was not strange of itself, but the Gaelic she used I had supposed was extinct as a spoken language: it was the Gaelic of scholars, pure, and with a distinctly archaic flavor. A woman from some secluded hill country, I thought, where the people still spoke the unadulterated tongue of their ancestors.

"We were speculating on its mystery," I answered in the same tongue, hesitantly, however, for though skilled in the more modern form taught in the schools, to match her use of the language was a strain on my knowledge of it.

She shook her head slowly. "I like not the dark man who was with you," she said somberly. "Who are you?"

"I am an American, though born and raised here," I answered. "My name is James O'Brien."

A strange light gleamed in her cold eyes.

"O'Brien? You are of my clan. I was born an O'Brien. I married a man of the MacDonnals, but my heart was ever with the folk of my blood."

"You live hereabouts?" I queried, my mind on her unusual accent.

"Aye, I lived here upon a time," she answered, "but I have been far away for a long time. All is changed—changed. I would not have returned, but I was drawn back by a call you would not understand. Tell me, would you open the cairn?"

I started and gazed at her closely, deciding that she had somehow overheard our conversation.

"It is not mine to say," I answered bitterly. "Ortali—my companion—he will doubtless open it and I am constrained to aid him. Of my own will I would not molest it."

Her cold eyes bored into my soul.

"Fools rush blind to their doom," she said somberly. "What does this man know of the mysteries of this ancient land? Deeds have been done here whereof the world reechoed. Yonder, in the long ago, when Tomar's Wood rose dark and rustling against the plain of Clontarf, and the Danish walls of Dublin loomed south of the river Liffey, the ravens fed on the slain and the setting sun lighted lakes of crimson. There King Brian, your ancestor and mine, broke the spears of the North. From all lands they came, and from the isles of the sea; they came in gleaming mail and their horned helmets cast long shadows across the land. Their dragon-prows thronged the waves and the sound of their oars was as the beat of a storm.

"On yonder plain, the heroes fell like ripe wheat before the reaper. There fell Jarl Sigurd of the Orkneys, and Brodir of Man, last of the sea kings, and all their chiefs. There fell, too, Prince Murrogh and his son Turlogh, and many chieftains of the Gael, and King Brian Boru himself, Erin's mightiest monarch."

"True!" My imagination was always fired by the epic tales of the land of my birth. "Blood of mine was spilled here, and, though I have passed the best part of my life in a far land, there are ties of blood to bind my soul to this shore."

She nodded slowly, and from beneath her robes drew forth something that sparkled dully in the setting sun.

"Take this," she said. "As a token of blood tie, I give it to you. I feel the weird of strange and monstrous happenings—but this will keep you safe from evil and the people of the night. Beyond reckoning of man, it is holy."

I took it, wonderingly. It was a crucifix of curiously worked gold, set with tiny jewels. The workmanship was extremely archaic and unmistakably Celtic. And vaguely within me stirred a memory of a long-lost relic described by forgotten monks in dim manuscripts.

"Great heavens!" I exclaimed. "This is—this must be—this *can* be nothing less than the lost crucifix of Saint Brandon the Blessed!"

"Aye." She inclined her grim head. "Saint Brandon's cross, fashioned by the hands of the holy man in long ago, before the Norse barbarians made Erin a red hell—in the days when a golden peace and holiness ruled the land."

"But, woman!" I exclaimed wildly, "I cannot accept this as a gift from you! You cannot know its value! Its intrinsic worth alone is equal to a fortune; as a relic it is priceless—"

"Enough!" Her deep voice struck me suddenly silent. "Have done with such talk, which is sacrilege. The cross of Saint Brandon is beyond price. It was never stained with gold; only as a free gift has it ever changed hands. I give it to you to shield you against the powers of evil. Say no more."

"But it has been lost for three hundred years!" I exclaimed. "How—where . . . ?"

"A holy man gave it to me long ago," she answered. "I hid it in my bosom—long it lay in my bosom. But now I give it to you; I have come from a far country to give it to you, for there are monstrous happenings in the wind, and it is sword and shield against the people of the night. An ancient evil stirs in its prison, which blind hands of folly may break open; but stronger than any evil is the cross of Saint Brandon which has gathered power and strength through the long, long ages since that forgotten evil fell to the earth."

"But who are you?" I exclaimed.

"I am Meve MacDonnal," she answered.

Then, turning without a word, she strode away in the deepening twilight while I stood bewildered and watched her cross the headland and pass from sight, turning inland as she topped the ridge. Then I, too, shaking myself like a man waking from a dream, went slowly up the slope and across the headland. When I crossed the ridge it was as if I had passed out of one world into another: behind me lay the wilderness and desolation of a weird medieval age; before me pulsed the lights and the roar of modern Dublin. Only one archaic touch was lent to the scene before me: some distance inland loomed the straggling and broken lines of an ancient graveyard, long deserted and grown up in weeds, barely discernible in the dusk. As I looked I saw a tall figure moving ghostily among the crumbling tombs, and I shook my head bewilderedly. Surely Meve MacDonnal was touched with madness, living in the past, like one seeking to stir to flame the ashes of dead yesterdays. I set out toward where, in the near distance, began the straggling window-gleams that grew into the swarming ocean of lights that was Dublin.

Back at the suburban hotel where Ortali and I had our rooms, I did not speak to him of the cross the woman had given me. In that, at least, he should not share. I intended keeping it until she requested its return, which I felt sure she would do. Now as I remembered her appearance, the strangeness of her costume returned to me, with one item which had impressed itself on my subconscious mind at the time, but which I had not consciously realized. Meve Mac-Donnal had been wearing sandals of a type not worn in Ireland for centuries. Well, it was perhaps natural that with her retrospective nature she should imitate the apparel of the past ages which seemed to claim all her thoughts.

I turned the cross reverently in my hands. There was no doubt that it was the very cross for which antiquarians had searched so long in vain, and at last in despair had denied the existence of. The priestly scholar, Michael O'Rourke, in a treatise written about 1690, described the relic at length, chronicled its history exhaustively and maintained that it was last heard of in the possession of Bishop Liam O'Brien, who, dying in 1595, gave it into the keeping of a kinswoman; but who this woman was, it was never known, and O'Rourke maintained that she kept her possession of the cross a secret, and that it was laid away with her in her tomb.

At another time my elation at discovering this relic would have been extreme, but, at the time, my mind was too filled with hate and smoldering fury. Replacing the cross in my pocket, I fell moodily to reviewing my connections with Ortali, connections which puzzled my friends, but which were simple enough.

Some years before I had been connected with a certain large university in a humble way. One of the professors with which I worked—a man named Reynolds—was of intolerably overbearing disposition towards those whom he considered his inferiors. I was a poverty-ridden student striving for life in a system which makes the very existence of a scholar precarious. I bore Professor Reynolds' abuse as long as I could, but one day we clashed. The reason does not matter; it was trivial enough in itself. Because I dared reply to his insults, Reynolds struck me and I knocked him senseless.

That very day he caused my dismissal from the university. Facing not only an abrupt termination of my work and studies, but actual starvation, I was reduced to desperation, and I went to Reynolds' study late that night intending to thrash him within an inch of his life. I found him alone in his study, but the moment I entered, he sprang up and rushed at me like a wild beast, with a dagger he used for a paperweight. I did not strike him; I did not even touch him. As I stepped aside to avoid his rush, a small rug slipped beneath his charging feet. He fell headlong and, to my horror, in his fall the dagger in his hand was driven into his heart. He died instantly. I was at once aware of my position. I was known to have quarreled, and even exchanged blows with the man. I had every reason to hate him. If I were found in the study with the dead man, no jury in the world would not believe that I had murdered him. I hurriedly left by the way I had come, thinking that I had been unobserved. But Ortali, the dead man's secretary, had seen me. Returning from a dance, he had observed me entering the premises, and, following me, had seen the whole affair through the window. But this I did not know until later.

The body was found by the professor's housekeeper, and naturally there was a great stir. Suspicion pointed to me, but lack of evidence kept me from being indicted, and this same lack of evidence brought about a verdict of suicide. All this time Ortali had kept quiet. Now he came to me and disclosed what he knew. He knew, of course, that I had not killed Reynolds, but he could prove that I was in the study when the professor met his death, and I knew Ortali was capable of carrying out his threat of swearing that he had seen me murder Reynolds in cold blood. And thus began a systematic blackmail.

I venture to say that a stranger blackmail was never levied. I had no money then; Ortali was gambling on my future, for he was assured of my abilities. He advanced me money, and, by clever wire-pulling, got me an appointment in a large college. Then he sat back to reap the benefits of his scheming, and he reaped full fold of the seed he sowed. In my line I became eminently successful. I soon commanded an enormous salary in my regular work, and I received rich prizes and awards for researches of various difficult nature, and of these Ortali took the lion's share—in money at least. I seemed to have the Midas touch. Yet of the wine of my success I tasted only the dregs.

I scarcely had a cent to my name. The money that had flowed through my hands had gone to enrich my slaver, unknown to the world. A man of remarkable gifts, he could have gone to the heights in any line, but for a queer streak in him, which, coupled with an inordinately avaricious nature, made him a parasite, a blood-sucking leech.

This trip to Dublin had been in the nature of a vacation for me. I was worn out with study and labor. But he had somehow heard of Grimmin's Cairn, as it was called, and, like a vulture that scents dead flesh, he conceived himself on the track of hidden gold. A golden wine cup would have been, to him, sufficient reward for the labor of tearing into the pile, and reason enough for desecrating or even destroying the ancient landmark. He was a swine whose only god was gold.

Well, I thought grimly, as I disrobed for bed, all things end, both good and bad. Such a life as I had lived was unbearable. Ortali had dangled the gallows before my eyes until it had lost its terrors. I had staggered beneath the load I carried because of my love for my work. But all human endurance has its limits. My hands turned to iron as I thought of Ortali, working beside me at midnight at the lonely cairn. One stroke, with such a stone as I had caught up that day, and my agony would be ended. That life and hopes and career and ambitions would be ended as well, could not be helped. Ah, what a sorry, sorry end to all my high dreams! When a rope and the long drop through the black trap would cut short an honorable career and a useful life! And all because of a human vampire who feasted his rotten lust on my soul, and drove me to murder and ruin.

But I knew my fate was written in the iron books of doom. Sooner or later I would turn on Ortali and kill him, be the consequences what they might. And I had reached the end of my road. Continual torture had rendered me, I believe, partly insane. I knew that at Grimmin's Cairn, when we toiled at midnight, Ortali's life would end beneath my hands, and my own life be cast away.

Something fell out of my pocket and I picked it up. It was the piece of sharp stone I had caught up off the cairn. Looking at it moodily, I wondered what strange hands had touched it in old times, and what grim secret it helped to hide on the bare headland of Grimmin. I switched out the light and lay in the darkness, the stone still in my hand, forgotten, occupied with my own dark broodings. And I glided gradually into deep slumber.

At first I was aware that I was dreaming, as people often are. All was dim and vague, and connected in some strange way, I realized, with the bit of stone still grasped in my sleeping hand. Gigantic, chaotic scenes and landscapes and events shifted before me, like clouds that rolled and tumbled before a gale. Slowly these settled and crystallized into one distinct landscape, familiar and yet wildly strange. I saw a broad bare plain, fringed by the gray sea on one side, and a dark, rustling forest on the other; this plain was cut by a winding river, and beyond this river I saw a city—such a city as my waking eyes had never seen: bare, stark, massive, with the grim architecture of an earlier, wilder age. On the plain I saw, as in a mist, a mighty battle. Serried ranks rolled backward and forward, steel flashed like a sunlit sea, and men fell like ripe wheat beneath the blades. I saw men in wolfskins, wild and shock-headed, wielding dripping axes, and tall men in horned helmets and glittering mail, whose eyes were cold and blue as the sea. And I saw myself.

Yes, in my dream I saw and recognized, in a semi-detached way, myself. I was tall and rangily powerful; I was shock-headed and naked but for a wolf hide girt about my loins. I ran among the ranks yelling and smiting with a red ax, and blood ran down my flanks from wounds I scarcely felt. My eyes were cold blue and my shaggy hair and beard were red.

Now for an instant I was cognizant of my dual personality, aware that I was at once the wild man who ran and smote with the gory ax, and the man who slumbered and dreamed across the centuries. But this sensation quickly faded. I was no longer aware of any personality other than that of the barbarian who ran and smote. James O'Brien had no existence; I was Red Cumal, kern of Brian Boru, and my ax was dripping with the blood of my foes.

The roar of conflict was dying away, though here and there struggling clumps of warriors still dotted the plain. Down along the river half-naked tribesmen, waist-deep in reddening water, tore and slashed with helmeted warriors whose mail could not save them from the stroke of the Dalcassian ax. Across the river a bloody, disorderly horde was staggering through the gates of Dublin.

The sun was sinking low toward the horizon. All day I had fought beside the chiefs. I had seen Jarl Sigurd fall beneath Prince Murrogh's sword. I had seen Murrogh himself die in the moment of victory, by the hand of a grim mailed giant whose name none knew. I had seen, in the flight of the enemy, Brodir and King Brian fall together at the door of the great king's tent.

Aye, it had been a feasting of ravens, a red flood of slaughter, and I knew that no more would the dragon-prowed fleets sweep from the blue North with torch and destruction. Far and wide the Vikings lay in their glittering mail, as the ripe wheat lies after the reaping. Among them lay thousands of bodies clad in the wolf hides of the tribes, but the dead of the Northern people far outnumbered the dead of Erin. I was weary and sick of the stench of raw blood. I had glutted my soul with slaughter; now I sought plunder. And I found it—on the corpse of a richly-clad Norse chief which lay close to the seashore. I tore off the silver-scaled corselet, the horned helmet. They fitted as if made for me, and I swaggered among the dead, calling on my wild comrades to admire my appearance, though the harness felt strange to me, for the Gaels scorned armor and fought half-naked.

In my search for loot I had wandered far out on the plain, away from the river, but still the mail-clad bodies lay thickly strewn, for the bursting of the ranks had scattered fugitives and pursuers all over the countryside, from the dark waving Wood of Tomar, to the river and the seashore. And on the seaward slope of Drumna's headland, out of sight of the city and the plain of Clontarf, I came suddenly upon a dying warrior. He was tall and massive, clad in gray mail. He lay partly in the folds of a great dark cloak, and his sword lay broken near his mighty right hand. His horned helmet had fallen from his head and his elf-locks blew in the wind that swept out of the west.

Where one eye should have been was an empty socket and the other eye glittered cold and grim as the North Sea, though it was glazing with approach of death. Blood oozed from a rent in his corselet. I approached him warily, a strange cold fear, that I could not understand, gripping me. Ax ready to dash out his brains, I bent over him, and recognized him as the chief who had slain Prince Murrogh, and who had mown down the warriors of the Gael like a harvest. Wherever he had fought, the Norsemen had prevailed, but in all other parts of the field, the Gaels had been irresistible.

And now he spoke to me in Norse and I understood, for had I not toiled as slave among the sea people for long bitter years?

"The Christians have overcome," he gasped in a voice whose timbre, though low-pitched, sent a curious shiver of fear through me; there was in it an undertone of icy waves sweeping along a Northern shore, as of freezing winds whispering among the pine trees. "Doom and shadows stalk on Asgaard and here has fallen Ragnarok. I could not be in all parts of the field at once, and now I am wounded unto death. A spear—a spear with a cross carved in the blade; no other weapon could wound me."

I realized that the chief, seeing mistily my red beard and the Norse armor I wore, supposed me to be one of his own race. But a crawling horror surged darkly in the depths of my soul.

"White Christ, thou hast not yet conquered," he muttered deliriously. "Lift me up, man, and let me speak to you."

Now, for some reason I complied, and as I lifted him to a sitting posture, I shuddered and my flesh crawled at the feel of him, for his flesh was like ivory—smoother and harder than is natural for human flesh, and colder than even a dying man should be.

"I die as men die," he muttered. "Fool, to assume the attributes of mankind, even though it was to aid the people who deify me. The gods are immortal, but flesh can perish, even when it clothes a god. Haste and bring a sprig of the magic plant—even holly—and lay it on my bosom. Aye, though it be no larger than a dagger point, it will free me from this fleshly prison I put on when I came to war with men with their own weapons. And I will shake off this flesh and stalk once more among the thundering clouds. Woe, then, to all men who bend not the knee to me! Haste; I will await your coming."

His lion-like head fell back, and feeling shudderingly under his corselet, I could distinguish no heartbeat. He was dead, as men die, but I knew that locked in that semblance of a human body, there but slumbered the spirit of a fiend of the frost and darkness.

Aye, I knew him: Odin, the Gray Man, the One-eyed, the god of the North who had taken the form of a warrior to fight for his people. Assuming the form of a human he was subject to many of the limitations of humanity. All men knew this of the gods, who often walked the earth in the guise of men. Odin, clothed in human semblance, could be wounded by certain weapons, and even slain, but a touch of the mysterious holly would rouse him in grisly resurrection. This task he had set me, not knowing me for an enemy; in human form he could only use human faculties, and these had been impaired by onstriding death.

My hair stood up and my flesh crawled. I tore off of my body the Norse armor, and fought a wild panic that prompted me to run blind and screaming with terror across the plain. Nauseated with fear, I gathered boulders and heaped them for a rude couch, and on it, shaking with horror, I lifted the body of the Norse god. And as the sun set and the stars came silently out, I was working with fierce energy, piling huge rocks above the corpse. Other tribesmen came up and I told them of what I was sealing up—I hoped forever. And they, shivering with horror, fell to aiding me. No sprig of magic holly should be laid on Odin's terrible bosom. Beneath these rude stones the Northern demon should slumber until the thunder of Judgment Day, forgotten by the world which had once cried out beneath his iron heel. Yet not wholly forgot, for, as we labored, one of my comrades said: "This shall be no longer Drumna's Headland, but the Headland of the Gray Man."

That phrase established a connection between my dream-self and my sleeping self. I started up from sleep exclaiming: "Gray Man's Headland!"

I looked about dazedly, the furnishings of the room, faintly lighted by the starlight in the windows, seeming strange and unfamiliar until I slowly oriented myself with time and space.

"Gray Man's Headland," I repeated, "Gray Man—Gray-min—Grimmin—*Grimmin's Headland*! Great God, the thing under the cairn!"

Shaken, I sprang up, and realized that I still gripped the piece of stone from the cairn. It is well known that inanimate objects retain psychic associations. A round stone from the plain of Jericho has been placed in the hand of a hypnotized medium, and she had at once reconstructed in her mind the battle and siege of the city, and the shattering fall of the walls. I did not doubt that this bit of stone had acted as a magnet to drag my modern mind through the mists of the centuries into a life I had known before.

I was more shaken than I can describe, for the whole fantastic affair fitted in too well with certain formless vague sensations concerning the cairn which had already lingered at the back of my mind, to be dismissed as an unusually vivid dream. I felt the need of a glass of wine, and remembered that Ortali always had wine in his room. I hurriedly donned my clothes, opened my door, crossed the corridor and was about to knock at Ortali's door, when I noticed that it was partly open, as if someone had neglected to close it carefully. I entered, switching on a light. The room was empty.

I realized what had occurred. Ortali mistrusted me; he

feared to risk himself alone with me in a lonely spot at midnight. He had postponed the visit to the cairn, merely to trick me, to give him a chance to slip away alone.

My hatred for Ortali was for the moment completely submerged by a wild panic of horror at the thought of what the opening of the cairn might result in. For I did not doubt the authenticity of my dream. It was no dream; it was a fragmentary bit of memory, in which I had relived that other life of mine. Gray Man's Headland—Grimmin's Headland, and under those rough stones that grisly corpse in its semblance of humanity—I could not hope that, imbued with the imperishable essence of an elemental spirit, that corpse had crumbled to dust in the ages.

Of my race out of the city and across those semi-desolate reaches, I remember little. The night was a cloak of horror through which peered red stars like the gloating eyes of uncanny beasts, and my footfalls echoed hollowly so that repeatedly I thought some monster loped at my heels.

The straggling lights fell away behind me and I entered the region of mystery and horror. No wonder that progress had passed to the right and to the left of this spot, leaving it untouched, a blind back-eddy given over to goblin-dreams and nightmare memories. Well that so few suspected its very existence.

Dimly I saw the headland, but fear gripped me and held me aloof. I had a vague, incoherent idea of finding the ancient woman, Meve MacDonnal. She was grown old in the mysteries and traditions of the mysterious land. She could aid me, if indeed the blind fool Ortali loosed on the world the forgotten demon men once worshiped in the North.

A figure loomed suddenly in the starlight and I caromed against him, almost upsetting him. A stammering voice in a thick brogue protested with the petulancy of intoxication. It was a burly longshoreman returning to his cottage, no doubt, from some late revel in a tavern. I seized him and shook him, my eyes glaring wildly in the starlight.

"I am looking for Meve MacDonnal! Do you know her? Tell me, you fool! Do you know old Meve MacDonnal?"

It was as if my words sobered him as suddenly as a dash of icy water in his face. In the starlight I saw his face glimmer whitely and a catch of fear was at his throat. He sought to cross himself with an uncertain hand.

"Meve MacDonnal? Are ye mad? What would ye be doin' with *her*?"

"Tell me!" I shrieked, shaking him savagely, "Where is Meve MacDonnal?"

"There!" he gasped, pointing with a shaking hand where dimly in the night something loomed against the shadows. "In the name of the holy saints, begone, be ye madman or devil, and l'ave an honest man alone! There—there ye'll find Meve MacDonnal—where they laid her, full three hundred years ago!"

Half-heeding his words I flung him aside with a fierce exclamation, and, as I raced across the weed-grown plain, I heard the sounds of his lumbering flight. Half-blind with panic, I came to the low structures the man had pointed out. And floundering deep in weeds, my feet sinking into musty mold, I realized with a shock that I was in the ancient grave-yard on the inland side of Grimmin's Headland, into which I had seen Meve MacDonnal disappear the evening before. I was close by the door of the largest tomb, and with an eerie premonition I leaned close, seeking to make out the deeply-carven inscription. And partly by the dim light of the stars and partly by the touch of my tracing fingers, I made out the words and figures, in the half-forgotten Gaelic of three centuries ago: "Meve MacDonnal—1565-1640."

With a cry of horror I recoiled and, snatching out the crucifix she had given me, made to hurl it into the darkness—but it was as if an invisible hand caught my wrist. Madness and insanity—but I could not doubt: Meve MacDonnal had come to me from the tomb wherein she had rested for three hundred years to give me the ancient, ancient relic entrusted to her so long ago by her priestly kin. The memory of her words came to me, and the memory of Ortali and the Gray Man. From a lesser horror I turned squarely to a greater, and ran swiftly toward the headland which loomed dimly against the stars toward the sea.

As I crossed the ridge I saw, in the starlight, the cairn, and the figure that toiled gnome-like above it. Ortali, with his accustomed, almost superhuman energy, had dislodged many of the boulders; and as I approached, shaking with horrified anticipation, I saw him tear aside the last layer, and I heard his savage cry of triumph, that froze me in my tracks some yards behind him, looking down from the slope. An unholy radiance rose from the cairn, and I saw, in the north, the aurora flame up suddenly with terrible beauty, paling the starlight. All about the cairn pulsed a weird light, turning the rough stones to a cold shimmering silver, and in this glow I saw Ortali, all heedless, cast aside his pick and lean gloatingly over the aperture he had made—and

I saw there the helmeted head, reposing on the couch of stones where I, Red Cumal, placed it so long ago. I saw the inhuman terror and beauty of that awesome carven face, in which was neither human weakness, pity nor mercy. I saw the soul-freezing glitter of the one eye, which stared wide open in a fearful semblance of life. All up and down the tall mailed figure shimmered and sparkled cold darts and gleams of icy light, like the northern lights that blazed in the shuddering skies. Aye, the Gray Man lay as I had left him more than nine hundred years before, without a trace of rust or rot or decay.

And now as Ortali leaned forward to examine his find, a gasping cry broke from my lips—for the sprig of holly worn in his lapel in defiance of "Nordic superstition," slipped from its place, and in the weird glow I plainly saw it fall upon the mighty mailed breast of the figure, where it blazed suddenly with a brightness too dazzling for human eyes. My cry was echoed by Ortali. The figure moved; the mighty limbs flexed, tumbling the shining stones aside. A new glint lighted the terrible eye and a tide of life flooded and animated the carven features.

Out of the cairn he rose, and the northern lights played terribly about him. And the Gray Man changed and altered in horrific transmutation. The human features faded like a fading mask; the armor fell from his body and crumbled to dust as it fell; and the fiendish spirit of ice and frost and darkness that the sons of the North deified as Odin, stood nakedly and terribly in the stars. About his grisly head played lightning and the shuddering gleams of the aurora. His towering anthropomorphic form was dark as shadow and gleaming as ice; his horrible crest reared colossally against the vaulting arch of the sky.

Ortali cowered, screaming wordlessly, as the taloned malformed hands reached for him. In the shadowy indescribable features of the Thing there was no tinge of gratitude toward the man who had released it—only a demoniac gloating and a demoniac hate for all the sons of men. I saw the shadowy arms shoot out and strike. I heard Ortali scream once—a single unbearable screech that broke short at the shrillest pitch. A single instant a blinding blue glare burst about him, lighting his convulsed features and his upward-rolling eyes; then his body was dashed earthward as by an electric shock, so savagely that I distinctly heard the splintering of his bones. But Ortali was dead before he touched the ground—dead, shriveled and blackened, exactly like a man blasted by a thunderbolt, to which cause, indeed, men later ascribed his death.

The slavering monster that had slain him lumbered now toward me, shadowy tentacle-like arms outspread, the pale starlight making a luminous pool of his great inhuman eye, his frightful talons dripping with I know not what elemental forces to blast the bodies and souls of men.

But I flinched not, and in that instant I feared him not, neither the horror of his countenance nor the threat of his thunderbolt dooms. For in a blinding white flame had come to me the realization of why Meve MacDonnal had come from her tomb to bring me the ancient cross which had lain in her bosom for three hundred years, gathering unto itself unseen forces of good and light, which war forever against the shapes of lunacy and shadow.

As I plucked from my garments the ancient cross, I felt the play of gigantic unseen forces in the air about me. I was but a pawn in the game—merely the hand that held the relic of holiness, that was the symbol of the powers opposed forever against the fiends of darkness. As I held it high, from it shot a single shaft of white light, unbearably pure, unbearably white, as if all the awesome forces of Light were combined in the symbol and loosed in one concentrated arrow of wrath against the monster of darkness. And with a hideous shriek the demon reeled back, shriveling before my eyes. Then with a great rush of vulture-like wings, he soared into the stars, dwindling, dwindling among the play of the flaming fires and the lights of the haunted skies, fleeing back into the dark limbo which gave him birth, God only knows how many grisly eons ago.

THE TOWER OF THE ELEPHANT

Weird Tales, March 1933

———

Torches flared murkily on the revels in the Maul, where the thieves of the east held carnival by night. In the Maul they could carouse and roar as they liked, for honest people shunned the quarter, and watchmen, well paid with stained coins, did not interfere with their sport. Along the crooked, unpaved streets with their heaps of refuse and sloppy puddles, drunken roisterers staggered, roaring. Steel glinted in the shadows where wolf preyed on wolf, and from the darkness rose the shrill laughter of women, and the sounds of scufflings and strugglings. Torchlight licked luridly from broken windows and wide-thrown doors, and out of those doors, stale smells of wine and rank sweaty bodies, clamor of drinking-jacks and fists hammered on rough tables, snatches of obscene songs, rushed like a blow in the face.

In one of these dens merriment thundered to the low smoke-stained roof, where rascals gathered in every stage of rags and tatters—furtive cut-purses, leering kidnappers, quick-fingered thieves, swaggering bravoes with their wenches, strident-voiced women clad in tawdry finery. Native rogues were the dominant element—dark-skinned, dark-eyed Zamorians, with daggers at their girdles and guile in their hearts. But there were wolves of half a dozen outland nations there as well. There was a giant Hyperborean

213

renegade, taciturn, dangerous, with a broadsword strapped to his great gaunt frame—for men wore steel openly in the Maul. There was a Shemitish counterfeiter, with his hook nose and curled blue-black beard. There was a bold-eyed Brythunian wench, sitting on the knee of a tawny-haired Gunderman—a wandering mercenary soldier, a deserter from some defeated army. And the fat gross rogue whose bawdy jests were causing all the shouts of mirth was a professional kidnapper come up from distant Koth to teach woman-stealing to Zamorians who were born with more knowledge of the art than he could ever attain.

This man halted in his description of an intended victim's charms, and thrust his muzzle into a huge tankard of frothing ale. Then blowing the foam from his fat lips, he said, "By Bel, god of all thieves, I'll show them how to steal wenches: I'll have her over the Zamorian border before dawn, and there'll be a caravan waiting to receive her. Three hundred pieces of silver, a count of Ophir promised me for a sleek young Brythunian of the better class. It took me weeks, wandering among the border cities as a beggar, to find one I knew would suit. And is she a pretty baggage!"

He blew a slobbery kiss in the air.

"I know lords in Shem who would trade the secret of the Elephant Tower for her," he said, returning to his ale.

A touch on his tunic sleeve made him turn his head, scowling at the interruption. He saw a tall, strongly made youth standing beside him. This person was as much out of place in that den as a gray wolf among mangy rats of the gutters. His cheap tunic could not conceal the hard, rangy lines of his powerful frame, the broad heavy shoulders, the massive chest, lean waist, and heavy arms. His skin was brown from outland suns, his eyes blue and smoldering; a shock of tousled black hair crowned his broad forehead. From his girdle hung a sword in a worn leather scabbard.

The Kothian involuntarily drew back; for the man was not one of any civilized race he knew.

"You spoke of the Elephant Tower," said the stranger, speaking Zamorian with an alien accent. "I've heard much of this tower; what is its secret?"

The fellow's attitude did not seem threatening, and the Kothian's courage was bolstered up by the ale, and the evident approval of his audience. He swelled with self-importance.

"The secret of the Elephant Tower?" he exclaimed. "Why, any fool knows that Yara the priest dwells there with the great jewel men call the Elephant's Heart, that is the secret of his magic."

The barbarian digested this for a space.

"I have seen this tower," he said. "It is set in a great garden above the level of the city, surrounded by high walls. I have seen no guards. The walls would be easy to climb. Why has not somebody stolen this secret gem?"

The Kothian stared wide-mouthed at the other's simplicity, then burst into a roar of derisive mirth, in which the others joined.

"Harken to this heathen!" he bellowed. "He would steal the jewel of Yara!—Harken, fellow," he said, turning portentously to the other. "I suppose you are some sort of a northern barbarian—"

"I am a Cimmerian," the outlander answered, in no friendly tone. The reply and the manner of it meant little to the Kothian; of a kingdom that lay far to the south, on the borders of Shem, he knew only vaguely of the northern races.

"Then give ear and learn wisdom, fellow," said he, pointing his drinking-jack at the discomfited youth. "Know that in Zamora, and more especially in this city, there are more bold thieves than anywhere else in the world, even Koth. If mortal man could have stolen the gem, be sure it would have been filched long ago. You speak of climbing the walls, but once having climbed, you would quickly wish yourself back again. There are no guards in the gardens at night for a very good reason—that is, no human guards. But in the watch-chamber, in the lower part of the tower, are armed men, and even if you passed those who roam the gardens by night, you must still pass through the soldiers, for the gem is kept somewhere in the tower above."

"But if a man *could* pass through the gardens," argued the Cimmerian, "why could he not come at the gem through the upper part of the tower and thus avoid the soldiers?"

Again the Kothian gaped at him.

"Listen to him!" he shouted jeeringly. "The barbarian is an eagle who would fly to the jeweled rim of the tower, which is only a hundred and fifty feet above the earth, with rounded sides slicker than polished glass!"

The Cimmerian glared about, embarrassed at the roar of mocking laughter that greeted this remark. He saw no particular humor in it, and was too new to civilization to understand its discourtesies. Civilized men are more discourteous than savages because they know they can be impolite without having their skulls split, as a general thing. He was bewildered and chagrined, and doubtless would have slunk away, abashed, but the Kothian chose to goad him further.

"Come, come!" he shouted. "Tell these poor fellows, who have only been thieves since before you were spawned, tell them how you would steal the gem!"

"There is always a way, if the desire be coupled with courage," answered the Cimmerian shortly, nettled.

The Kothian chose to take this as a personal slur. His face grew purple with anger.

"What!" he roared. "You dare tell us our business, and intimate that we are cowards? Get along; get out of my sight!" And he pushed the Cimmerian violently.

"Will you mock me and then lay hands on me?" grated the barbarian, his quick rage leaping up; and he returned the push with an open-handed blow that knocked his tormenter back against the rude-hewn table. Ale splashed over the jack's lip, and the Kothian roared in fury, dragging at his sword.

"Heathen dog!" he bellowed. "I'll have your heart for that!"

Steel flashed and the throng surged wildly back out of the way. In their flight they knocked over the single candle and the den was plunged in darkness, broken by the crash of upset benches, drum of flying feet, shouts, oaths of people tumbling over one another, and a single strident yell of agony that cut the din like a knife. When a candle was relighted, most of the guests had gone out by doors and broken windows, and the rest huddled behind stacks of wine-kegs and under tables. The barbarian was gone; the center of the room was deserted except for the gashed body of the Kothian. The Cimmerian, with the unerring instinct of the barbarian, had killed his man in the darkness and confusion.

2.

The lurid lights and drunken revelry fell away behind the Cimmerian. He had discarded his torn tunic, and walked through the night naked except for a loincloth and his high-strapped sandals. He moved with the supple ease of a great tiger, his steely muscles rippling under his brown skin.

He had entered the part of the city reserved for the temples. On all sides of him they glittered white in the starlight—snowy marble pillars and golden domes and silver arches, shrines of Zamora's myriad strange gods. He did not trouble his head about them; he knew that Zamora's religion, like all things of a civilized, long-settled people, was intricate and complex, and had lost most of the pristine essence in a maze of formulas and rituals. He had squatted for hours in the courtyards of the philosophers, listening to the arguments of theologians and teachers, and come away in a haze of bewilderment, sure of only one thing, and that, that they were all touched in the head.

His gods were simple and understandable; Crom was their chief, and he lived on a great mountain, whence he sent forth dooms and death. It was useless to call on Crom, because he was a gloomy, savage god, and he hated weaklings. But he gave a man courage at birth, and the will and might to kill his enemies, which, in the Cimmerian's mind, was all any god should be expected to do.

His sandaled feet made no sound on the gleaming pave.

No watchmen passed, for even the thieves of the Maul shunned the temples, where strange dooms had been known to fall on violators. Ahead of him he saw, looming against the sky, the Tower of the Elephant. He mused, wondering why it was so named. No one seemed to know. He had never seen an elephant, but he vaguely understood that it was a monstrous animal, with a tail in front as well as behind. This a wandering Shemite had told him, swearing that he had seen such beasts by the thousands in the country of the Hyrkanians; but all men knew what liars were the men of Shem. At any rate, there were no elephants in Zamora.

The shimmering shaft of the tower rose frostily in the stars. In the sunlight it shone so dazzlingly that few could bear its glare, and men said it was built of silver. It was round, a slim perfect cylinder, a hundred and fifty feet in height, and its rim glittered in the starlight with the great jewels which crusted it. The tower stood among the waving exotic trees of a garden raised high above the general level of the city. A high wall enclosed this garden, and outside the wall was a lower level, likewise enclosed by a wall. No lights shone forth; there seemed to be no windows in the tower—at least not above the level of the inner wall. Only the gems high above sparkled frostily in the starlight.

Shrubbery grew thick outside the lower, or outer wall. The Cimmerian crept close and stood beside the barrier, measuring it with his eye. It was high, but he could leap and catch the coping with his fingers. Then it would be child's play to swing himself up and over, and he did not doubt that he could pass the inner wall in the same manner. But he hesitated at the thought of the strange perils which were said to await within. These people were strange and mysterious to him; they were not of his kind—not even of the same blood as the more westerly Brythunians, Nemedians, Kothians and Aquilonians, whose civilized mysteries had awed him in times past. The people of Zamora were very ancient, and, from what he had seen of them, very evil.

He thought of Yara, the high priest, who worked strange dooms from this jeweled tower, and the Cimmerian's hair prickled as he remembered a tale told by a drunken page of the court—how Yara had laughed in the face of a hostile prince, and held up a glowing, evil gem before him, and how rays shot blindingly from that unholy jewel, to envelop the prince, who screamed and fell down, and shrank to a withered blackened lump that changed to a black spider which scampered wildly about the chamber until Yara set his heel upon it.

Yara came not often from his tower of magic, and always to work evil on some man or some nation. The king of Zamora feared him more than he feared death, and kept himself drunk all the time because that fear was more than he could endure sober. Yara was very old—centuries old, men said, and added that he would live forever because of the magic of his gem, which men called the Heart of the Elephant, for no better reason than they named his hold the Elephant's Tower.

The Cimmerian, engrossed in these thoughts, shrank quickly against the wall. Within the garden someone was passing, who walked with a measured stride. The listener heard the clink of steel. So after all a guard did pace those gardens. The Cimmerian waited, expected to hear him pass again, on the next round, but silence rested over the mysterious gardens.

At last curiosity overcame him. Leaping lightly he grasped the wall and swung himself up to the top with one arm. Lying flat on the broad coping, he looked down into the wide space between the walls. No shrubbery grew near him, though he saw some carefully trimmed bushes near the inner wall. The starlight fell on the even sward and somewhere a fountain tinkled.

The Cimmerian cautiously lowered himself down on the inside and drew his sword, staring about him. He was shaken by the nervousness of the wild at standing thus unprotected in the naked starlight, and he moved lightly around the curve of the wall, hugging its shadow, until he was even with the shrubbery he had noticed. Then he ran quickly toward it, crouching low, and almost tripped over a form that lay crumpled near the edges of the bushes.

A quick look to right and left showed him no enemy in sight at least, and he bent close to investigate. His keen eyes, even in the dim starlight, showed him a strongly built man in the silvered armor and crested helmet of the Zamorian royal guard. A shield and a spear lay near him, and it took but an instant's examination to show that he had been strangled. The barbarian glanced about uneasily. He knew that this man must be the guard he had heard pass his hiding-place by the wall. Only a short time had passed, yet in that interval nameless hands had reached out of the dark and choked out the soldier's life.

Straining his eyes in the gloom, he saw a hint of motion through the shrubs near the wall. Thither he glided, gripping his sword. He made no more noise than a panther stealing through the night, yet the man he was stalking heard. The Cimmerian had a dim glimpse of a huge bulk close to the wall, felt relief that it was at least human; then the fellow wheeled quickly with a gasp that sounded like panic, made the first motion of a forward plunge, hands clutching, then recoiled as the Cimmerian's blade caught the starlight. For a tense instant neither spoke, standing ready for anything.

"You are no soldier," hissed the stranger at last. "You are a thief like myself."

"And who are you?" asked the Cimmerian in a suspicious whisper.

"Taurus of Nemedia."

The Cimmerian lowered his sword.

"I've heard of you. Men call you a prince of thieves."

A low laugh answered him. Taurus was tall as the Cimmerian, and heavier; he was big-bellied and fat, but his every movement betokened a subtle dynamic magnetism, which was reflected in the keen eyes that glinted vitally, even in the starlight. He was barefooted and carried a coil of what looked like a thin, strong rope, knotted at regular intervals.

"Who are you?" he whispered.

"Conan, a Cimmerian," answered the other. "I came seeking a way to steal Yara's jewel, that men call the Elephant's Heart."

Conan sensed the man's great belly shaking in laughter, but it was not derisive.

"By Bel, god of thieves!" hissed Taurus. "I had thought only myself had courage to attempt *that* poaching. These Zamorians call themselves thieves—bah! Conan, I like your grit. I never shared an adventure with anyone, but by Bel, we'll attempt this together if you're willing."

"Then you are after the gem, too?"

"What else? I've had my plans laid for months, but you, I think, have acted on a sudden impulse, my friend."

"You killed the soldier?"

"Of course. I slid over the wall when he was on the other side of the garden. I hid in the bushes; he heard me, or thought he heard something. When he came blundering over, it was no trick at all to get behind him and suddenly grip his neck and choke out his fool's life. He was like most men, half-blind in the dark. A good thief should have eyes like a cat."

"You made one mistake," said Conan.

Taurus' eyes flashed angrily.

"I? I, a mistake? Impossible!"

"You should have dragged the body into the bushes."

"Said the novice to the master of the art. They will not change the guard until past midnight. Should any come searching for him now, and find his body, they would flee at once to Yara, bellowing the news, and give us time to escape. Were they not to find it, they'd go beating up the bushes and catch us like rats in a trap."

"You are right," agreed Conan.

"So. Now attend. We waste time in this cursed discussion. There are no guards in the inner garden—human guards, I mean, though there are sentinels even more deadly. It was their presence which baffled me for so long, but I finally discovered a way to circumvent them."

"What of the soldiers in the lower part of the tower?"

"Old Yara dwells in the chambers above. By that route we will come—and go, I hope. Never mind asking me how. I have arranged a way. We'll steal down through the top of the tower and strangle old Yara before he can cast any of his accursed spells on us. At least we'll try; it's the chance of being turned into a spider or a toad, against the wealth and power of the world. All good thieves must know how to take risks."

"I'll go as far as any man," said Conan, slipping off his sandals.

"Then follow me." And turning, Taurus leaped up, caught the wall and drew himself up. The man's suppleness was amazing, considering his bulk; he seemed almost to glide up over the edge of the coping. Conan followed him, and lying flat on the broad top, they spoke in wary whispers.

"I see no light," Conan muttered. The lower part of the tower seemed much like that portion visible from outside the garden—a perfect, gleaming cylinder, with no apparent openings.

"There are cleverly constructed doors and windows," answered Taurus, "but they are closed. The soldiers breathe air that comes from above."

The garden was a vague pool of shadows, where feathery bushes and low spreading trees waved darkly in the starlight. Conan's wary soul felt the aura of waiting menace that brooded over it. He felt the burning glare of unseen eyes, and he caught a subtle scent that made the short hairs on his neck instinctively bristle as a hunting dog bristles at the scent of an ancient enemy.

"Follow me," whispered Taurus. "Keep behind me, as you value your life."

Taking what looked like a copper tube from his girdle, the Nemedian dropped lightly to the sward inside the wall. Conan was close behind him, sword ready, but Taurus pushed him back, close to the wall, and showed no inclination to advance, himself. His whole attitude was of tense expectancy, and his gaze, like Conan's, was fixed on the shadowy mass of shrubbery a few yards away. This shrubbery was shaken, although the breeze had died down. Then two great eyes blazed from the waving shadows, and behind them other sparks of fire glinted in the darkness.

"Lions!" muttered Conan.

"Aye. By day they are kept in subterranean caverns below the tower. That's why there are no guards in this garden."

Conan counted the eyes rapidly.

"Five in sight; maybe more back in the bushes. They'll charge in a moment—"

"Be silent!" hissed Taurus, and he moved out from the wall, cautiously as if treading on razors, lifting the slender tube. Low rumblings rose from the shadows and the blazing eyes moved forward. Conan could sense the great slavering jaws, the tufted tails lashing tawny sides. The air grew tense—the Cimmerian gripped his sword, expecting the charge and the irresistible hurtling of giant bodies. Then Taurus brought the mouth of the tube to his lips and blew powerfully. A long jet of yellowish powder shot from the other end of the tube and billowed out instantly in a thick green-yellow cloud that settled over the shrubbery, blotting out the glaring eyes.

Taurus ran back hastily to the wall. Conan glared without understanding. The thick cloud hid the shrubbery, and from it no sound came.

"What is that mist?" the Cimmerian asked uneasily.

"Death!" hissed the Nemedian. "If a wind springs up and blows it back upon us, we must flee over the wall. But no, the wind is still, and now it is dissipating. Wait until it vanishes entirely. To breathe it is death."

Presently only yellowish shreds hung ghostlily in the air; then they were gone, and Taurus motioned his companion forward. They stole toward the bushes, and Conan gasped. Stretched out in the shadows lay five great tawny shapes, the fire of their grim eyes dimmed forever. A sweetish cloying scent lingered in the atmosphere.

"They died without a sound!" muttered the Cimmerian. "Taurus, what was that powder?"

"It was made from the black lotus, whose blossoms wave in the lost jungles of Khitai, where only the yellow-skulled priests of Yun dwell. Those blossoms strike dead any who smell of them."

Conan knelt beside the great forms, assuring himself that they were indeed beyond power of harm. He shook his head; the magic of the exotic lands was mysterious and terrible to the barbarians of the north.

"Why can you not slay the soldiers in the tower in the same way?" he asked.

"Because that was all the powder I possessed. The obtaining of it was a feat which in itself was enough to make me famous among the thieves of the world. I stole it out of a caravan bound for Stygia, and I lifted it, in its cloth-of-gold bag, out of the coils of the great serpent which guarded it, without awaking him. But come, in Bel's name! Are we to waste the night in discussion?"

They glided through the shrubbery to the gleaming foot of the tower, and there, with a motion enjoining silence, Taurus unwound his knotted cord, on one end of which was a strong steel hook. Conan saw his plan, and asked no questions as the Nemedian gripped the line a short distance below the hook, and began to swing it about his head. Conan laid his ear to the smooth wall and listened, but could hear nothing. Evidently the soldiers within did not suspect the presence of intruders, who had made no more sound than the night wind blowing through the trees. But a strange nervousness was on the barbarian; perhaps it was the lion-smell which was over everything.

Taurus threw the line with a smooth, ripping motion of his mighty arm. The hook curved upward and inward in a peculiar manner, hard to describe, and vanished over the jeweled rim. It apparently caught firmly, for cautious jerking and then hard pulling did not result in any slipping or giving.

"Luck the first cast," murmured Taurus. "I—"

It was Conan's savage instinct which made him wheel suddenly; for the death that was upon them made no sound. A fleeting glimpse showed the Cimmerian the giant tawny shape, rearing upright against the stars, towering over him for the death-stroke. No civilized man could have moved half so quickly as the barbarian moved. His sword flashed frostily in the starlight with every ounce of desperate nerve and thew behind it, and man and beast went down together.

Cursing incoherently beneath his breath, Taurus bent above the mass, and saw his companion's limbs move as he strove to drag himself from under the great weight that lay limply upon him. A glance showed the startled Nemedian that the lion was dead, its slanting skull split in half. He laid hold of the carcass, and by his aid, Conan thrust it aside and clambered up, still gripping his dripping sword.

"Are you hurt, man?" gasped Taurus, still bewildered by the stunning swiftness of that touch-and-go episode.

"No, by Crom!" answered the barbarian. "But that was as close a call as I've had in a life noways tame. Why did not the cursed beast roar as he charged?"

"All things are strange in this garden," said Taurus. "The lions strike silently—and so do other deaths. But come— little sound was made in that slaying, but the soldiers might have heard, if they are not asleep or drunk. That beast was in some other part of the garden and escaped the death of the flowers, but surely there are no more. We must climb this cord—little need to ask a Cimmerian if he can."

"If it will bear my weight," grunted Conan, cleansing his sword on the grass.

"It will bear thrice my own," answered Taurus. "It was woven from the tresses of dead women, which I took from their tombs at midnight, and steeped in the deadly wine of the upas tree, to give it strength. I will go first—then follow me closely."

The Nemedian gripped the rope and crooking a knee about it, began the ascent; he went up like a cat, belying the apparent clumsiness of his bulk. The Cimmerian followed. The cord swayed and turned on itself, but the climbers were not hindered; both had made more difficult climbs before. The jeweled rim glittered high above them, jutting out from the perpendicular of the wall, so that the cord hung perhaps a foot from the side of the tower—a fact which added greatly to the ease of the ascent.

Up and up they went, silently, the lights of the city spreading out further and further to their sight as they climbed, the stars above them more and more dimmed by the glitter of the jewels along the rim. Now Taurus reached up a hand and gripped the rim itself, pulling himself up and over. Conan paused a moment on the very edge, fascinated by the great frosty jewels whose gleams dazzled his eyes—diamonds, rubies, emeralds, sapphires, turquoises, moonstones, set thick as stars in the shimmering silver. At a distance their different gleams had seemed to merge into a pulsing white glare; but now, at close range, they shimmered with a million rainbow tints and lights, hypnotizing him with their scintillations.

"There is a fabulous fortune here, Taurus," he whispered; but the Nemedian answered impatiently, "Come on! If we secure the Heart, these and all other things shall be ours."

Conan climbed over the sparkling rim. The level of the tower's top was some feet below the gemmed ledge. It was flat, composed of some dark blue substance, set with gold that caught the starlight, so that the whole looked like a wide sapphire flecked with shining gold dust. Across from the point where they had entered there seemed to be a sort of chamber, built upon the roof. It was of the same silvery material as the walls of the tower, adorned with designs worked in smaller gems; its single door was of gold, its surface cut in scales, and crusted with jewels that gleamed like ice.

Conan cast a glance at the pulsing ocean of lights which spread far below them, then glanced at Taurus. The Nemedian was drawing up his cord and coiling it. He showed Conan where the hook had caught—a fraction of an inch of the point had sunk under a great blazing jewel on the inner side of the rim.

"Luck was with us again," he muttered. "One would think that our combined weight would have torn that stone out. Follow me; the real risks of the venture begin now. We are in the serpent's lair, and we know not where he lies hidden."

Like stalking tigers they crept across the darkly gleaming floor and halted outside the sparkling door. With a deft and cautious hand Taurus tried it. It gave without resistance, and the companions looked in, tensed for anything. Over the Nemedian's shoulder Conan had a glimpse of a glittering chamber, the walls, ceiling and floor of which were crusted with great white jewels which lighted it brightly, and which seemed its only illumination. It seemed empty of life.

"Before we cut off our last retreat," hissed Taurus, "go you to the rim and look over on all sides; if you see any soldiers moving in the gardens, or anything suspicious, return and tell me. I will await you within this chamber."

Conan saw scant reason in this, and a faint suspicion of his companion touched his wary soul, but he did as Taurus requested. As he turned away, the Nemedian slipt inside the door and drew it shut behind him. Conan crept about the rim of the tower, returning to his starting point without having seen any suspicious movement in the vaguely waving sea of leaves below. He turned toward the door—suddenly from within the chamber there sounded a strangled cry.

The Cimmerian leaped forward, electrified—the gleaming door swung open and Taurus stood framed in the cold blaze behind him. He swayed and his lips parted, but only a dry rattle burst from his throat. Catching at the golden door for support, he lurched out upon the roof, then fell headlong, clutching at his throat. The door swung to behind him.

Conan, crouching like a panther at bay, saw nothing in the room behind the stricken Nemedian, in the brief instant the door was partly open—unless it was not a trick of the light which made it seem as if a shadow darted across the gleaming floor. Nothing followed Taurus out on the roof, and Conan bent above the man.

The Nemedian stared up with dilated, glazing eyes, that somehow held a terrible bewilderment. His hands clawed at his throat, his lips slobbered and gurgled; then suddenly he stiffened, and the astounded Cimmerian knew that he was dead. And he felt that Taurus had died without knowing what manner of death had stricken him. Conan glared bewilderedly at the cryptic golden door. In that empty room, with its glittering jeweled walls, death had come to the prince of thieves as swiftly and mysteriously as he had dealt doom to the lions in the gardens below.

Gingerly the barbarian ran his hands over the man's half-naked body, seeking a wound. But the only marks of violence were between his shoulders, high up near the base of his bull-neck—three small wounds, which looked as if three nails had been driven deep in the flesh and withdrawn. The edges of these wounds were black, and a faint smell as of putrefaction was evident. Poisoned darts? thought Conan—but in that case the missiles should be still in the wounds.

Cautiously he stole toward the golden door, pushed it open, and looked inside. The chamber lay empty, bathed in the cold, pulsing glow of the myriad jewels. In the very center of the ceiling he idly noted a curious design—a black eight-sided pattern, in the center of which four gems glittered with a red flame unlike the white blaze of the other jewels. Across the room there was another door, like the one in which he stood, except that it was not carved in the scale pattern. Was it from that door that death had come?—and having struck down its victim, had it retreated by the same way?

Closing the door behind him, the Cimmerian advanced into the chamber. His bare feet made no sound on the crystal floor. There were no chairs or tables in the chamber, only three or four silken couches, embroidered with gold and worked in strange serpentine designs, and several silver-bound mahogany chests. Some were sealed with heavy golden locks; others lay open, their carven lids thrown back, revealing heaps of jewels in a careless riot of splendor to the Cimmerian's astounded eyes. Conan swore beneath his breath; already he had looked upon more wealth that night than he had ever dreamed existed in all the world, and he grew dizzy thinking of what must be the value of the jewel he sought.

He was in the center of the room now, going stooped forward, head thrust out warily, sword advanced, when again death struck at him soundlessly. A flying shadow that swept across the gleaming floor was his only warning, and his instinctive sidelong leap all that saved his life. He had a flashing glimpse of a hairy black horror that swung past him with a clashing of frothing fangs, and something splashed on his bare shoulder that burned like drops of liquid hellfire. Springing back, sword high, he saw the horror strike the floor, wheel and scuttle toward him with appalling speed—a gigantic black spider, such as men see only in nightmare dreams.

It was as large as a pig, and its eight thick hairy legs drove its ogreish body over the floor at headlong pace; its four evilly gleaming eyes shone with a horrible intelligence, and its fangs dripped venom that Conan knew, from the burning of his shoulder where only a few drops had splashed as the thing struck and missed, was laden with swift death. This was the killer that had dropped from its perch in the middle of the ceiling on a strand of its web, on the neck of the Nemedian. Fools that they were not to have suspected that the upper chambers would be guarded as well as the lower!

These thoughts flashed briefly through Conan's mind as the monster rushed. He leaped high, and it passed beneath him, wheeled and charged back. This time he evaded its rush with a sidewise leap, and struck back like a cat. His sword severed one of the hairy legs, and again he barely saved himself as the monstrosity swerved at him, fangs clicking fiendishly. But the creature did not press the pursuit; turning, it scuttled across the crystal floor and ran up the wall to the ceiling, where it crouched for an instant, glaring down at him with its fiendish red eyes. Then without warning it launched itself through space, trailing a strand of slimy grayish stuff.

Conan stepped back to avoid the hurtling body—then ducked frantically, just in time to escape being snared by the flying web-rope. He saw the monster's intent and sprang toward the door, but it was quicker, and a sticky strand cast across the door made him a prisoner. He dared not try to cut it with his sword; he knew the stuff would cling to the blade, and before he could shake it loose, the fiend would be sinking its fangs into his back.

Then began a desperate game, the wits and quickness of the man matched against the fiendish craft and speed of the giant spider. It no longer scuttled across the floor in a direct charge, or swung its body through the air at him. It raced about the ceiling and the walls, seeking to snare him in the long loops of sticky gray web-strands, which it flung with a devilish accuracy. These strands were thick as ropes, and Conan knew that once they were coiled about him, his desperate strength would not be enough to tear him free before the monster struck.

All over the chamber went on that devil's dance, in utter silence except for the quick breathing of the man, the low scuff of his bare feet on the shining floor, the castanet rattle of the monstrosity's fangs. The gray strands lay in coils on the floor; they were looped along the walls; they overlaid the jewel-chests and silken couches, and hung in dusky festoons from the jeweled ceiling. Conan's steel-trap quickness of eye and muscle had kept him untouched, though the sticky loops had passed him so close they rasped his naked hide. He knew he could not always avoid them; he not only had to watch the strands swinging from the ceiling, but to keep his eye on the floor, lest he trip in the coils that lay there. Sooner or later a gummy loop would writhe about him, python-like, and then, wrapped like a cocoon, he would lie at the monster's mercy.

The spider raced across the chamber floor, the gray rope waving out behind it. Conan leaped high, clearing a couch—with a quick wheel the fiend ran up the wall, and the strand, leaping off the floor like a live thing, whipped about the Cimmerian's ankle. He caught himself on his hands as he fell, jerking frantically at the web which held him like a pliant vise, or the coil of a python. The hairy devil was racing down the wall to complete its capture. Stung to frenzy, Conan caught up a jewel chest and hurled it with all his strength. It was a move the monster was not expecting. Full in the midst of the branching black legs the massive missile struck, smashing against the wall with a muffled sickening crunch. Blood and greenish slime spattered, and the shattered mass fell with the burst gem-chest to the floor. The crushed black body lay among the flaming riot of jewels that spilled over it; the hairy legs moved aimlessly, the dying eyes glittered redly among the twinkling gems.

Conan glared about, but no other horror appeared, and he set himself to working free of the web. The substance clung tenaciously to his ankle and his hands, but at last he was free, and taking up his sword, he picked his way among the gray coils and loops to the inner door. What horrors lay within he did not know. The Cimmerian's blood was up, and since he had come so far, and overcome so much peril, he was determined to go through to the grim finish of the adventure, whatever that might be. And he felt that the jewel he sought was not among the many so carelessly strewn about the gleaming chamber.

Stripping off the loops that fouled the inner door, he found that it, like the other, was not locked. He wondered if the soldiers below were still unaware of his presence. Well, he was high above their heads, and if tales were to be believed, they were used to strange noises in the tower above them—sinister sounds, and screams of agony and horror.

Yara was on his mind, and he was not altogether comfortable as he opened the golden door. But he saw only a flight of silver steps leading down, dimly lighted by what means he could not ascertain. Down these he went silently, gripping his sword. He heard no sound, and came presently to an ivory door, set with bloodstones. He listened, but no sound came from within; only thin wisps of smoke drifted lazily from beneath the door, bearing a curious exotic odor unfamiliar to the Cimmerian. Below him the silver stair wound down to vanish in the dimness, and up that shadowy well no sound floated; he had an eery feeling that he was alone in a tower occupied only by ghosts and phantoms.

3.

Cautiously he pressed against the ivory door and it swung silently inward. On the shimmering threshold Conan stared like a wolf in strange surroundings, ready to fight or flee on the instant. He was looking into a large chamber with a domed golden ceiling; the walls were of green jade, the floor of ivory, partly covered by thick rugs. Smoke and exotic scent of incense floated up from a brazier on a golden tripod, and behind it sat an idol on a sort of marble couch. Conan stared aghast; the image had the body of a man, naked, and green in color; but the head was one of nightmare and madness. Too large for the human body, it had no attributes of humanity. Conan stared at the wide flaring ears, the curling proboscis, on either side of which stood white tusks tipped with round golden balls. The eyes were closed, as if in sleep.

This then, was the reason for the name, the Tower of the Elephant, for the head of the thing was much like that of the beasts described by the Shemitish wanderer. This was Yara's god; where then should the gem be, but concealed in the idol, since the stone was called the Elephant's Heart?

As Conan came forward, his eyes fixed on the motionless idol, the eyes of the thing opened suddenly! The Cimmerian froze in his tracks. It was no image—it was a living thing, and he was trapped in its chamber!

That he did not instantly explode in a burst of murderous frenzy is a fact that measures his horror, which paralyzed him where he stood. A civilized man in his position would have sought doubtful refuge in the conclusion that he was insane; it did not occur to the Cimmerian to doubt his senses. He knew he was face to face with a demon of the Elder World, and the realization robbed him of all his faculties except sight.

The trunk of the horror was lifted and quested about, the topaz eyes stared unseeingly, and Conan knew the monster was blind. With the thought came a thawing of his frozen nerves, and he began to back silently toward the door. But the creature heard. The sensitive trunk stretched toward him, and Conan's horror froze him again when the being spoke, in a strange, stammering voice that never changed its key or timbre. The Cimmerian knew that those jaws were never built or intended for human speech.

"Who is here? Have you come to torture me again, Yara? Will you never be done? Oh, Yag-kosha, is there no end to agony?"

Tears rolled from the sightless eyes, and Conan's gaze strayed to the limbs stretched on the marble couch. And he knew the monster would not rise to attack him. He knew the marks of the rack, and the searing brand of the flame, and tough-souled as he was, he stood aghast at the ruined deformities which his reason told him had once been limbs as comely as his own. And suddenly all fear and repulsion went from him, to be replaced by a great pity. What this monster was, Conan could not know, but the evidences of its sufferings were so terrible and pathetic that a strange aching sadness came over the Cimmerian, he knew not why. He only felt that he was looking upon a cosmic tragedy, and he shrank with shame, as if the guilt of a whole race were laid upon him.

"I am not Yara," he said. "I am only a thief. I will not harm you."

"Come near that I may touch you," the creature faltered, and Conan came near unfearingly, his sword hanging forgotten in his hand. The sensitive trunk came out and groped over his face and shoulders, as a blind man gropes, and its touch was light as a girl's hand.

"You are not of Yara's race of devils," sighed the creature. "The clean, lean fierceness of the wastelands marks you. I know your people from of old, whom I knew by another name in the long, long ago when another world lifted its jeweled spires to the stars. There is blood on your fingers."

"A spider in the chamber above and a lion in the garden," muttered Conan.

"You have slain a man too, this night," answered the other. "And there is death in the tower above. I feel; I know."

"Aye," muttered Conan. "The prince of all thieves lies there dead from the bite of a vermin."

"So—and so!" the strange inhuman voice rose in a sort of low chant. "A slaying in the tavern and a slaying on the roof—I know; I feel. And the third will make the magic of which not even Yara dreams—oh, magic of deliverance, green gods of Yag!"

Again tears fell as the tortured body was rocked to and fro in the grip of varied emotions. Conan looked on, bewildered.

Then the convulsions ceased; the soft, sightless eyes were turned toward the Cimmerian, the trunk beckoned.

"Oh man, listen," said the strange being. "I am foul and monstrous to you, am I not? Nay, do not answer; I know. But you would seem as strange to me, could I see you. There are many worlds besides this Earth, and life takes many shapes. I am neither god nor demon, but flesh and blood like yourself, though the substance differ in part, and the form be cast in different mold.

"I am very old, oh man of the waste countries; long and long ago I came to this planet with others of my world, from the green planet Yag, which circles forever in the outer fringe of this universe. We swept through space on mighty wings that drove us through the cosmos quicker than light, because we had warred with the kings of Yag and were defeated and outcast. But we could never return, for on Earth our wings withered from our shoulders. Here we abode apart from earthly life. We fought the strange and terrible forms of life which then walked the Earth, so that we became feared, and were not molested in the dim jungles of the east, where we had our abode.

"We saw men grow from the ape and build the shining cities of Valusia, Kamelia, Commoria, and their sisters. We saw them reel before the thrusts of the heathen Atlanteans and Picts and Lemurians. We saw the oceans rise and engulf Atlantis and Lemuria, and the isles of the Picts, and the shining cities of civilization. We saw the survivors of Pictdom and Atlantis build their Stone Age empires, and go down to ruin, locked in bloody wars. We saw the Picts sink into abysmal savagery, the Atlanteans into apedom again. We saw new savages drift southward in conquering waves from the Arctic Circle to build a new civilization, with new kingdoms called Nemedia, and Koth, and Aquilonia and their sisters. We saw your people rise under a new name from the jungles of the apes that had been Atlanteans. We saw the descendants of the Lemurians who had survived the cataclysm, rise again through savagery and ride westward, as Hyrkanians. And we saw this race of devils, survivors of the ancient civilization that was before Atlantis sank, come once more into culture and power—this accursed kingdom of Zamora.

"All this we saw, neither aiding nor hindering the immutable cosmic law, and one by one we died; for we of Yag are not immortal, though our lives are as the lives of planets and constellations. At last I alone was left, dreaming of old times among the ruined temples of jungle-lost Khitai, worshipped as a god by an ancient yellow-skinned race. Then came Yara, versed in dark knowledge handed down through the days of barbarism, since before Atlantis sank.

"First he sat at my feet and learned wisdom. But he was

not satisfied with what I taught him, for it was white magic, and he wished evil lore, to enslave kings and glut a fiendish ambition. I would teach him none of the black secrets I had gained, through no wish of mine, through the eons.

"But his wisdom was deeper than I had guessed; with guile gotten among the dusky tombs of dark Stygia, he trapped me into divulging a secret I had not intended to bare; and turning my own power upon me, he enslaved me. Ah, gods of Yag, my cup has been bitter since that hour!

"He brought me up from the lost jungles of Khitai where the gray apes danced to the pipes of the yellow priests, and offerings of fruit and wine heaped my broken altars. No more was I a god to kindly jungle-folk—I was slave to a devil in human form."

Again tears stole from the unseeing eyes.

"He pent me in this tower which at his command I built for him in a single night. By fire and rack he mastered me, and by strange unearthly tortures you would not understand. In agony I would long ago have taken my own life, if I could. But he kept me alive—mangled, blinded, and broken—to do his foul bidding. And for three hundred years I have done his bidding, from this marble couch, blackening my soul with cosmic sins, and staining my wisdom with crimes, because I had no other choice. Yet not all my ancient secrets has he wrested from me, and my last gift shall be the sorcery of the Blood and the Jewel.

"For I feel the end of time draw near. You are the hand of Fate. I beg of you, take the gem you will find on yonder altar."

Conan turned to the gold and ivory altar indicated, and

took up a great round jewel, clear as crimson crystal; and he knew that this was the Heart of the Elephant.

"Now for the great magic, the mighty magic, such as Earth has not seen before, and shall not see again, through a million million of millenniums. By my life-blood I conjure it, by blood born on the green breast of Yag, dreaming far-poised in the great blue vastness of Space.

"Take your sword, man, and cut out my heart; then squeeze it so that the blood will flow over the red stone. Then go you down these stairs and enter the ebony chamber where Yara sits wrapped in lotus-dreams of evil. Speak his name and he will awaken. Then lay this gem before him, and say, 'Yag-kosha gives you a last gift and a last enchantment.' Then get you from the tower quickly; fear not, your way shall be made clear. The life of man is not the life of Yag, nor is human death the death of Yag. Let me be free of this cage of broken blind flesh, and I will once more be Yogah of Yag, morning-crowned and shining, with wings to fly, and feet to dance, and eyes to see, and hands to break."

Uncertainly Conan approached, and Yag-kosha, or Yogah, as if sensing his uncertainty, indicated where he should strike. Conan set his teeth and drove the sword deep. Blood streamed over the blade and his hand, and the monster started convulsively, then lay back quite still. Sure that life had fled, at least life as he understood it, Conan set to work on his grisly task and quickly brought forth something that he felt must be the strange being's heart, though it differed curiously from any he had ever seen. Holding the still-pulsing organ over the blazing jewel, he pressed it with both hands, and a rain of blood fell on the stone. To his surprize, it did not run off, but soaked into the gem, as water is absorbed by a sponge.

Holding the jewel gingerly, he went out of the fantastic chamber and came upon the silver steps. He did not look back; he instinctively felt that some sort of transmutation was taking place in the body on the marble couch, and he further felt that it was of a sort not to be witnessed by human eyes.

He closed the ivory door behind him and without hesitation descended the silver steps. It did not occur to him to ignore the instructions given him. He halted at an ebony door, in the center of which was a grinning silver skull, and pushed it open. He looked into a chamber of ebony and jet, and saw, on a black silken couch, a tall, spare form reclining. Yara the priest and sorcerer lay before him, his eyes open and dilated with the fumes of the yellow lotus, far-staring, as if fixed on gulfs and nighted abysses beyond human ken.

"Yara!" said Conan, like a judge pronouncing doom. "Awaken!"

The eyes cleared instantly and became cold and cruel as a vulture's. The tall silken-clad form lifted erect, and towered gauntly above the Cimmerian.

"Dog!" His hiss was like the voice of a cobra. "What do you here?"

Conan laid the jewel on the great ebony table.

"He who sent this gem bade me say, 'Yag-kosha gives a last gift and a last enchantment.'"

Yara recoiled, his dark face ashy. The jewel was no longer crystal-clear; its murky depths pulsed and throbbed, and curious smoky waves of changing color passed over its smooth surface. As if drawn hypnotically, Yara bent over the table and gripped the gem in his hands, staring into its shadowed depths, as if it were a magnet to draw the shuddering soul from his body. And as Conan looked, he thought that his eyes must be playing him tricks. For when Yara had risen up from his couch, the priest had seemed gigantically tall; yet now he saw that Yara's head would scarcely come to his shoulder. He blinked, puzzled, and for the first time that night, doubted his own senses. Then with a shock he realized that the priest was shrinking in stature—was growing smaller before his very gaze.

With a detached feeling he watched, as a man might watch a play; immersed in a feeling of overpowering unreality, the Cimmerian was no longer sure of his own identity; he only knew that he was looking upon the external evidences of the unseen play of vast Outer forces, beyond his understanding.

Now Yara was no bigger than a child; now like an infant he sprawled on the table, still grasping the jewel. And now the sorcerer suddenly realized his fate, and he sprang up, releasing the gem. But still he dwindled, and Conan saw a tiny, pigmy figure rushing wildly about the ebony tabletop, waving tiny arms and shrieking in a voice that was like the squeak of an insect.

Now he had shrunk until the great jewel towered above him like a hill, and Conan saw him cover his eyes with his hands, as if to shield them from the glare, as he staggered about like a madman. Conan sensed that some unseen magnetic force was pulling Yara to the gem. Thrice he raced wildly about it in a narrowing circle, thrice he strove to turn and run out across the table; then with a scream that echoed faintly in the ears of the watcher, the priest threw up his arms and ran straight toward the blazing globe.

Conan saw Yara clamber up the smooth, curving surface, impossibly, like a man climbing a glass mountain. Now the priest stood on the top, still with tossing arms, invoking what grisly names only the gods know. And suddenly he sank into the very heart of the jewel, as a man sinks into a sea, and Conan saw the smoky waves close over his head. Now he saw him in the crimson heart of the jewel, once more crystal-clear, as a man sees a scene far away, tiny with great distance. And into the heart came a green, shining winged figure with the body of a man and the head of an elephant— no longer blind or crippled. Yara threw up his arms and fled as a madman flees, and on his heels came the avenger. Then, like the bursting of a bubble, the great jewel vanished in a rainbow burst of iridescent gleams, and the ebony tabletop lay bare and deserted—as bare, Conan somehow knew, as the marble couch in the chamber above, where the body of that strange transcosmic being called Yag-kosha and Yogah had lain.

The Cimmerian turned and fled from the chamber, down the silver stairs. So mazed was he that it did not occur to him to escape from the tower by the way he had entered it. Down that winding, shadowy silver well he ran, and came into a large chamber at the foot of the gleaming stairs. There he halted for an instant; he had come into the room of the soldiers. He saw the glitter of their silver corselets, the sheen of their jeweled sword-hilts. They sat slumped at the banquet board, their dusky plumes waving somberly above their drooping helmeted heads; they lay among their dice and fallen goblets on the wine-stained lapis lazuli floor. And he knew that they were dead. The promise had been made, the word kept; whether sorcery or magic or the falling shadow of great green wings had stilled the revelry, Conan could not know, but his way had been made clear. And a silver door stood open, framed in the whiteness of dawn.

Into the waving green gardens came the Cimmerian, and as the dawn wind blew upon him with the cool fragrance of luxuriant growths, he started like a man waking from a dream. He turned back uncertainly, to stare at the cryptic tower he had just left. Was he bewitched and enchanted? Had he dreamed all that had seemed to have passed? As he looked he saw the gleaming tower sway against the crimson dawn, its jewel-crusted rim sparkling in the growing light, and crash into shining shards.

AUTUMN

Weird Tales, April 1933

———

Now is the lyre of Homer flecked with rust,
  And yellow leaves are blown across the world,
And naked trees that shake at every gust
  Stand gaunt against the clouds autumnal-curled.

Now from the hollow moaning of the sea
  The dreary birds against the sunset fly,
And drifting down the sad wind's ghostly dree
  A breath of music echoes with a sigh.

The barren branch shakes down the withered fruit,
  The seas faint footprints on the strand erase;
The sere leaves fall on a forgotten lute,
  And autumn's arms enfold a dying race.

MOONLIGHT ON A SKULL

Weird Tales, May 1933

———

Golden goats on a hillside black,
    Silken gown on a wharf-side trull,
Screaming girl on a silver rack—
    What are dreams in a shadowed skull?

I stood at a shrine and Chiron died,
    A woman laughed from the purple roofs,
And he burned and lived and rose in his pride
    And shattered the tiles with clanging hoofs.

I opened a volume dark and rare,
    I lighted a candle of mystic lore—
Bare feet throbbed on the outer stair
    And book and candle sank to the floor.

Ships that reel on the windy sea,
    Lovers that take the world to wife,
What may the Traitress hold for me
    Who scarce have lifted the veil of life?